To: Dan[e]
Thanks for b[eing]
person to talk to
you enjoy my work
for supporting me.

Carmen

Secrets of A Bayou Mystique

By

Dr. Carman S. Clark, Ed.D

authorHOUSE™

1663 LIBERTY DRIVE, SUITE 200
BLOOMINGTON, INDIANA 47403
(800) 839-8640
WWW.AUTHORHOUSE.COM

First published by AuthorHouse 03/07/05

ISBN: 1-4184-7947-0 (e)
ISBN: 1-4184-7948-9 (sc)

Library of Congress Control Number: 2004099691

Printed in the United States of America
Bloomington, Indiana

This book is printed on acid-free paper.

FOREWORD

If this book could be summed up in a few words, it would state, "Never underestimate the healing power of the human spirit." The spirit is the place where love lives and breathes and it is designed to heal all emotional wounds. The main character of this book was the victim of a sexual predator and child abuse. But, holding on to the spirit of love for herself, her family and her faith, she found a way to break its traumatic hold on her life. As a spiritual mystery, her life history will challenge both science and sensibility. As a one-time silent sufferer, her life experience highlights the devastating effects that sexual abuse, incest and child abuse can enact on its victims. And as a crusader for justice, her personal triumph over this menace offers hope and solutions for dealing with this epidemic evil and exposes the kind of family secrets that allows this behavior to continue. The names of all the characters are fictional but the story is based on real events. Perhaps some specifics of her experience will be personalized in the life story of a neighbor, friend, sister, brother, cousin, co-worker, associate, minister, entertainer, partner, spouse, or child. The story, for the most part, is being narrated by the author. However, woven into the narrative are some insightful references to the psychopathology and personality profiles of the sex offender, child abuser, enablers, and the victim and the author will occasionally shift from first person to third person in order to explain certain dynamics. The main character has decided to share her story in order to raise public awareness of sexual abuse trauma and child abuse to a more personal level in hopes that healing is made possible to many who are hurting. As the narrator, it is the author's greatest desire that something in this story will be helpful to others who are suffering from the traumatic effects of predatory sexual abuse and child abuse as well as provide insight into how to recognize and deal effectively with the traumatic injuries of this evil menace, the sexual predator and the people who support them. It is vital that we understand what the victims of these people endure. There is an evil that men (and women) do which when mentioned strikes an immediate chord of repulsion and rage in the hearts of decent people. This evil is so reprehensible that even the prison population ranks the people who commit such offenses as lower than murderers, thieves and serial killers. Such is the rank of a sexual predator and their abuse of victims causes them to be considered the lowest scum of the earth. Sexual abuse trauma causes untold damages to the victims. The traumatic effects can last a lifetime because such an insidious violation is psychologically overwhelming, affecting a person's ability to cope, trust, and love. All victims of sexual predators suffer in some way. Some manage to heal; but for others, the pain lingers without resolve. In the wake of sexual trauma and abuse, many victims become stuck in a quagmire of confusion, trying to undo the effects of the trauma. This story highlights that struggle. By definition, sexual abuse occurs when someone forces an unwanted sexual activity on another more vulnerable person, by any means necessary. There are three key points to keep in mind in reference to this descriptive behavior of the sex offender. One, they will use *force* to in order to violate a person, refusing to hear or accept the word "no" by eliminating or overpowering a person's resistance. Two, their sexual encroachments are *unwanted*. Under any normal circumstance, their targeted victim would not consent to or be interested in them in a sexual manner. And three, they *use any means necessary* to violate someone else's body, usually through coercion, manipulation, threats, or force. A sexual predator in pursuit of a victim is relentless. They will not be stopped; they must be caught. So many people, men, women and children, from all walks of life, religions, cultures, race and all socioeconomic backgrounds suffer in an abysmal silence, muted into self-isolation by the wicked acts of a sexual predator. As if there is a creeping menace languishing inside their bitter souls, these people, both men and women, follow their sinister conscious to desecrate all of innocence. The sexual predator views the body of a vulnerable child or person as an object of opportunity and secretly plots to defile it as mockery to innocence. They target vulnerability for destruction, treating someone else's body as if they are entitled to use it for whatever perversion they want. Sexual predators make a conscious choice to violate someone else's purity as if it is their personal right, acting like the only reason a child or person was born was to fulfill the predator's filthy, cannibalistic sexual perversion. They are nasty, selfish, arrogant, insecure, egotistical, extremely manipulative and sociopathic mutant forms of a greater evil and regardless of what anyone else says, they are an unwelcomed menace to society and one form of proof that evil does exist. There is no such thing as a "nice" child molester. The damages a sexual predator cause in the wake of alleviating their filthy indiscretion are incalculable and their victims are sometimes scarred for life in every way imaginable. If you show these monsters compassion, you may be setting yourself up to be manipulated and used as a tool to justify their evil. Because, no matter what sob story they try to force feed us, there is no excusing the fact that they *pre-meditated* their attack. This is a story about survival, determination, resilience, tragedy and triumph. It highlights both pain and passion; elevates purpose over loss; and encourages an invisible army of silent sufferers to come out from the shadows and speak out against such evil. There is hope for silent sufferers and that hope lives inside the collective power of love.

Precious memories, how they linger,

How they ever flood my soul;

In the stillness of the midnight,

Sacred secrets will unfold.

J.B.F. Wright

INTRODUCTION

I am not psychic. I am not a medium. The voice of God does not speak to me. No unseen or otherworldly entity speaks through me or tells me to do stuff. I am an educated, born-again Christian, mother and wife who has lived a bizarre life experience. This book is part of a culmination of a journey through this maze called life. It is a life defined by hurt, providence, and the unconventional; a life that sometimes feels like it began some time "between then and now," ending up somewhere "between here and there;" a life rife and scarred by bitter turmoil and the evils that men do; predictably, unpredictable; laced with unexpected twists and turns, teeming with extreme situations, eerie dreams and spiritual visions; a life lived as if I am a spirit borrowing a body. Making sense of it all has been a daunting task.

I am a medical scientist, used to viewing reactions within the confines of a test tube. I hold several clinical specialties in laboratory medicine, biopsychology and forensics. Entertaining fantasy is not one of my favorite pastimes. I love science because, for the most part, it is predicable, practical, and verifiable. Compared to science, odd dreams, visions, and other experiences I've dealt with are contradictory. But, I have come to understand that both science and the unusual coexist, verifying the existence of each other. For a long time, I tried to fuse the realities of both without success. I now understand both from its own perspective, seeing science and spirituality as two sides of the same coin. I realize that they are a dichotomy of separate and equal parts of the same reality.

I grew up in a small town on the south side of America in a place where spirituality, visions, and prophecy were accepted norms. No one explained such things. We were told to accept them. Well, I didn't want to just accept someone's opinion. I questioned everything because even as a child, I knew that bizarre experiences were not consistent with everyday life. I wanted answers. After leaving home, I searched for years trying to understand the meaning of some really weird experiences because the scientist in me needed answers. I learned some interesting revelations.

Occasionally, someone comes along and steps boldly into the spotlight of skepticism, and presents the spiritual and the unbelievable in a way that is hard to deny. A few personalities have done so with convincing certainty. Several people referred interesting authors and their writing to me such as Edgar Cayce's discourse on the Akashic Files; Dr. Maurice Rawlings' book, Beyond Death's Door; Dr. James Moody, Jr.'s book, Life After Life and Dannon Brinkley's book, Saved By the Light. Their information has confirmed some things but, I still have many questions.

My name is Suzaunna and this is my story. I was named after my paternal great-grandmother. She was not known to posses any spiritual gifts; as a matter of fact, my mother remembers her as being cold and mean-spirited. I never met her in person. She died before I was born. But I did meet her under unusual circumstances. I'll explain later. As a child, I was *different*. During infancy and childhood, I saw people who had either shadows or light surrounding them and I could see people no one else could see. Like a deja vu memory, I knew many things about my mother's family that no one had ever told me. Some of the details are sketchy and some cannot be confirmed. But based on some peculiar experiences, I felt like I knew this family and had lived with them *before* I was born. Let me explain what I mean.

I have never lived on a farm or in the country. But my mother was shocked when I described memories of walking down a country dirt road I wasn't supposed to know about, visiting a farmhouse I didn't know existed, playing with a red water pump the family had never owned, looking inside a deep water well on a farm I've supposedly never visited, sitting on a front porch shelling peas, cleaning and cutting okra, shucking corn and doing other things no one she knows had ever taught me to do.

I described how I used to sit on the concrete steps of a large house and watch members of this family slaughter cows, pigs, and chickens for food. They acted like they didn't see me and according to my grandmother, her generation had stopped slaughtering their own meat long before I was born. My mother did not teach me how to do much of anything. Like people who are born with artistic talent, I showed up in the world prepared for certain challenges of the environment. My mother still holds her breath each time I start a sentence with "I remember when…"

As for her opinion of the prebirth farm memories, "That's impossible!," she has said more often than I can remember. "You never lived on a farm! You haven't even been to a farm," she has insisted.

"Yes, I have mother," I would respond and explain in specific detail everything I remembered. One day we were having a conversation about farms and I volunteered my knowledge of canning vegetables.

"Who taught you how to can vegetables?" she asked. "I didn't."

"No mother, I said, you did not." "I don't know her name but I can describe her for you. She was short and stocky, standing only about 4'11" in height. She had dark brown, almost black skin, and piercing brown eyes. She always wore a scarf on her head, an apron wrapped around her dress, and a deep scowl on her face. She frowned a lot."

"That sounds like Mom-mom Suzaunna," my mother said.

"My great-grandmother?" I asked.

"Yes, she said, my daddy's momma." She's the one you are name after. She was a mean old lady."

"Yes," I interrupted, "I remember y'all telling me that when I was little. Does anyone have a picture of her?" I was curious.

"No," my mother said. "But you couldn't have met her. She died when I was only fifteen years old. How did you know what she looked like?"

"Well, mother," I stated, "I didn't exactly meet her in person. "Remember the old rocking chair mamma had in the kitchen? When I was about three, one day while I was sitting in it, I fell asleep and I saw Mom-mom Suzaunna in a dream. I didn't know who she was until you named her." My mother's expression changed.

"What's wrong?" I asked.

"That was mom-Suzaunna's rocking chair," she whispered. When I first heard this, a cold chill swept over me. The details of this dream are still vivid.

In the dream, Mom-Suzaunna was sitting in a rocking chair on the front porch of a farmhouse, with a large cast iron pot in her lap, brimming with shelled peas. At her feet were ears of corn and a silver tin tub filled with uncut okra and green beans. Several young women were sitting on the porch steps and around the foot of the rocking chair, but I don't remember who they were.

Mom-mom Suzaunna was teaching all of us how to shell peas, clean and cut okra, snap green beans and shuck corn. The dream takes an interesting turn, which I will talk about later. Realizing that I may have seen my great-grandmother was intriguing to me; but, for my mother, it was scary. Over the years, my mother has been put in the position of corroborating several detailed accounts of my childhood dreams and other bizarre memories, such as the one we talked about just recently.

On Easter of 2002, I asked her, "Mom, do you remember con-Toot?" I remembered con-Toot as the thin, frail dark-skinned old woman who pierced my ears.

"You remember con-Toot?" My mother almost whispered in disbelief.

"Yes, I do. She lived right across the street from your mother-in-law's house." "Right?" I inquired.

"Yeah," was all she said.

That familiar look of confusion appeared on her face, so I described the house and the events of that day. I remember that day quiet well. The house was a small, one room shack sitting atop four concrete stilts. I don't know who was with me but I remember standing on concrete steps waiting for someone to answer the door. Greeted by an unsmiling stare and the strong aroma of pipe tobacco, con-Toot appeared. She opened the door and let us in. Once inside, she picked me up and sat me on a tall chair, while patting me on the head like I was a puppy.

"Don't do that! Stop touching me!" I countered, squirming in agitation. I didn't exactly say those words, but I felt them. After I calmed down, I saw the items laid out on a small section of counter space between the sink and the stove; two small pieces of navy blue string, a sewing needle, a long piece of broom straw and a jar of Vaseline. She worked silently. Taking the sewing needle, she burned the tip of it on an open flame of her stove and cooled it by licking her forefinger and her thumb and dabbing the hot needle between them. She put a piece of blue string in the needle and stuck the needle through my ear lobes, left the string in the new hole, then rubbed my ears with Vaseline.

I didn't feel any pain. She picked up the broom straw, broke it into two small pieces, and burned the tips on the open flame. The tips of the straw were needlepoint fine. I remember seeing the molded pieces of straw with black sharp tips and yellow centers, but I don't remember how she made the tips so pointed. Anyway, she oiled the straw pieces with Vaseline, and passed them through my newly pierced ears, spinning them in circles. Speaking for the first time since we arrived, she coached whoever was with me to "spin the straw every hour for seven days to help the piercing take."

It was dark in that house. She did all of this by the light of an open flame on her gas-powered stove and a small daylight flowing window above the sink. She never smiled. The entire house was visible from the chair. It was sparsely furnished with a small table, four chairs, including the one I sat in, the stove, a rusting refrigerator, and a closed door to the left. Someone named Jackie also lived there. I saw her as she peaked at me from just over the right shoulder of con-Toot and introduced herself.

"Hello," she said, "My name is Jackie." I just looked at her and smiled. Con-Toot acted as if she didn't even hear or see her. Jackie didn't stay long but I don't know where she went. After the introduction, she disappeared. There was no one else in the room except me, con-Toot and the person who brought me there. No one walked out the front door. That was the only time I ever saw the ninety-year old, con-Toot. My mother was stunned by my recollection of details. I did go to con-Toot, she confirmed. And yes, she did pierce my ears.

"But, who told you con-Toot was ninety years old?," she inquired.

"No one. I just knew."

"Mother, who was Jackie?" I asked.

"How did you know Jackie?" she inquired.

"She introduced herself to me while I was getting my ears pierced," I stated.

"That's not possible!" My mother shot back. "Jackie was con-Toot's daughter; but she got sick and died of an illness long before you were born. Furthermore, when your ears were pierced, you were just a baby, barely a year old. There's no way you could know such things."

"Mother," I continued, "how did I know con-Toot's name?"

"I must have mentioned it in conversation," she said.

"Then who is Jackie? You've never mentioned anyone named Jackie." I was adamant. "How would I know details such as the color of the string and the other items Con-Toot used to pierce my ears? Or the contents inside the house, including the peeling tile on the floor and the smell of pipe tobacco? I didn't even know she had a daughter named after her father!" I was getting agitated.

"How did you know she was named after her daddy?," mother whispered in disbelief. "Because her daddy's name was Jack and she was named Jackie; do you remember mentioning that too?" I inquired.

"No, we didn't talk about con-Toot after she pierced your ears and she died a short time afterwards. Her husband, Jack, died before his daughter did. You were in that house only once at a young age, as a baby. But, you're not supposed to remember such things," she stood there shaking her head in disbelief. "How in the world did you remember all of that?" I think I scared my mother so much we haven't talked about that conversation again.

I didn't talk about most of these dreams and memories until I became an adult, because given the volatile nature of the environment I grew up in, no one would have believed me. My mother knew I was "different." Her own mother told her so. But she had no idea just how different I was. I didn't tell her until I was well into my thirties that these and other memories had started revealing themselves to me when I was a small child. One day, while sitting in great-grand mother's old rocking chair, scenes started unfolding like movies on a screen. At first, I thought this was normal. I was a toddler and it was fun to sit in that chair and see things happening. But some of those dreams were so bizarre, I still don't know what to make of them.

For instance, in one of those dreams I remember seeing this adult figure, who looked like me, standing in the middle of a paved road, clothed in a long white dress, looking at both Con-Toot's house and my mother's future mother-in-law's house, which were across the road from each other. The whole scene stands within the contrast of a deep shade of gray that resembled an intensely gray sky just before a rainstorm. The hue was so rich and intense that everything was illuminated in this space. Beneath this strange cloudless sky, I stood there, turning my head from side-to-side in curiosity, viewing both houses with the consciousness of an adult long before I ever entered Con-Toot's home and eons before my mother would even meet her new mother-in-law.

In addition to the dreams, cautions and predictions were constant. I saw things happening before their time, including the deaths of certain people. As an adolescent, I had documented everything in a little red diary, but that diary met a tragic end. (I'll explain this in greater detail later in this book). Several years ago, I started keeping journals of bizarre dreams and experiences. They are filled with information that is so hard to believe.

I've recorded names, addresses, phone numbers, odd places, scenes flashing as if a camera is taking pictures, crime scenes, and hauntings. Sometimes people speak to me in my dreams and confess things, disclosing information and disturbing details I don't want to know about. I've also seen lives in review. Throughout all of these experiences, a sixth sense has helped me navigate my way through inexplicable events.

I've talked with other individuals who have had a strange and overwhelming feeling that a loved-one was sick or in trouble. Some people described seeing recently deceased relatives appear to reassure the family that all is well. Others talked about having had an out-of-body experience and the impressions that experience left on them. I was amazed at how many people struggle with trying to make sense of their own unusual experiences. This is the story of my life.

After years of trying ignore these odd happenings, I have decided that my life has been what it is and I cannot change any of it. I am not an artist by any stretch of the imagination. The extent of my artistic talent starts and stops with "paint-by-numbers" pictures bought at the dollar store. However, a talented sketch artist could easily capture and breathe life into most of the details of the dreams and experiences. Trying to make sense of this has not been easy. In an attempt to distance myself from this unusual gift, I pursued a career in science. Science made sense to me; these dreams, experiences, visions, and strange memories did not. So, I embraced the concrete nature of science because it kept me grounded and gave me an escape from the acute feeling of being different.

As a scientist, I had been trained to look for objective confirmations and had convinced myself that **ALL** things must have a basis in reality in order to be accepted. However, science did not take away the experiences, it confirmed them. I was humbled by the realism that some things must be believed before they can be seen; that sometimes faith overrules reason; and fact is often stranger than fiction.

Having survived chaos, a series of tragic and horrifying circumstances, suicide attempts, and near-death experiences, I thank God that I am still alive. I was hesitant to record what happened to me after age ten because I was a victim of child abuse whose traumatic effects can distort reality. Because the unusual experiences did not stop during the abuse, for years I questioned my own sanity, even going into therapy to make sure I was not psychotic or insane because of the abuse.

A well-respected psychologist assured me that I was fine. Weathering the storms and ripple effects of shattered dreams, repulsive incest, beatings and child abuse, has made me strong. I believe it is a miracle that I didn't go insane. But, my story has its skeptics because there is an uneasy alliance between secular psychology and spirituality. With the exception of paranormal psychology, most mental health professionals would prefer to keep the details and subjective experiences of spirituality out of the therapeutic setting unless the experience negatively affects social, employment and personal functioning. As an adult, I have not been hindered by these subjective experiences. It has been suggested, however that the dreams were perhaps little more than an imaginary safety net I probably invented when I couldn't cope with stress. If so, they were some pretty powerful and accurate safety nets.

Many people have had unusual experiences and are afraid to talk about them for fear of being labeled psychologically impaired. This label is an unfair. Law enforcement officials around the country have successfully used the unnatural abilities of psychics to help solve crimes and most of the world believes in some type of spirituality. The experts will always have an opinion. I can respect that and I welcome the skepticism. If their words make sense, I will accept them. If their words are insulting, I will ignore them.

My experiences are firmly rooted in the memories of infancy and preadolescent development. Most of the details can be confirmed. But, even as I have maintained firm footing in a scientific reality, these strange occurrences stand out in deference to the practicalities of life. To have viewed both the spiritual and the scientific side-by-side, and acknowledging the accounts of other credible people, I am convinced that man is indeed a dual entity of both body and spirit.

While this physical body is not designed to completely embrace the realities of a spiritual existence, the body acts like a "wireless receiver" that intermittently shifts our attention to a spiritual presence. All of my life, I've tried to keep both feet on the ground, rooted in faith, but firmly anchored in reality. But as bizarre as it may appear, everything you will read is based on true events. I started out talking about Con-Toot and Mom-mom Suzaunna because both of these memories represent the dual nature of how situations have occurred to me. I saw Mom-mom Suzaunna in a dream; Con-Toot was a real memory-both were accurate. I don't have any special powers. I just felt it was time to leave the safety of science and share what I know with others. Something in my experiences, as in all shared experiences, may contain a message of hope that could help someone else.

CHAPTER ONE

Have you ever walked through the bayou on a full moonlit night? Croaking frogs, screeching crickets and cackling katydids create the distinct sounds of the bayou orchestra. As you catch glimpses of the moon darting in and out of view; make your way past the floating logs of alligator bodies; watch the moccasins form S-curls in the still, foggy waters; and smell the musky aroma of wet moss and algae along your traveling path; skipping along carefree and barefoot through the cool grass, when suddenly there is absolute silence.

The noise just STOPS... and a skin-crawling chill lingers in the air. You stop dead in your tracks; eyes open so wide, they hurt; and a cold sweat breaks out on your forehead. The eerie stillness dares you to move. The air is too thick to breathe; the trees are not moving; the sounds of darkness stop; and you swear something or someone just floated through the darkness, circling the stillness of the trees, right before your eyes; no doubt. This is the ambience of the bayou; mysterious, breathtaking, beautiful, paralyzing. This is a place that can toy with the imagination like a twilight zone experience. Amid the hanging gray moss, playing peekaboo with a full moon's light, you almost *expect* something odd to happen. This is the "bayou's mystique;" My birthright.

Some of the residents of the bayou are as spooky as the ambience. *There is something about their eyes.* Most of them have had experiences that would be hard for outsiders to understand. If you ask them about this, they will tell you; speaking cautiously of family curses, demon possessions, faith-healings and ghostly sightings. But you have to ask because they will not volunteer anything, especially to outsiders. These are not things "good Christian folk" discuss with just anyone. A lot remains unexplained in these parts. The elders of my community are quiet, modest people, descendants of slaves and settled nomads of the trail of tears. Many members of my family have lived past one hundred years old. The Crowe family is unique that way.

The oldest elder, uncle Walter, lived to be one hundred and fifteen years old. He died in 1989, stubborn as the day he was born, and still cloaked in his right mind only a few days after he was spotted on top of a ladder picking apples in a California grove. I don't know how he made it all the way to California. But rumor has it that he just went to sleep one night and crossed over into eternity. Some of the elders in my family were interesting that way. Back in the old days, when they got tired of living, they would just lay down and die. They had survived slavery, biting racism, and dodged lynchings; it was only fitting that they controlled a most important rhythm of their own lives. And in due time, in their time, the rhythm moved on. In my family, elders were retired ceremoniously.

The elder, at a time of their choosing, usually at age eighty or older, decides that they have worked long enough. It is time for the community to take care of them until their death. Festive preparations begin and at the start of the ceremony, the retiree is escorted to a place of honor usually in the front and center of the room, and seated in a crafted rocking chair, built by a male family member. As a seven-year-old child I was summoned to such an event; a retirement ceremony, of uncle Walter's great aunt, Taunte-Dane.

I walked through the screened door of my great-uncle Natro's house and stood frozen and speechless before this beautiful one hundred and seven-year-old female icon! Her facial tone was a beautiful combination of African and Native-American features. She had smooth bronze-colored skin, not one wrinkle in her face, the longest, blackest, silkiest hair I had ever seen; and glistening white teeth. She sat straight up in her rocking chair with her shoulders pulled back, head held high and her nose slightly tilted to the ceiling. She was absolutely regal. I felt like I was in the presence of royalty.

Every member of the family must attend the ceremony and everyone including the children is required to say something to the retiring elder as a show of respect. Somebody had to push me up to her chair. Mesmerized by the sheer brilliance of my great, great, great aunt, I approached her rocking chair, speechless. I didn't know what to say. Somehow, I managed a feeble, almost inaudible "hello." "Come, child," she commanded.

After stepping closer to her, she reached for my face with slightly trembling hands and began to trace her wrinkled and gnarled fingers down the trellis of my long pigtails. "Ah! Suzaunna. This is you child," she said.

"Yes ma'am, it's me," I answered with respect.

Then she touched my clothes. "Red, you are wearing red."

"Yes ma'am," I answered with similar reverence.

"Good," she says.

"Don't look into her eyes; don't look into her eyes!" Those words rang in my head like a bad mantra. It is disrespectful to look the elders in the eyes. I don't know why, but for some reason, I looked. "Whew!" I remember thinking. "No one noticed!" Or so I thought. I felt so bad after I looked because what I saw made me hang my head in sadness and shame. I felt like I had done something wrong. Someone pulled me aside and said, "It's Okay, Suzaunna. I saw what you did. It's not your fault; Taunte-Dane is blind. Her eyes have been this way for a long time." And with that, I was escorted out of her presence, to stand with the other children.

After asking questions about her, I learned that Taunte-Dane had lost her sight to glaucoma. Her eyes were discolored with no sign of a pupil. But, she could see colors by simply touching a piece of cloth. Taunte-Dane had also been bedridden with what they believed was cancer. Unable to do for herself, she developed bedsores so severe, they ate holes in the flesh of her back. Hospitals did not accept colored people in those days. Without treatment, she died at home surrounded by the love her family.

I remember when she died. One sunny day, as some of us stood around the bed and others prepared warm soapy water to clean the sores on her back, her eyes opened wide, she sat straight up in bed, said good-bye to everyone, laid back down, closed her eyes and died. Her rhythm moved on. That's the way I remembered it. But there was something else. The family was puzzled about something.

How did I know Dane? They all wanted to know.

"I met her at the ceremony," was all I could say during another retirement ceremony honoring my grandfather's sister.

"No, that's impossible! Dane died before you were born," my mother insisted.

"Then, who am I describing? I asked.

"Her name was Taunt-Dane." I continued. "That's what everybody at the ceremony called her. She was tall, thin and she had on a white dress."

"What you are describing is true; I just don't know how you could have been there since you weren't born yet. I was only five years old when Dane died. And as for uncle Natro's house, you've never been inside that house." My mother was thoroughly confused. So was I, but I didn't let her know that.

"Yes, I have been inside of Uncle Natro's house," I said.

"When? I never took you there," Mother insisted.

"Mother, I don't remember when I was there but, let me describe what I saw. Uncle Natro had two beautiful large reddish-brown colored dogs, Springer Spaniels named Mike and Molly. They were sitting in the front yard as I approached the steps and they lifted their heads and looked right at me. Someone opened the screened door and I walked inside the house. Taunt-Dane was sitting in the center of the room in a light-oak colored rocking chair.

The living room was to the left where the men were; around the corner from the living room was Taunte-Dane's bedroom; the dining room table was directly behind her, in the center of the room and the dining room semi-circled into the kitchen where all the women were standing. There was a lot of food in the kitchen. The children were lined against a back door that led to a screened-in back porch, whose concrete steps led to a backyard that had a clothesline in it. Uncle Natro's wife and several other people I did not recognize were also there. Did I leave anything out?"

She was speechless. My description of the house, the ceremony, Dane, and even the dogs were accurate. But it all happened when my mother was just a toddler. This was confusing to me. I couldn't understand how I knew such things. How could I have lived in this time and space before my own birth? It was an eerie thought.

There were memories I tried to keep to myself because I could not explain them or understand how I knew certain things. I needed answers. But, there were none. No one could explain what was happening to me. Beginning at age three, from the seat of my great-grandmother's old rocking chair, one-by-one, the memories revealed themselves. I always knew when a dream was about to happen. As soon as I would sit in the rocking chair, the room would start spinning and I would "zone out." I guess everybody thought I was sleeping. This next memory is as haunting as all the others.

Seated in the old rocking chair one day, I dreamed that I was walking down a concrete sidewalk, which led up to the steps of a hospital. The driveway was made up of large smooth, colorful gravel rocks. Around back, amid a piercing blue sky, stood a huge magnolia tree, bold and beautiful in the middle of a well-manicured, grass-covered courtyard. Rays of the sun flowed through its leaves, creating a halo around its foliage. It was a beautiful day. I was a child wearing a white dress. Someone was holding my right hand and I don't remember whom. We walked past the tree and up three gray-discolored wooden steps and entered through the right side of the double doors of the hospital.

The paste-colored speckled floor and green walls were shiny and clean. There was a smoky haze swirling inside a strange tunnel of light, up and down a long hallway and a low, steady, humming sound coming from somewhere. I heard many voices and sounds, but didn't see any people... not at first. But then, out of nowhere, a tall, stocky white nurse wearing a white dress, white shoes, white panty hose and a pointed white hat, came careening around a corner right toward us. She was in a big hurry! She may have seen us because she scooted over to one side of the hallway like she was trying not to bump into us, holding on to her hat like it was going to fly off.

At the same time she was headed for us, I heard the shrill of screeching tires and the distinct sounds of a violent car crash, just outside a window to my left; and suddenly, several people came running down the hallway headed right for us. A tall white man with black-framed glasses wearing a white physician's coat and several other people dressed in hospital clothes followed closely behind him; while yet another, much thinner nurse was pushing a wheelchair in front of her, like she was trying to get to someone. We did not have time to get out of the way! It didn't matter; all of them went right *through* us. I could hear a lot of commotion, but couldn't make out a single word.

Suddenly, there was silence. Still holding the hand of someone who is to my right, I get an eerie feeling,...like I'm being watched. Then I saw him. Off to my left, parked against the wall, beneath the window, sitting in a wheelchair, was a little white male child of about six years old. He was frightening to look at. He had a lot of blood in his sandy brown hair. His forehead had a big hole in it, a large cracked opening that was dripping blood everywhere. His face and neck were scraped and dirty, liked he'd been dragged and his nose was bleeding profusely.

One of his hands was mangled and the sheet that covered him from the chest down was drenched in blood where his legs were supposed to be. Just beneath the sheets, I noticed that both of his legs had been ripped from his body below the knees, leaving only dangling shreds of torn flesh. He was pale, his eyes were sunken, but wide open, and both lips were cut and swollen. He was staring right at me. I felt so sorry for him. We stared at each other until I disappeared into that swirling circle of light at the end of the hallway. I don't know who he was.

During a conversation about medicine one day, I inquired innocently about the hospital I saw in the dream. I was shocked by what my mother told me. I had dreamed that I visited a hospital where my mother said at age seventeen, she had tried to get a job as a nurse's aide. She had also worked there for a month as a cook. She said she has never taken me to that hospital and I was too young to even remember when it was torn down. On a visit back home, I took her to the exact location where the hospital used to be. She has confirmed the details of the hospital and the courtyard as I remembered them, but remains confused about how I knew the things I did.

When I first started talking about these memories, I was engaged in a conversation with relatives. They were not spoken of in the context of a sudden memory; I was contributing to the conversation as one who was a living part of each situation; much like having a conversation about the current weather. Imagine my own shock and surprise when relatives told me that my presence during those times was impossible because I was not even an actual human being. I had not been born yet. Mother was five years old when Taunte-Dane died and seventeen when she sought a job at the hospital.

I was not born until she turned twenty years old. The hospital was torn down a few years after I was born. The oldest of my three younger brothers was born in that hospital. I didn't know that detail until my mother told me. But all the other details I shared about the hospital building were accurate. These memories and many others like them are hardwired into my brain, playing over and over again like movie reviews. The details I remember are astounding to me; I just wish I knew *how* and *why* I know such things.

CHAPTER TWO

There were two types of religious people in my community. There were those who faced spirituality with faith and confidence. These were the faith healers, prayer warriors, and ministers who conversed with God as if speaking to a friend which they tried to teach others to do. Elders too far along in years to be trifling explained the bible with words of wisdom. They often spoke with patience and compassion. They had a calming effect on people and were good listeners.

And then there were the "church people." From as far back as my childhood days will take me, inside the old Saint James Baptist Community Church, I watched in amazement as the minister yelled his sermon at the congregation; coughing, and hacking like he was choking on something; jumping, running in circles, even tap-dancing in jubilation, waving his hands over his head; screaming at this unseen power; yelling, demanding and commanding Him to do stuff. The sermon resembled an entertaining minstrel show.

There was always intense passion in the minister's voice; but it seemed to solicit the kind of call-and-response from the congregation that one would expect to hear at a rap concert. But, something curious usually happened. As soon as the hooping and hollering stopped, so did the cheering and excitement; as if there was nothing else to be excited about. I used to wonder what happened to the spirit? Why did the people stop cheering? These were the ones I called the "church people."

They were always quick to talk about God but never willing to discuss the reality of the spirit. I had an inquisitive mind that extended beyond the boundaries of the bible and the pulpit. I wanted someone to tell me what my dreams meant. I wanted to know where was God when life hurt? What happens to evil people? What happens when we die? The church people

7

were the loudest voices in the church and seemed to know a lot. But as a child, when I asked these questions to the church people I was told to "pray about it." But more questions emerged. Pray to whom? To what? What does God look like? How will I know when he is speaking to me? The more questions I asked the more confused I became.

Sometimes I found myself praying to this mysterious, formless entity, an invention I made up in my own mind called God who presented as more of a "genie in a bottle" than anything else. It was confusing. There had to be more to God than this. I didn't want a God I could control and the church people seemed all too eager to maintain control over this unseen force by avoiding any real discussions beyond their dogmatic rhetoric. They would say stuff like, "You can't question God, it's a sin." "God don't want you to know what he looks like; it's not important." "Evil people go to heaven just like everybody else." "You ask too many questions." This one was my favorite. "It's not for you to know."

None of them ever said, "I don't know." They were impatient and made up answers. I felt like a nuisance around them, so I shied away from talking to them. The quiet elders admitted they did not have all the answers, but always offered words of encouragement. After a while, I gave up asking spiritual questions and resigned to being an observer. And whether it was a church revival with visiting ministers or the local preacher, they all continued to scream their requests at God.

I used to think that maybe God was deaf or heaven was so far away we had to shout to be heard. GOD!, they would shout, scaring me out of my skin, YOU NEED TO COME DOWN HERE AND DELIVER US! Or GOD, YOU NEED TO HEAL THIS PERSON RIGHT NOW! Or the more infamous, GOD, TOUCH THEM! TOUCH ME! MAKE YOUR PRESENCE KNOWN TO US SO WE CAN WORSHIP YOU!

I think if something out of the ordinary did happen, these loud mouth ministers would be the first ones leading the stampede out of the building! Sometimes even today, sitting in church, when I see and hear such things, fighting the urge to cover my ears to reduce the noise, I shake my head in confusion and sorrow. I wish I could ask these people, especially so-called prayer leaders and some ministers, "WHO ARE YOU YELLING AT?"

I thought God was a peaceful, loving spirit who loves to converse with humanity, specifically through thoughtful prayer. I understand prayer as a quiet conversation whether personal or intercessory. Did I misinterpret that part? If not, then somebody please explain, WHY ARE THEY YELLING AT GOD?! SCREAMING, DEMANDING, and INSISTING that he obeys what they command? Where is the respect?

No one likes to be yelled at and from what I understand, God is close enough to hear thoughts and whispers. Praying in public is not for me, because there is something genuine about the privacy of the moment. But to the ordained whose job it is to pray and preach, why do some of you yell so much? I was told by the elders and discovered for myself that on a personal level, we can all converse with God the same way we talk to a close friend and that this is the key to respecting what He has to say. I believe they were right.

Maybe these religious people yelled so much because having a heartfelt conversation with God is risky. "You're only as sick as your secrets," the elders used to say. "Loud noise drowns out secrets we don't want known." "People yell," they'd say, "because they don't want you to hear what they're not saying." I thought they made a good point. We live with pain, anguish, confusion, and disappointment in our daily lives. Frustration boils over when prayers go unanswered and patience wears thin. We don't like to suffer. So the path of least resistance is to scream at the one power we hold responsible for both good and evil and demand intervention.

In this defining moment comes the realization that no one controls God. We cannot tell him what to do and yelling commands won't hasten a response. This is a helpless feeling. Most of the time, in the midst of the screaming and complaining, we forget to mention how our own choices may have brought us to the place we now find ourselves in. We don't always want to accept personal responsibility for the self-made predicaments that often complicate our lives, myself included.

But, someday the personal spirit that lives in all of us will have some explaining to do. We will have to answer to hidden deeds. Those loud mouth ministers and the church people never mentioned anything like this. This is what the elders meant when they told me to listen for what is not being said. I had to learn for myself that there is no need to scream and yell at God. To get his attention, all that is required is honest and sincere prayer.

When I watched the screaming minstrel shows that went on in the pulpit; people shouting phony praises at this distorted figment of imagination on Sunday and cursing one another out the other six days of the week; church people hiding behind layers of compressed pain and insincere prayer, demanding to be forgiven for things they had already judged unforgivable in someone else; I concluded that maintaining a personal relationship with this awesome spirit, this powerful God who transforms from within, even if it means seeing my secret, not-so-pretty side, was a good thing. This is a spiritual transformation; a choice to change from within; where the heart is; where the soul lives; in the spirit, where God is best understood.

It takes significant effort to rise above the "noise" of hypocrisy, complacency, spiritual indifference, and Christian fear, including my own, to see that what most of us want is inner peace. But I learned the hard way that winning inner peace will cost you your inner pain. The elders laid the foundation for my understanding of peace. I gravitated toward these humble souls of the church community because church people and loud mouth ministers were scary.

To my impressionable mind, they made God appear scary and distant. From age eleven to seventeen, my life was anything but peaceful. Having to struggle against the fiendish cruelty of a predatory personality, peace was so elusive that many times I wanted to curse God and die because he wouldn't come to my rescue. When I needed Him most and didn't know how to find Him, gently spoken words of wisdom, coming from the quiet ones, were sometimes all the hope I had to hold on to.

Like so many others, I've lived through some ominous moments. There were days when I would lash out, enraged that such a powerful presence would leave me vulnerable to resident evil. At times I gave up on hope and life, weighted down by despondency so heavy, it hurt to breathe. I have approached this mysterious entity we call God, broken in body and spirit, crawling on hands and knees, crying out in confusion, begging to know "*why must life be so painful.*" Somewhere during the struggle, the reality of a spirit got lost in my search for peace and understanding. And this was the reality I needed to know more about.

From the deepest depths of despair, when the walls surrounding me were slippery with tears and there was no way out except to find strength from within, I had to learn the value of reliance on the spirit. The realization of believing something before it can be seen became undeniable when I had to acknowledge that something greater than a physical body sustained me during my darkest hours. In the physical helplessness of the moment, when I cried out from the personal depths within, my soul's desire found its God. In order to survive the wicked crimes of a predatory personality, I leaned hardest on the strongest part of my being, my spirit, which could withstand such ruthless pressure.

During these times, I learned some valuable lessons. I understand now that when a broken body can't stand on its own, the spirit holds it together. When tired, overburdened shoulders give under the weight of grief and turmoil, the spirit nurtures all life. That unseen virtue of power, the spirit, cannot be bought or sold. Reliance on the spirit brings chaos into clear focus. Your personal spirit holds you together when your world starts falling apart. It is our spirit that moves mountains, heals open wounds, fills empty voids, mends broken hearts, and destroys all evil menace. This is the greatest part of us that connects with the most powerful virtue of what God is. God is spirit.

At some critical times in my life, I chose to ignore this strength and that choice almost cost me my life. But in my search to reestablish a firm foundation, the words of those humble, faithful souls provided the wisdom for my faith. They uttered simple phrases like "hold on" and "troubles don't last always" which had a powerful effect on my agonized soul. It is because of them and the spirit that God is, I understand a very important proverb: what happens *to* a person is not as significant as what happens *inside* them.

Their wisdom has carried me through this journey called life. I believe the spirit of God was there all along, throughout my childhood, speaking to me through the peaceful centers of those elders who chose to personalize His message of love. As for those loud mouth ministers and the "church people," well… they just scared me.

Spiritual things scare people, too. It's like death; you don't talk about it; just accept it; and let it be. But, stuff that other people considered bizarre was a natural occurrence to the elders of my community. The bayou mystique is stubborn about revealing her secrets; and as I discovered, some secrets are healings in disguise. In this closed community, nurtured by the wisdom of the quiet elders, spirituality and divine ordination merged with ease.

They believed in the Bible, King James Version, but were neither Jesus-freaks nor religious zealots who stomped around provoking angry rattlesnakes, knocking people out with laying on of hands, or casting judgments of damnation. They were more sensible and wisely merged God with common sense. They didn't know how special they were. For many years after the abolition of slavery, few residents left the community. I don't know how uncle Walter ended up in California.

There were some deeply rooted fears. For instance, pursuing a college education was acceptable, but not encouraged. It was believed, at one time that leaving the sanctity of the community would result in you "forgetting where you came from" or worse, you may never come back. You see, being only a few generations removed from slavery, restricted mobility had become deeply rooted in the culture. Black folk were not encouraged to stray far from home; slavery had embedded in the minds of the elders that it was too dangerous. So for generations, the children were encouraged to stay close to home.

Elders made it mandatory that we graduate from the local high school, but for a while, employment prospects were often limited to landing a job working as a field hand picking cotton, yams, sugarcane and other produce. Until 1974, white men would drive rusted out school buses and old pickup trucks displaying the confederate flag somewhere on the vehicle, into suburban black neighborhoods, picking up workers for the fields.

Some of the children they picked up were as young as ten years old. Old habits died hard. As the years went by, employment opportunities expanded. The young women were encouraged to work as maids in white folk houses or grocery store cashiers at the local grocery store; and the young men sought employment as a janitor at one of the local schools or factory worker at the local tire-making plant. With the average all brick, 3-bedroom, 2 baths, home priced at only $10,000.00, all of these jobs supported a modest living. We had our poor, but there was no poverty. When families could not do for one another or themselves, the church stepped in.

For almost my entire childhood, the community was segregated. As a matter of fact, the whole town had clear territorial boundaries defined by the town railroad track. Whites lived on one side of the train tracks and blacks lived on the other. We even had separate swimming pools and recreational facilities. Except for two modest black-owned, grocery stores, one of which was owned by my mother and her husband, everybody shopped either on the town's main street or on the white side of town where most of the banks, clothing stores and boutiques were.

Voting was a hard fought battle for the people of my community. Strange stories of intimidation abounded. It was legal, but discouraged. Even for those brave souls who boldly exercised their right to vote, the process was often ridiculed as a waste of time. Once again, from the seat of the old rocking chair, I remember one particular daydream experience where I was sitting between at least five people in the front seat of someone's old pickup truck, being driven deep into a bayou marsh. I could see gray moss hanging from the trees as the truck passed beneath them. I was too short to see over the dashboard, but I could smell the bayou. When the truck stopped, everybody piled out facing a small wooden, well-lit, square building that was sitting in mud atop some square concrete stilts.

We had to walk in dark-colored mud to get to the building. It sat so high off the ground, we had to climb concrete steps to get inside. Someone is holding my hand leading me up the stairs into the building. The building didn't have a door. It had a cutout entrance that spilled onto a muddy, unstained, faded wooden floor. As we are walking up the steps, to my right stood a fat, hairy white man wearing blue overalls and no shirt, holding a rifle in his hand, like he was guarding the door.

I stood off to the left side of the entrance and made an intriguing observation. When Black people walked in through the door, a white man carrying a rifle in his right hand, would come up to him or her, put his left hand on a shoulder and walk with them over to a box which sat on a funny-looking table that leaned forward on shiny, silver, skinny legs. There were at least four of these funny-looking tables separated by a curtain.

The white man would point to something on a piece of paper, whisper into the black person's ear and the black person would write something in that space. After a Black person finished writing where he or she was told, the white man gave him or her some money and escorted them out of the building. I didn't know this at the time, but they were sabotaging the voting process. For the brave souls who showed up to exercise their right to vote, it was indeed an exercise in futility. I didn't give this dream much thought until many years later.

One evening the church sponsored a debutante ball, which was being held in a building in a nearby bayou town. As my mother turned down a dirt road surrounded by swamplands and bayou moss trees, I got an eerie feeling that I had visited this place before. As soon as she drove up to the building, I recognized it immediately.

"This used to be a voting place," I said to her. "People used to come here to vote."

"Yeah, we used to vote here. But, how did *you* know that?" She asked. "You've never been here before."

"Yes, I have." I countered with a bruised adolescent ego. "I remember seeing black people come in and out of here while these mean-looking white men holding shotguns and rifles stood over them while they voted and then escorted them out of the building. One of them acted like a guard at the door."

I was speaking so fast, I could hardly catch my breath. Walking toward the building, which now had a door, I walked up those familiar concrete steps, stepped inside and I felt like I had drifted back in time.

"Suzaunna, slow down! How did you get way out here without me knowing about it? Did someone bring you here?" She had a concerned look on her face.

"No. I mean yes, I mean…I don't know how I got here. I just know I've been here before. Look, I'll even show you where the voting booths and the curtains were."

Now I was getting scared. I didn't know how to explain how a twelve-year-old girl ended up 30 miles away from home at a voting place, deep inside the bayou, several years earlier. There was no way to explain that. I just needed to find something; some type of proof that I was telling the truth, because now the other girls and my cousin were all staring at me like I was some kind of freak and it was making me uneasy.

"Look! Look at the ceiling! That's where the curtains were!" I thought I had vindicated myself. The hooks where the curtain had hung were still intact. But my mother was not impressed.

"That still does not explain how you got here." She said.

I just shrugged my shoulders, shut my mouth and sat down at a table with the other girls, feeling confused.

I don't know how I got there. I don't know whose truck I was in; I don't remember who was in the truck with me. I don't even remember who the driver was. The more I thought about it, I realized that except for the person who was holding my hand, no one was in charge of me during that time; I wandered about watching everything and everybody, uninterrupted and unnoticed. Nobody questioned me or approached me; like they didn't even see me.

"Did you really see this place before, like you said?" One of the other girls inquired. "Leave her alone. She's weird." Those were the caustic words of a rival cousin. "Shut up!" I shot back rolling my eyes at her till they hurt. We didn't like each other; so she was enjoying this moment. "No." I directed my attention to the inquiring mind. "I probably just dreamed it all up." And with that, I ended the conversation. I just wanted this moment to go away. After that, I never told anyone about my dreams; I wrote them down in my diary instead.

CHAPTER THREE

There were many entries in my diary. For example, this next entry stands out as the most bizarre of them all. I remember this dream as if it occurred yesterday. Wrapped in the security of an old rocking chair, I drifted into what looked like a cold day. There was ice and frost on the ground. In the dream, I was an adult, staring at a small shed with a shiny tin roof. It stood only about 10 yards away from a large willow tree. It was nighttime; the stars were glowing. I looked at this structure with interest because I had never seen one before. As I stared at the front of it, I noticed a silver handle on the door and a wooden latch that kept the door closed.

I think to myself, "I wonder what's in here?" And with only a thought,…I am inside. There is a hole in the middle of this structure. And there are worms crawling around inside the hole. That was a disgusting sight. I think, "I want to get out of here"…and again, with only a thought,…I am out of the structure. But as I gazed at the front of it, trying to make sense of my surroundings, a daytime scenery appears to my right, just above the roof, and I am watching a tall black man use a shovel to dig a hole at the place I exist. I watched him saw and cut and nail wood together to make the walls of this building.

I watched him and other men lift and place the walls of this building over a wooden seat where the hole is. Then another scene appears, to my left. It is still daytime, but close to sunset. A large truck with an enormous flatbed is backing up into the yard, carrying a house. The house is placed on concrete blocks and the truck drives away. The porch of the house is facing the little building I am next to. I exist beneath a nighttime, star-lit sky; yet, the scenes are happening in daylight. I can see both day and night at the same time. Within the nighttime scene, a little girl of about 8 years old runs out to the small building in a big hurry. The thought occured to me. "I *know* her." Indeed, I did. She was my mother.

Passages like this one can paralyze an open-minded, logical thinker. One can almost hear the obvious question, **"what do you mean she was your mother?"** If I could explain "how" I knew, I would. Therein lies the mystery. So much is credited to the "deja vu" mystique; that mysterious aura of having that "I've-been-here-before" or "I've-seen-this-before" feeling. No hard evidence exists to support the claim; just that irrefutable nagging feeling of confirmation that is hard to ignore. I felt fully conscious, mature, almost divine, as I watched this little girl, my mother, run toward the outhouse.

I can recall several significant events that speak to an unusual nature. I was a strange child. I was the infant who rarely cried; the toddler with an incredible memory; the child who stood off from the crowd. Always the observer, a child of few words, I watched people all the time and wondered about their behaviors. Humans fascinated me and between the ages of two and ten, I would look at other humans as if I were a visitor in a strange world.

One of my earliest memories is laying on a bed as an infant, staring up at several faces that were staring down at me. I had an adult-like awareness that is hard to explain. A tradition in our family was that if you visited someone who had just given birth, everyone who sees or holds the newborn baby for the first time, must put a piece of string from their clothing inside the infant's undershirt, so it touches the body. This ritual was believed to keep the infant from getting colic. I did not like some of these people touching me. Some of these people were bad. They had swirling, dark smoky shadows surrounding them and a "bad" look in their eyes; but a brilliant light surrounded the others.

I have always been aware of a strange dual existence. While living this physical life, I have vivid memories of a spiritual one. Sometimes the two worlds collide. This is the weirdest feeling. As a small child, I took an old JC Penney catalog and some blunted school scissors, sat in a corner of my mother's small apartment house, beneath portraits of John F. Kennedy and the "white Jesus" and began cutting out and creating my own paper doll families complete with pets, home appliances and wardrobes, many years before I would even play with real paper dolls.

My grandmother would just look at me and shake her head. I watched her point to me sometimes and say to my mother, "that one is different." I waded through life in a haze and *felt different* all the time; like I didn't belong here...in *this* world. Day-to-day living in my little community was marked by strange happenings, unexplained events and unusual sightings and I absorbed all of it as if it were normal. As a toddler, I saw things that were supposed to scare me, but they didn't. Instead, I was intrigued; fascinated by the events in this world. There were plenty of situations to hold my interest.

For most of the 1960's, the people in my community rarely went to hospitals. Growing up in the rural south during that time, the hospital "no coloreds" sign was still the psychological norm in these parts. Therefore, when we got sick, we went to a faith healer. These were people believed to have extraordinary powers of healing the sick just by "laying hands" on them while praying for them to be healed. In 1968, at age four, I contracted a severe case of round worms.

These parasites (superstitiously) believed to be the result of eating too much candy, had gotten so bad in my system, my mother would literally pull some of these creatures out of my rectum with her hand and I can remember watching them wiggle and squirm in the toilet. (I probably got them from eating improperly cooked infested meat). I don't remember experiencing too much pain, but my mother knew I needed medical attention.

Going to a medical doctor was not an option. My grandmother worked for a doctor as a housekeeper and baby-sitter; but for some reason, he was not an option either. So my mother took me to see Con-Gwin, one of the most powerful faith healers in the community. We were greeted at the screened door by a stocky young black woman, with mysterious eyes, whose name I don't remember. Someone told me this was Con-Gwin's adopted daughter. When we walked in, she was sitting in a small-overstuffed chair facing the door. Con-Gwin had thick white, woolly hair and powerful gray eyes with a penetrating stare. She looked at you as if she could see inside you.

When we walked into her home, there was a feeling of power and omnipotence, and she was greatly respected within the community. Once inside, my mother greeted her. She nodded and simply said, "Give me the child" as if she already knew which one of us was sick. My mother placed me in con-Gwin's lap and I noticed the younger woman backing up into the shadows, as if trying to stay out of sight. Con-Gwin raised her right hand to silence my mother from saying anything, closed her eyes and began to pray. She touched my belly and then moved her hand as if she had been bitten. She stopped praying and motioned for the young woman to give her a ball of string that was in a basket on the floor.

After cutting a length of string from the ball with her teeth, she began wrapping segments of the string around her finger, rubbing the string against my bare belly and praying while I watched the segments turn into knots, without losing contact with my skin. I heard her pray for a "binding" of the evil that was making me sick. She made seven knots (that's what she told my mother) in that string and then put it around my neck, tying the two loose ends together, praying without ceasing. After she ended her prayer, I violated that rule in our culture, again. Children are never to look the elders in the eyes; it is considered disrespectful.

I am not sure why I did it, but I looked Con-Gwin right in the eyes. She smiled at me; but then the power in her eyes shifted and I saw moving white clouds, blue skies, and other things I have a hard time describing. Some people say the eyes are the windows to the soul. If this is true, then I saw something I can't explain. I do remember at the moment I looked into her eyes, something from within her eyes took hold of me and; I suddenly lurched forward, feeling like I had been punched in the chest with a sharp object; my small frame jerked forward and I settled back with a Thud! Then…silence and calm. Maybe this was just part of the healing process. My mother must have figured as much; she did not intervene.

Something had just happened to me; I *felt* it but I didn't know what *it* was. I think I received more than a healing from round worms that day. The young woman stood off in a corner of the room, in the shadows, almost out of sight, watching everything, during the whole session and came out when it was time for us to leave. My mother had told me that Con-Gwin did not touch money. She didn't like the way it felt. So, all of her customers put their money in a crystal glass ashtray where the young woman would pick it up, wave her right hand over the paper, brush it off like it was dirty, fold it in half and put the money in a change purse.

Just before we left, Con-Gwin told my mother "Do not remove the string; it will fall off by itself in seven days and she will be healed." That's exactly what happened. My mother did not explain to Con-Gwin why we were there. Con-Gwin just knew. Her powers were legendary. Poor eyesight, severe pain, headaches, muscle aches, no matter what you brought to her, she could heal it. Her gift made her the most respected faith healer in the community. I don't know how old she was when she died. But to this day, my experience with her has remained my most compelling testimony to the power of healing.

Soon after this experience, I was sitting in the old rocking chair when I had this unusual dream. Within the backdrop of a familiar, intensely gray sky that enhanced and illuminated everything else, I am an adult dressed in a brilliant white dress and standing on the concrete driveway of a green house with dark colored bricks. The house faces a major highway. Across the highway are acres of open field. There is an eerie stillness in this place.

When I turn to face the house, someone approaches from my right and walks pass me.

She looked like an older version of the child in the rocking chair. The young adolescent female walks across the driveway and steps into the well-landscaped, grass-covered front yard of the house. As soon as she does, a huge, dark, menacing figure bolts through the front door, onto the lawn, gets right up on her as if he is going to hit her and confronts the quiet stranger.

"What do you want?" he snarls. "Get out of this place!" "We don't want you here!"

"I'm just passing through," she said very gently. "I won't be staying."

"Then leave now!" the sinister figure shouted. "We don't want your kind here!"

"I told you, I am just passing through." She was patient with this hostile existence. "I shall not pass this way again," she warned.

"Get out!" he muttered through clenched teeth.

She stares deep into his vicious green eyes and finds no light in him-only darkness. "There are others here," she stated. "Where are the others?"

"You cannot have them," this time he growled. "They belong to me."

"No, they belong to someone else," she stated firmly. "You know of whom I speak. I will go now. It is time. But like the dust of the earth, this too shall pass."

The stranger moves on, walking through the front yard, and does not look back. She disappears into a circle of light. The dark, angry figure watches her walk away and fades back inside the house. All is quiet again. I awaken to the smell of frying bacon.

CHAPTER FOUR

My grandmother's house was a virtual playground. The rooms were huge, the hallways had many twists and turns; but the old rocking chair in the kitchen was my favorite space. My great-grandmother's rocking chair was big, warm, and secure. It was fun to sit in because I could see all kinds of things when I climbed inside. As far back as I can remember I always dreamed about something every time I sat in that chair. I always knew when a dream was about to happen because the room would start spinning, I would get dizzy and just pass out, but always stayed fully conscious and aware of everything.

Sitting in that chair one day, I zoned out and found myself in a bedroom staring at a hole in the ceiling and being able to see inside an attic without stepping one foot up there. I could see right through to the tin roof ceiling. When I did get inside, with only a thought,...I found myself staring at rays of sunlight streaking through holes in the tin roof, competing with floating dust particles for attention. The attic had lots of neat stuff in it.

Trunks filled with clothes and jewelry were wide open, ready for curious little hands; and a three-piece crushed red velvet Victorian living room furniture set collected cobwebs in one corner of the attic. It was dusty up there. I don't remember how old I was; but I felt much older and more mature than the child who loved to sit in that chair. I used to play hide-and-seek in the house, by myself, crawling underneath enormous solid steel bed frames and sinking into the deepest, darkest corner. Or I would be a busybody, foraging through the pine-scented, chef faros, playing dress up with pearl necklaces, gaudy clip-on earrings and church hats. Strange how I usually walked around the house unchallenged and unnoticed by everyone; ...like I wasn't supposed to be there yet.

The house had an eerie feel to it; like we'd met before. I knew a lot about this house without anyone ever telling me about its history. I knew where the house used to be before it was moved to the city. Nobody had to tell me. The house was originally located deep inside the woods, surrounded by tall tress and shrubs and not visible from the dirt road that wound in front of it.

I believe it was originally built for someone else, because, in another dream, I remember standing outside the house, staring way up toward the roof; not as a child, but as an adult draped in a glowing white dress that flowed in a nondescript wind. The house was surrounded by darkness, the window trims on the house were painted white and the rest of the house was a pale gray. Everything glowed against the looming darkness. There was a loud humming sound coming from somewhere. I began moving toward the house. Before I entered, I looked around at the trees that surrounded it. But then scenes started shifting in a "then-and-now" kind of way.

I saw that the lawn would eventually become the new backyard of its future resting place. An L-shaped vegetable garden in the far back and right hand corner of the yard flourished with green peppers, red peppers, tomatoes, green onions, cabbage and tall stalks of corn. The garden ended with stalks of corn growing several feet near the willow tree. I turned and entered the house by walking "through" a screened in porch and notice an old white washing machine sitting off to the right. It looked out of place.

Inside the house, White Victorian-laced linens lined the glass paned cabinets with a toy-like tea set on display but quickly became glass-pained cabinets housing common plates and glasses. Two kerosene lamps were sitting on the cabinets, but one of them quickly became a silver meat grinder. The floor was tiled with a floral pattern of pink and white flowers and there was a large rocking chair in the middle of the kitchen floor. There was also a large black furnace with burning wood and flames inside at the rear of the house; but not in any particular room. There was a fireplace in the room next to the kitchen, with a sitting stool and two chairs.

At the back of the house, was a large bedroom that had two beds and a light oak colored, vanity with a large mirror on it, a large pink and white flower painted above the mirror, and no pictures on the walls. As I wandered through that house, looking around, examining every room, a woman appeared. I saw her leaning against a doorpost, in the room with the wooden vanity, staring at me. I had first seen her in the kitchen, but she vanished when I looked at her.

Here she was again, standing in the doorway of the room with the vanity inside. She looked like she was about 21 years old and was wearing a low-cut, long Victorian style dress with lots of lace and satin frills on it. It was one of those dresses that ballooned out on the bottom like an opened umbrella. She had dark brown or black wavy hair that was pinned up and back in a bun as independent strings of wavy hair flowed against her shoulders.

She was pale and had a painful expression on her face…and she was transparent. We stared at each other for a moment; but I turned away and continued studying the house. She followed me but didn't speak. She just watched me. I awakened sitting in the old rocking chair, motionless, eyes wide open, staring into space. This dream like all the others, was so vivid, it felt more like a memory than a dream.

When I was not sitting in the chair, I was foraging around looking for stuff to get into. But, there was one particular room that was eerie. It was the same room I had seen in my dream; the same room with the transparent young woman and the vanity in it. Even if my grandmother was around, I avoided going in that room. Something was uninviting and unnerving about it. I stood in its doorway one day with my fingers locked behind my back, rocking back and forth heel-to-toe saying to myself, "I've been in this room before; it's always so cold in here. I don't like this room." Peeking around the doorway, I wondered, "Where is the pale woman in the big dress?"

Even my mother insisted that as a child, she felt a presence in this room, like it was haunted. I used to stand in its doorway and just stare inside. One time while staring inside this room, I saw a group of about five black people, all dressed in church clothes, standing between the two beds, near a back wall of the room talking to one another. But something was wrong with them.

I could see right *through* them; these were *ghostly figures*. Their lips were moving; but, I couldn't hear what they were saying. One of them, a woman, noticed me standing in the doorway. She turned her head toward me in a creepy gesture, stared for a moment and then resumed her ghostly fellowship with the others. I found out later that part of my grandmother's house, a section of the kitchen, was used as a funeral parlor before it was moved from the country to the city.

Many families had wakes in this house, where families and friends would put a relative in a pine coffin box and sit up with a dead relative overnight to see if the person would "wake up." If they did not wake up, they were buried. I think some of these spirits stayed in the house. The old rocking chair sat near the spot where many coffins were placed.

The year was 1967 and I was three years old. This time I wasn't in the rocking chair. I was just wandering around the house. Upon hearing a lot of commotion just beyond the door of the creepy room that led to a porch and a backyard, I stepped inside the room, and stared out the window pained door. Chills crept across my arms. "It's so cold in here," I thought. I was drawn toward the commotion.

Neighbors across the street, Ms. Risa and her son Carlton were arguing. She was standing in the doorway yelling at him. "Carlton, come in de house…rat now! Put dat gun down an come in de house! Carlton, you hear me tawkin' to you?" She started screaming at him.

"No! I'm not comin in. I need some money. I'm not comin in." Carlton was serious.

Somebody had called the police and two officers arrived with blaring sirens, to find Carlton waving a handgun in the air and threatening to shoot himself.

"Get away from me or I'll shoot myself!" "Get away from me, now!" The whole time he is waving the gun in the air.

"Sir, please put the gun down." The police tried to reason with him, as they barricaded themselves behind their car doors.

"No! Don't come near me or I'll shoot myself!" That would be Carlton's last warning to them. When one of the police officers motioned toward him, he put the gun to his side and pulled the trigger. POW! And shot himself in the right side. "Get away from me! Don't come near me! I'll shoot myself again," he warned. He started staggering and bleeding profusely.

"Suzaunna, Get away from the window! NOW!" My grandmother was screaming at me. "Get away from that door!" she yelled. My teeth were grinding uncontrollably and I stood petrified, unable to move. Every part of my little body shook when I heard that gun go off. It was terrifying to see this man shoot himself. He was still standing, bleeding from his side, waving the gun in the air, while the two police officers shielded themselves behind their car doors and pointed their guns at him. Everything started happening in slow motion as Carlton lifted the gun to his head.

"No! Don't! I heard a desperate whisper rise from deep inside of myself.

"Get away!" Carlton was shouting at the police. "Get away from me!" POW!

I shut my eyes tight, turned away from the window, and bolted out of that room, feeling my way against the walls, tripping over the two sewing machines in the hallway, almost knocking myself out and slid, headfirst, beneath a large brass bed in another room. I sat there out of breath, with my eyes shut tight, arms hugging my knees, moaning, trembling and shaking, rocking back and forth.

In all the commotion, I forgot that I had been standing in the "creepy" room. I had to make sense of this horrible scene. "It was that room," I reasoned. "Something in that room made him do that to himself." I think someone coaxed me out from under the bed with the promise of ice cream. I never went back in there alone nor did I ever find out what became of Carlton.

On another day, I climbed inside the chair and "zoned out." I saw myself standing in the doorway of that creepy room, wearing a familiar gray dress that had red plaid, white lace-trimmed collars. My arms were folded behind my back and I was rocking back and forth on the toes and heels of a pair of shiny patent leather loafers, looking at that tall man, wondering why was he laying on his back in one of the beds. He was dressed in a black suit and a white shirt, and laid so still, I thought he was asleep.

Although I couldn't understand why he was sleeping with his shoes on, I refused to go in there and find out. "Mamma is going to be mad when she finds him in her bed with his shoes on," I thought. So I left the room and sat on the kitchen floor and started playing by myself. In this dream, three different themes emerge, and I will try to explain this as best I can

First, the adult figure, a brilliant, glowing entity, was standing behind the old rocking chair as if watching over the physical child who was zoned out in its seat. And encircled by glowing light, was the form of a little girl wearing the gray dress, sitting on the floor, leaning against the rocking chair and playing with a rag doll. This was a very bizarre memory because each time any of the three reacted, I felt it.

Somewhere in this zone, a shuffling movement startled me, the little girl on the floor. And even though I was zoned out in the rocking chair, I was awake in a conscious sense; aware of this entire strange situation. When I turned toward the sound, I was looking down at a pair of large black shoes. My sights trailed north, as I started to look up, very slowly, to figure out whom this was. I noticed he was wearing black pants, white shirt, black coat, a hat and wait…he has no eyes!

The man from the bed in that creepy room, was standing in the doorway of the kitchen and the living room (which was adjacent to the creepy room) swaying slowly back and forth as if he were about to fall over either backward or on top of me. I could only see the whites of his eyes and it scared me. Suddenly, WHOOSH!!! A rush of energy rages past me and I saw at least three or four people come out of nowhere, rushing toward this man. They went right *through* me; like I wasn't even there! They grabbed his arms, held him around the head, and across his chest and dragged the man backward into the creepy room and my body in the chair starts to tremble.

The scene shifts...but the adult figure was still there, watching me...like a guardian, and I was aware of all events around me. I witnessed several men dressed in black, come into mamma's house and go into that creepy room. They came out a short time later carrying a large box on their shoulders and walk outside followed by women dressed in white. This time I was dressed in a plain white dress, holding on to my great-grandmother's apron and stayed close to her side. Everything was so silent, so still. I didn't even hear footsteps.

The group walked out into a field and stopped near a huge tree. I know this tree. I've seen it before. "Oh, now I remember," I thought. That was the tree I passed on the dirt road leading to Mom-Suzaunna's porch! Another huge pecan tree stood off in the distance. But there was something unclean about this tree. "Don't touch it!" The whispers came from the lady in white who had stood behind the rocking chair. I scanned the environment.

We were in an open field a good distance from the house. The large tree loomed beneath a full moon, cloudless sky. Someone had put ropes around a large extended branch of the tree. The loop end of four ropes lay flat against several planks of wood that stretched across a large hole in the ground. Several of the men, standing on either side of the deep hole, slid the large box over the loops and lifted the box into the air, while some others removed the planks of wood. Then they began to lower the box into this hole in the ground. It was too quiet! Nobody said a word; like it was forbidden. But suddenly, breaking the silence, I hear "scratching" sounds coming from inside the box. Peeking from behind my great-grandmother's dress, looking into a deep hole where the box was going down inside of, I saw the top of the box shake and heard the soft scratching turn into loud banging.

BANG! BANG! BANG! The top of that box rattled and shook. Something or someone wanted out of that box! BANG! BANG! And I awoke with a jump! The adult dressed in white was gone; the child who played on the floor was gone. I woke up alone and trembling. That was scary. Something bad happened that day; something too ugly for words. Having one of those "I remember when..." moments, I asked my grandmother about this situation one day, during a conversation about funerals.

She had no knowledge that something so horrible had taken place in this house. After thinking about it, I didn't expect her to remember. This happened before she moved into this house. My family cannot confirm every detail of my memories. I believe some things I've seen happened long before they even lived in that house. But, one thing is consistent. My mother has confirmed the existence of people, long deceased relatives I had never met in person and had never seen pictures of. These dream experiences were common.

CHAPTER FIVE

I introduced Mom-mom Suzaunna and the old rocking chair at the beginning of the book. Here is the rest of the story. One day I was sitting in Mom Suzaunna's old rocking chair and next thing I know, that familiar dizziness hits, and Zoom! I am watching the reviews of lives in progress. Two little girls and I, all of us about six years old and all dressed in brilliant white dresses, are walking along a tree-lined country dirt road, inside the bayou. We have on white socks, patent-leather shiny shoes and white bows in our hair. The three of us are chattering, laughing and skipping along this dirt road and stop only when we get to a little country store nestled on a corner, beneath a large moss-covered tree.

The front of the store has three wooden steps that lead to a small porch. I opened the screen door, using the silver metal handle and we skip inside. There is stuff everywhere, even hanging from the ceiling. Jars of pickles, crates of dried peppers and jugs of cookies line the front of the counter. "Here you go" a jolly, round, white man with pink cheeks calls the three of us over to the counter, hands each of us a huge cookie from the jug and watches as we skip out of his store. We didn't have any money, but we were happy to have the cookie. We skipped along until we came to a dirt path that detoured left off the dirt road.

Scenes in the dream started moving in slow motion. There was a farmhouse off in a distance, sitting in the middle of a huge field. Partly surrounding the yard was a fence made of barbed wire and rotting wood. I saw two massive pecan trees, one in front of the house and one off to the right side. The path wound alongside a large pecan tree and up to the steps of a farmhouse. The house was in the middle of a field, alone.

I departed from my companions and skipped down the dirt path heading toward the farmhouse. No neighbors in sight. On the way, I stopped, paused and gazed at that massive tree on my left. Something about this tree wasn't right. It sent chills across my arms. I scurried along, increasing my pace with each step, trying to put some distance between me and the shadows that swirled around the base of the tree. A red water pump sat in the front yard. "There is a well and running water around here somewhere," I remember thinking. When I get to the steps of the house, a dark-skinned, short, old woman was sitting in a rocking chair shelling peas.

"Come on, Suzaunna," the old woman calls out to me. I climbed the steps, maneuvering between other girls who are sitting at the foot of her rocking chair. I stood right in front of her; that's why I remember what she looked like. "This is what you do," she began and shows me how to clean and cut okra; shell peas; snap beans; and shuck corn. All the produce was being put in silver tin tubs and cast iron pots. As I am standing on the porch gazing out into open land, taking a break from the labor, I capture another vision. A wagon train emerges. The caravan is headed this way. Someone who knows me is on one of these wagons.

It is important to remember that I am still in the midst of a dream. With only a thought, I am a part of the wagon trail caravan. But there is trouble. Robbers are ambushing the wagons and stealing from the travelers. One wagon driver in particular catches my attention. His horses are frightened and he is trying to regain control of them. But he loses control of the wagon and falls off; directly into the path of his own wagon and is run over by one of the huge wagon wheels. As I kneel beside him, cradling his head in my lap, I notice that I am wearing clothes of that time, with an apron. The man is trying to speak to me; but I think he is dying.

Someone comes up behind me and shoots me in the head and I watch myself fall right next to him; he is still clutching his hat. I don't know who he was, but I felt like I was supposed to. As the vision begins to fade, I look up to see others who are standing over us, looking down at us. They don't speak; they just stare and I am jolted awake. The faces of these people were so vivid, that I would recognize them anywhere.

Years later, when I was eight years old, the vision returned. While visiting one of my grandfather's sisters, great-aunt Lou, I decide to take a walk outside in the backyard. As I approach the third concrete step, I started feeling dizzy so I sat down. I didn't even have time to look around. I zoned out right there on the step with my head in my lap. I can see myself standing up, almost in slow motion, and face a dirt path, which leads to a barn. To my right is a pigpen surrounded by a wooden fence, with a sow and piglets wallowing in mud and a trough with slop inside. Next was a wired fence that has chickens and a coup with hay-filled nesting sites, a rooster, and cute baby chicks scurrying around on the ground.

Further down is an open, empty pen. I don't know what was supposed to be here. As I walk in the direction of the barn, something compels me to look to my left. I saw endless rows of fields with nothing growing in it. It was vast and barren; a virtual dust bowl. When I got to the barn and looked inside, I saw horse saddles and thick rope hanging on the barn walls. There was hay everywhere. I don't remember seeing cows or horses. But I did see an old wagon with a missing a wheel. As a matter of fact, the wheel was leaning up against the wagon. The first thing I thought of was, that wagon looks familiar. I went over and touched the wheel and that's when it happened. With my hand on that wheel, like a flash of lightning, a new vision emerges in a bubble, like a distant movie review.

I saw the wagon-trail scene of the dying man again, with his head in my lap. His hat lay beside him, clutched in his hand and his lips were moving. His lips are moving slowly as if he is trying to tell me something, but I could not hear him. I still do not know who this man was. I remember coming to my senses with a jolt. Saliva was seeping out of the corner of my mouth. I sat on the step for a moment, trying to shake off the dizziness. When my vision cleared, I looked up, and right in front of me was the dirt path. There was the sow and her piglets wallowing in the mud; the chicken coup; the rooster; the empty pen; the sun-dried open field to my left; and the barn. It was all here, just like in the vision. I followed the path to the barn; and as I peeked around the corner to my right, hay was everywhere; on the ground, on the stairs, in the rafters; caught in the crevices of the horse's saddle; tangled in the thick rope both which hung on huge nails in the wall; there was even tons of hay in the back of the wagon. The Wagon!? My heart almost skipped a beat.

I noticed that there is a wheel missing. "Where is the missing wheel?" I wondered. I started looking around, frantically trying to find that wheel. Could the vision, the dream, whatever it was…could it be true? I **had** to know. Then, I saw it, leaning against the wagon just like in the dream. The wheel! By now my heart was pounding. Something magnetic was pulling me toward that wheel, to touch it. But, I didn't want to touch it. I was afraid I would see the dying man again. I slowly backed away from the wagon, with my eyes glued to the wheel and ran back to the house. That was an unusual experience. But nothing prepared me for what was about to happen next.

Every two years we have a family reunion. For years, the elders rented summer camps and cabins to host the event. One year, two elders and my mother decided to pool their resources and buy property for us to have a permanent place to host our reunions. The land was bought in a nearby town. I had never seen this property but had imagined it to be a large plot of land where the men would eventually build the structures needed to house attendants of the family reunion. My mother had told me there was an old farmhouse on the land. It had long been condemned; but they had plans to tear it down and restore it to its original form. I never gave the situation much thought.

The following year, I decided to spend Thanksgiving with my grandmother; so we drove to her home for the holidays. It was the end of pecan-picking season and I asked my mother if she would mind accompanying several of us in picking up the last fruits of the pecan trees that had fallen to the ground. First we went to an old apartment home I used to live in and still have nightmares about; where my doll disappeared; where that bloody sack was probably still buried.

When we arrived there, I stood at the mouth of the garage and gazed into its darkness. The feeling was surreal. Although everyone was walking into the garage to get to the backyard, I refused to go inside. Instead, I went through two neighbors' backyards, around the back of a third house and through a small alley to avoid going through that garage.

Even as an adult, I was still haunted by the events of that horrifying day involving this garage. "Maybe it never happened," I whispered out loud to myself. I put my head down, trying to avoid looking at that creepy garage and caught up with everybody else. After getting to the backyard where everybody was busy picking pecans, I couldn't stop staring at the old storage shed where I used to see people float past the window. The place still felt haunted. "...Or maybe it did happen" I was struggling with my conscious. "Stop," I told myself, "just don't think about it."

Then, my mother got another idea. On the land purchased by the elders, there was an even bigger pecan tree that was sure to have shed pecans all over the ground. I was too happy to leave this place. Everyone piled back into cars and drove to what was affectionately called "the property." As soon as we turned onto a gravel road, I became spellbound by what I was seeing. Everything looked familiar. Enormous oak trees on one side and thick blackberry bush on the other shadowed the dirt and gravel road. *I knew this place from somewhere.*

Without thinking what I was saying, I asked my mother, "Where is the little grocery store?" Her exact words to me were, "We just passed it. It used to be just down the road, on the left; but it has been closed for a long time now. As a matter of fact, it closed long before you were bor..." she stopped in mid-sentence.

"You mean before I was born?" I asked.

"How did you know there was a store on this road? This is the first time you've ever been here." My mother was curious.

"I don't know; lucky guess." I lied. I didn't want to talk about it. Images of the three little girls skipping down the dirt road faded in and out of consciousness like a reborn memory. When we arrived at "the property," which was fenced in with rotting wood and barbed wire, something within me moved. The first thing I said was, "Where is the other tree? There used to be a large tree to the left, in front of the house. What happened to it?" My mother answered. "That tree either fell down or was chopped down. This happened years ago."

By now I am getting strange looks and I tried to ignore the stares. "She's still weird as hell," she whispered under her breath. It was my rival cousin again. "Shut up before I predict something about you," I snarled with indignation. She still got on my nerves. With that threat, she got as far away from me as possible. But just to make sure I was not kidding myself, I walked up to the spot where it was supposed to be and there it was; a dead, barely visible stump of a long deceased tree. In the eerie stillness, drifting in a subtle breeze, I caught the faint sound of tapping on that wooden coffin lid.

When I looked up, I saw the house. While everyone else danced around, with white plastic buckets in hand, picking pecans under an enormous pecan tree, I walked slowly toward the house, half acknowledging the dirt path, now grown over with tall grass, which led to the steps of the front porch. The porch, the front screened door, the window leading to the tiny bedroom where she died; I remembered everything.

"Come on, Suzaunna." I could still hear the echo in my ear; and see her sitting in that old rocking chair with a large bowl of freshly shelled peas in her lap. I made a move toward the steps and one of my cousins stopped me, yelling from across the yard. "No!", he yelled. "Don't go up there! It's too dangerous! The wood's all rotted out and you gonna go right through the porch." I had been here before. I was on that porch and inside the house. I knew this house because I had seen it in a dream. Mom-mom Suzaunna had been here too.

I turned to my mother and said, "I've been in this house before."

"Describe it." She challenged.

And I did. I closed my eyes, mentally putting myself back in the old rocking chair and I described where every room was located. I even said to my mother, "if we go around back, you will see a small kitchen window. You will find a tractor parked beneath the window and you will see a small stream several feet away from the back of the house." Sure, enough, we walked around back and there was the small window, the tractor and the stream.

"You are weird," my mother said. I just shrugged my shoulders.

What's even more extraordinary is I remember when my great-grandmother died. But I'm not sure if she died in this house. I remember that she passed away in a small room. There was a window in the room and a braided rug on the floor. She was covered with a thick quilt that she had made, because the "fever" had made her sick. She complained that she was "hot and cold" at the same time.

Sweat was pouring out of her skin. I stood right next to her as she held my hand, rubbing and patting my hand, telling me "don worry, sha. Everythin' gonna be awright." The elders used to warn us to "never let a dying person pat your hand; it means they want to take you with them." Every time they said this, I thought about my great-grandmother, because, in the dream, she died holding my hand.

This memory troubles me sometimes. Given all the weird happenings that occurred before adolescence, I wonder…what does all of this mean. Although my great-grandmother died before I was born, I remember talking with her and learning from her. I have never seen a portrait of her but when I described her for my mother; she told me exactly who this woman was. A special feeling waves over me when I think about her; this old woman whose name I carry. It's odd feeling so close to someone I've known only in spirit.

Everyone was sitting around the table drinking coffee one day, and the conversation drifted to when my grandmother first moved to the "city." I remembered details about the move, so I joined the conversation. I told my mom, aunt and grandmother what I could recall, because after all, I was there too. I was caught off guard by what happened next.

My grandmother just stared at me; my aunt was silent; but, my mom's mouth dropped open and her eyes got wide. As I mentioned before, my maternal grandmother's house was moved from its country spot to the city. I remember the move quiet well, but I was always careful not to mention too many spooky details. Even though they were aware of the bayou's ambience, they didn't like to talk about it. On this day, I told everything.

Several dreams from the rocking chair had already shown me everything I needed to know about this house. A truck with a large head and a long tail backed up and lifted the house up and moved it from its country space to its new rural home. I watched some men dig the front ditch deep and set large round concrete tubing in the crevices. Two men placed large planks over the concrete circles and used this as a makeshift driveway so the truck could back up and place the house on its concrete stilts. When the house was set down, it was placed backward, with the porch facing the wrong direction, something my grandmother was not happy about.

I talked earlier about seeing myself standing outside the house in the yard staring at the house with its tin roof and hollowed-out windows. I've already spoken about standing in the backyard, underneath a large, beautiful willow tree, where ten yards away my grandfather had built an outhouse, complete with a wooden latch, held in place by a single nail. I mentioned being inside the outhouse on a cold night and remember seeing frost on the ground and the latch.

I don't know how, but I knew this was the January. It was an awareness that is difficult to explain. I was born in January. But, I don't know exactly what month the house was moved. One of these dreams focused on the interior of the house. I talked earlier about being on the porch behind the wooden screened door, where I saw a strange white, bulky tub-looking machine with rolling pins on top of it. It was an old washing machine. Inside the washing machine was a silver washboard. A large tin tub sat at the foot of the washing machine. I went *through* the next door and entered an enormous kitchen. There was a hole in the ceiling. Around a corner, to my left, two sewing machines were in the hallway.

There was a bedroom room with a large wrought iron frame, thick mattresses and a large quilt draped over the bed. I could see underneath the bed without bending down. The closet in this bedroom had only a piece of cloth for a door, so I look behind the curtain and notice there is another hole in the ceiling. That's where the fireplace I saw in one of my other dreams, used to be. The fireplace did not survive the move. The furnace stayed inside the house for a while, then it too was removed and replaced first with a hot water heater, then a bathroom.

My mother of course, was stunned when I told her I knew about the hole in the kitchen ceiling, the fireplace and the large black furnace. She did confirm that both the fireplace and the furnace had been in the house. However, both had been removed while she was still a child. There was a hole in the kitchen ceiling, which led to another part of the attic. I remember watching men climb inside this part of the attic using a ladder. She said there was no hole in kitchen ceiling. I disagreed.

I distinctly remember some men climbing a ladder to get inside the attic from inside the kitchen. The hole may have been sealed before I was born, but I do remember where it was. It's almost as if I saw details of this house even before my mother was born and before my grandmother bought it. For a long time, I had moved about the home uninterrupted and thought it strange that no one ever spoke to me or came around to stop me.

In another one of these strange dreams, the field of vision shifted and I remember watching my grandfather put a tile rug down on the floor in the same room I liked to play in. The large bed was gone. The chef faro with all the jewelry in it was gone. I was watching my grandfather install the first indoor bathroom this house would ever know. He had a strange way of doing things. He used to put nails in his mouth, pointed end first and carried his hammer on his left side. He would reach across his body with his right hand to retrieve his hammer and put nails into the floor. He took away my favorite bedroom playground and my crawl space to put in a bathtub, a toilet and a sink. I remember thinking in a childlike manner, "I want my room back."

I stood right next to him and watched him work. He never noticed I was there. I stood right next to my grandfather while he and some men tore down the outhouse and poured dirt and concrete into the hole that used to be the toilet. No one noticed that a little girl was watching everything they did. The most intriguing part of these dreams and memories is this: when I told my mother and grandmother what I remembered most about the house, they were speechless. I spoke of these memories as I would the birth of my children. But, the first time I talked about this, it would be as an adult and my mother turned a shade of pale gray and looked at me as if she had just seen a ghost.

"You could not have remembered the move," she insisted. "I was only eight years old when that house moved."

She was clearly spooked so I decided to have a little fun. "I know you were only eight mother, I saw you."

"You what?" she asked with a puzzled look on her face. She looked like somebody had smacked her upside the head.

"I saw you when you were eight years old," I continued. "I watched you run out to the outhouse. Looked like you were in a big hurry, too."

I couldn't help but smile. This was so amusing in a witty kind of way. Here I am telling my mother I saw her when she was eight years old. She stared into empty space without blinking for about five minutes trying to figure all this out. I repeated all the details I could recall and several times she stopped me in mid-sentence. My mother and I disagree on some of the details of the house. She doesn't remember the hole in the kitchen ceiling. No one knows who the woman I saw in the big umbrella dress was. That was okay by me. I was kind of glad they couldn't confirm everything. Knowing all those strange details made me feel weird and I didn't like it.

CHAPTER SIX

One day we were talking about the move again and the conversation took an interesting turn. My mother was always questioning me about this house. I felt like I was being interrogated. I understand her intrigue. It is sometimes difficult to comprehend the impossible. My mother was eight years old when the house was moved. Obviously I had not been born yet. I have to admit, these memories are spooky. At the time the house was moved, my uncle Jerome was only an infant. I didn't see a baby in the house.

While we were discussing the details of the move for the one-hundredth time, I started talking about my grandfather again. I remember how I used to stand right next to him holding my hands behind my back, rocking back and forth, wearing these patent leather shoes, with white lace socks, and a gray dress with red plaid collars that were trimmed in white, satin lace.

"You remember that dress, Suzaunna?" my mother asked.

"Yes, I do," I told her. This time I actually thought about what I was saying. "Wait a minute!" I was shocked into confusion. That dress, the shoes,…what the…? What I had just described was a dress my grandmother tailored for me in 1968 when I was four. She had dressed me up and had my picture taken in those clothes. But, there was one problem. The picture was in black and white.

There are no color photos of me in that dress. I spoke of details that I could not have possibly remembered unless someone had described them for me or I saw them myself. For the first time, I began to feel afraid. Where was all of this coming from? *Who was I?* My mother was insistent. There was no way I could have known any details of the house, the outhouse, or the way Poppa did his carpentry work without actually being there. But, I pressed on.

I repeated my stories about the clothes in the large trunks and the red crushed velvet furniture that were in the attic. I reminded her about the large black furnace that had been located in the back of the house, and how someone used to put wood inside to keep fire burning. Weird, you say? Now you know how I feel. After that conversation, nobody talked about the house anymore. That little gray dress with the red plaid, circular lace trimmed collars, disappeared by the time I reached age five. I saw the details of that little dress in a dream, while seated the old rocking chair.

As well as being an incredible seamstress, my grandmother was an expert farmer. To the right of the outhouse, beneath the willow tree, ever singing and humming old Negro spirituals, she created a beautiful vegetable garden. She grew stalks of corn at least six feet high; tomatoes; green peppers; green onion; parsley; red peppers; and cabbage. I used to walk right alongside her, dressed in white, and holding on to her apron, while she inspected her garden. She would open an ear of corn, take out a kernel and taste it to see if the corn was ripe for picking. She didn't notice I was there holding on to her apron.

Sometimes on Sunday mornings, my grandmother would take me to church with her. This was one such Sunday...or so I thought. After services, the stewards and members of the Eastern Star would get together and sell plate lunches to raise extra money for church. My grandmother was famous for her homemade pies. On one particular Sunday, I was in the kitchen with my grandmother hanging out with her while she sold plate lunches and pies. Hungry church members formed a line in front of the counter and waited their turn to buy the food.

On days when I went with her to the kitchen, I usually got in the way, sometimes getting caught underneath my grandmother's feet causing her to trip over me, but she usually just kept right on working and did not pay any attention to my intrusion. True to form on this particular Sunday, I was being my usual "you're in the way again" self; holding on her apron string, watching her sell food. But this time, she moved about as if I wasn't even there. Most people just waved and smiled at me and kept going.

Today, all of them ignored me; except for this one rather tall, black man who came up to the counter, clutching a hat in his hand, put both fists down, leaned over the counter into the kitchen, and began to stare at me. He looked like the dying man on the wagon trail. I darted behind my grandmother to escape his gaze and peeked around the other side to see if he was gone. He was still there. His expression had not changed. He looked angry about something. What was interesting however was people kept coming to the counter to buy food and walk right up the place where he was leaning over the counter.

Everyone went right through him. "Who is this strange man and what does he want?" I wondered. I darted behind my grandmother again and peeked around the other side. This time he was gone. That was a good thing, because I needed to use the bathroom. "Mama, I gotta go pee-pee." I really had to go. "Go on, Sue," she said, without moving her lips and off I went.

I knew how to get there by myself. On my way there, something interesting happens. As I am walking and weaving through the crowd of hungry people making my way to the bathroom, something odd occurs to me. The hallway is crowded with people, but I am not bumping into them, and *they're still moving past me*. Many people floated past me dressed in different kinds of clothing. Some looked like they were wearing old slave clothing. Males had on torn, dirty shirts and pants that stopped several inches above the ankles.

Females wore oversized dresses and head kerchiefs. Others were dressed much neater with vests and white frilly shirts. All of them were black and some looked like African slaves. They were hovering past me; some went right through me. Others floated, while some shuffled. They all had a blank stare on their faces and none of them appear happy. Some looked right at me but most of them ignored me.

I don't know who they were or where they were going. But I did notice that I could still see the walls and the floor right through them. I went inside and used the bathroom, which I don't remember doing. When I came out, these people were still floating down the hallway. I just joined the fray until I got back with my grandmother. Strangely enough, I was not afraid, not even of the mean looking man who just stared at me. When I returned to my grandmother, he had returned. I felt like he knew something about me that I didn't know and I was very much intrigued.

At one point I started playing peek-a-boo with him, closing my eyes really tight and then suddenly, popping them open to see if he was still standing there, staring at me. (This was a cute little game one of my aunt's used to play with me.) The man didn't move nor did he crack a smile. He was not amused. He looked so familiar. Eventually he just faded away. This was probably another dream. The church kitchen I saw was not built until some time in the mid seventies. When I had this experience, I felt like I was only four or five years old, still in the late nineteen sixties.

The old man clutching his hat; happy memories of a great-grandmother I never met; recurring visits to my grandmother's house before I was born; watching memories unfold like movie reviews on a canvas screen;

ghostly sightings; hauntings; childhood experiences that defy plausible explanation; I remember them plain as day. Sometimes I sit up well into the early morning hours, trying to make sense of everything. But, this is all too weird for me.

What am I supposed to do with all of this? What does it all mean? Another significant recollection comes to mind involves one of my grandmother's sisters. Once again, from the seat of the old rocking chair and without warning, I am in someone's front yard. My grandmother's sister, Aunt Toni used to live two houses down. I remember going over there. The front yard was nothing but dirt. The steps leading to the porch were concrete and five steps high off the ground and the porch was red and large. I remember going inside; but I didn't open the door. I simply stepped right through a screened door.

On the right hand side of the room was a large floor model machine that had moving pictures on it. It also had pink plastic over the glass face, giving the moving picture a strange hue. The walls were an orange-brown color and a semi-half bar separated the kitchen from the den. I could see clear out the back door and into the backyard, right where two metal poles held a piece of wire between them. Clothing was hanging on the wire.

There was a bathroom inside the short, narrow hallway with two bedrooms on either side of it. No one was home. The significance of this is this was my Uncle Lyle and Aunt Toni's first house. According to my mother, they moved into that house in the early fifties. By the time I was born, they had moved to another home. I was not even supposed to know they had lived there because no one talked about any of this until I asked about it.

There was something strange, but powerful about the old rocking chair. From its creaking, wooden frame, rocking back and forth, I watched my grandmother work magic in her kitchen. She would attach a metal meat grinder to the kitchen cabinet, insert whole chunks of meat into the top and turn the wooden/silver steel crank handle until strings and rows of meat flowed into a waiting bowl or inside an attached skin casing, where she would tie both ends in knots and turn the links into sausage.

Sometimes she would mix rice, onions, and seasonings in with the meat, grind all of it together and make boudin. She would pluck freshly slaughtered chickens of feathers in the huge kitchen sink, gut them open, and using her bare hands, rotate the raw skin over an open flame, singing off any residue of remaining feathers. Southern fried chicken, gumbo, stew, and a host of other dishes were prepared with the versatile yard bird.

Using beef from slaughtered cows, pork from pigs, meat from turkey, duck, deer, rabbit, turtle and even squirrel, my grandmother could prepare a meal with ease; a virtual genius at her craft. It didn't matter that she only had a third grade education. She continues to make homemade pies, bread, cakes and other delicacies using recipes that exist only in her heart.

She never measured anything. And having watched her maneuver around a kitchen with such grace, I learned to combine ingredients without the aid of measuring devices. I've observed my grandmother mixing cold remedies that could rival any modern-day cold remedy. She designed a breathing system so sophisticated it could emulate the modern-day humidifier. Her farming techniques were so genuine; she could have managed her own produce industry. I have the greatest amount of respect for this grand woman.

To have watched my grandmother, her siblings, the other elders, and my grandfather's family navigate through life using skills honed first in mother Africa and perfected in slavery, was a bittersweet history lesson in survival and an irony of genius. They survived on instincts and skills that defied the horrors of the Diaspora. For the first several years of my life, almost everyday, my grandfather's brother, pop-pop Schukle, would sit on an old, wooden Coca-Cola crate and tell us stories of his life as a child; of growing up a black male child in the Deep South.

With tears streaming down his face, he would create visual images of hiding in tall grass, out of sight of angry lynch mobs of white men who routinely raped black women and hung black men from trees, sometimes just for sport. His own grandfather had been lynched over a farming dispute with a white farmer, and his body wrapped in the "federate (confederate) flag," abandoned and left to rot, in an open field.

The elders would stare off into a distant past, into empty space and speak with a dryness that would send shivers all over me, causing the hair on my arms to rise and bristle as they told stories of white men digging up the fresh bodies of recently buried black folks and carrying them off "somewhere." They also spoke of many mornings of returning to a place where a body lay in its wooden coffin, after a ceremonial wake, kinfolk returning to bring the homemade coffin to its burial place, only to find the body laying on the floor, stripped of its clothing, stomped on, sliced into pieces, shot up, smeared with human waste, or desecrated in some other horrifying and humiliating manner. "God don't like ugly," my grandmother would remind us.

It is no secret that medicine owes some credit to the many stolen bodies of black folks which taught them basic anatomy and physiology. Forced into adjusting to the present chaos and making peace with fate, these elder people of color had know a history of being used and brutalized into forced labor by a sadistic subpopulation of white people whose only reason for existence, in the mind of some people in my community, was to bring evil into the world. One elder whispered to me one day his opinion that when Satan got kicked out of heaven, the angels who fell with him was white people and everybody else learned to be evil by watching them, further instilling in me a fear of white people. Of course, this was not true. This was an irrational side of bayou mysticism. Many white people did do some evil things to the people of my community, but we didn't need them to keep the evil going.

Despite the elders influence, simmering just beneath the surface of gaity, a slow burn of psychological pain emerged demonstrated by patterns of relating that encouraged my people toward being deliberately mean to one another; dehumanizing one another with names unfit for any animal. I noticed how they dared one another to take offense to insults, name-calling, or even deliberate injustices, such as stealing and lying. A common phrase I used to hear the adults say to each other was "you took it from the white folk, so you better take it from me."

Black pride symbols, black history books, and slogans like "black is beautiful" and "I am somebody" took some of the sting out of internal rage, but somewhere along the evolutionary time line of post-slavery, virtues like honor, esteem, and compassion were getting hopelessly lost and replaced with mistrust, disrespect and self-hate. There was so much agony and anger; so much fear and degradation and sometimes we acted like we hated each other. Competition was a form of "bonding" as long as no one finished first. It seems a people with a shattered past and an uncertain future, powerless to attack their oppressor, turned instead on one another and themselves; obvious chosen paths of least resistance.

I learned later in life that the younger generation's negative attitudes toward each other, waning disrespect for elders, and a chronic indifference toward God was unacceptable to the elders and a microcosm of the larger society. The elders had survived so much; fought so hard for so long; had been stripped of an inheritance they had built and lost it all to thievery and insolence. The main thing succeeding generations had to do to become great was emulate the very thing that had kept the elders striving - staying strong in spirit.

In over 150 years since the end of slavery, there has been significant change in our attitudes towards each other and race relations. But, we can do better. Those bold survivors of the Diaspora and the protégés who succeeded them are in danger of becoming a distant memory to the rest of the world, lost in the shadows of a hopelessly evil and diabolical time in American history. But the rhythm, the strength and the resilience they instilled within the hearts and spirits of succeeding generations, survives. They lived so we could be born. At the very least, we owe them a day of remembrance and respect.

CHAPTER SEVEN

In the late 60's, my mother married a man from another town; an outsider to our close-knit community. Some people did not like this family. They had a reputation for doing violent things, especially fighting. And they looked funny. Everybody in my family had dark brown skin; these people looked like my "coffee milk." Little did I realize, a sinister darkness had found its way into my world and I would soon discover the meaning of evil. The abuse from my stepfather's side of the family began early in life. When my mother married her husband, things changed. For some strange reason, only for a short period of time, I was taken from my grandmother's care and placed in the care of his mother.

From my first day in that house, my name was "little black dog." It was obvious this mulatto woman with beautiful, creamy, colored skin and long silky black hair, hated my deep, dark chocolate skin. I was NEVER referred to by name. I was the little black dog who was not allowed to sit on the furniture, sit on the rug on the floor or touch any part of her home. She had a special place to put a little black dog. I was shoved into a small v-shaped corner space in the hallway where she kept dirty clothes and cleaning rags. I was told to sit on top of that smelly heap, with a ceiling-to-floor curtain pulled in front of me, because that's where dirty little black dogs were supposed to stay.

I was very young, perhaps only four years old, but I remember this as if it were yesterday. I would arrive early in the morning and as soon as my mother would leave, that mean old woman would grab me by the back of neck, shove me into that corner and pull the curtain in front of my face. I was forced to sit there all day. She would never feed me because she didn't feed little black dogs. This was a vile woman with mean eyes. She cooked every day. Red beans and grits were her favorite foods. But she would never give me anything to eat. I remember getting so hungry that I would hold my knees up to my stomach to try and control the hunger pains. Going to the bathroom was another torture. Her bathroom light had a string attached to a chain-link control switch and I couldn't reach it.

She had already told me that she was not going to waste her electricity turning on the light for me so I learned to use the bathroom in the dark. I would also sneak and drink water from the bathroom sink to ease hunger pains. Just before my mother would stop by to pick me up at the end of a workday, she would yank me by the arm from that dirty pile of clothes and make me sit in front of the television if it were cold outside or out on the front step if the weather was warm.

Sitting on the front steps was not so bad because I could look right across the street and see the house of the old lady who had pierced my ears. I was forbidden to move, so I didn't go over there; but I distinctly remember wondering why she never came to the door. Sitting on those concrete steps holding my face in my hands, while periodically rubbing my pierced ears, I would reminisce back to the time I was in her house and I wondered if Jackie was still there. "She was nice to me," I used to say to myself.

One day, I was sitting in my corner when this short, round, dark-skinned old woman with big boobs, wearing a white apron around a dark colored dress, appeared, peeking at me from behind the curtain. She looked like the old woman on the porch; the one in the rocking chair. She said to me, "Your momma has pecans. When you get home, put some pecans in your pocket. Take a cloth and wrap some pecans inside and bring them with you so you will have somethin' to eat when you come here." And then she vanished. She was right.

When I got home, my mother had gotten a bucket of pecans from my grandmother. I did what the old woman said and I didn't go hungry that day. As a matter of fact, I started bringing cookies, crackers and other food the mean old woman never found and never went hungry again. I also noticed that when I had to go to the bathroom, I would hear a click! And the light would come on by itself and turn off when I was done. I didn't ask any questions and I was never afraid. But, I hated that house.

One day a child's curiosity got the best of me and I ventured out from behind that curtain. I decided to explore the rest of the house. It was a creepy place. In the first room, there were at least six, 4 and 1/2-foot dolls, white dolls, with blonde hair and blue eyes, draped in plastic, hanging on dark-blue painted the walls. Their eyes seemed to follow me. This was spooky. The next room was little more than a corner that housed a huge, rusting wrought iron bed.

That bed sat at least three feet off the linoleum floor. There was a little stepping stool off to the side. One side of the bed was pushed up against a wall, looking like the bed had been shoved into that corner with tremendous force. Then to my left was a long room that had ten beds in it, five on each side. The room resembled a military basic training dormitory barracks and all the beds were neatly made. The entire house was spotless. There was a door behind the house, which lead to a backyard. A BACKYARD!? Wow! I got excited. I wanted so much to go into the backyard and run around, do cartwheels, fall down and roll around in the grass. I could do this at my "real" grandmother's house. The excitement was short-lived. A painful loneliness crept in with an icy reminder that I was now a "little black dog" with no freedom.

I missed my "real" grandmother and stood there feeling a heavy sense of loneliness unlike anything I was used to feeling. Just as my eyes began to water and I was about to start crying, I heard footsteps. SHE was coming and I was not in my corner. I scurried around, bouncing back and forth in the large room like a frightened rabbit, trying to decide if I should hide underneath one of those beds or if I could get back to that corner before she realized I was gone.

I took my chances on the corner. I tiptoed back through the rooms-none of them had doors. I saw her in her room, which was directly across from my little corner. While her back was turned, I darted back into my corner and sat back on top of those dirty, smelly rags and dirty laundry. My heart was pounding from fright but I was so happy to be back in that nasty corner! The old woman never hit me; but the energy around her was evil.

Her behavior baffled me. I couldn't understand why she was so mean to me. I used to wonder, "What did I do wrong?" When she was not eating and watching soap operas on television, she would prance around her living room in house shoes and a robe in a drunken stupor, dancing and singing at the top of her lungs, cursing at me and calling out to me, "you little nasty black dog!" The tone in her voice was unearthly.

After a while, I went back to live with my maternal grandmother. I couldn't be happier. I guess that mean old lady couldn't take having a little black dog in her house anymore. I didn't like her anyway. As I got older, I was forced to drive the old bat to doctor's appointments, pick up her medication, bring her groceries, and sit with her while she rambled on about nothing. She had siblings in the town, but people rarely visited her. She never apologized to me for how she treated me. But, I was told that a few days before she died of a painful liver disease in the hospital, she asked for me.

After I left that mean old woman's house and returned to be with my grandmother, I don't remember seeing my mother that much. It's as if she had disappeared from my life. It didn't bother me and for some reason, I didn't miss her. My grandmother's house was a safe-haven now, and besides, I could go outside and turn cartwheels in the backyard. I found out later that my grandmother wanted me to stay with her and complained bitterly about me being sent to that mean old woman's house. Someone had told me that she did not like my mother's new husband or his family.

I didn't even know *where* mother was living until one day I was sitting in my great-grandmother's rocking chair and zoned out. Walking inside a tunnel, in a familiar swirling haze, surrounded by an aura of light, I saw myself moving down the hallway of a run down building that had many rooms. My mother called this building "the cottage." For some strange reason, in the dream, I had entered from the rear of the building.

I was moving inside this circle of light, going from room to room, looking inside. The rooms were painted mint green. Each room had a bed, a small table and a window. The beds were rusted, heavy wrought iron with rounded foot ends and heavy springs that held heavy blue and gray striped mattresses, high off the floor. Only one room was neat. The beds in the other rooms were unmade. As I am moving down this hallway, I came upon one room that is right next to the front door, on the right, as you enter the building. The door is partially opened, so I peak inside. The room had a shadowy, dark hue, a bad feeling and an irritating low humming sound. The bed is not made and the room is a bloody mess.

The sheets were all wrinkled and the entire bed and the walls were soaked and stained with blood. Something within me screams and I could feel my body shaking or jerking as if I am trying to wake up. As I begin to back away from the scene, I hear a familiar voice coming from a room across the hall from this horrible scene. As I get closer to the room and peer inside, I see a man and a woman sitting together on a couch with watercolor patterns. A gas heater is blazing fire beneath a window. I hear him yelling at her. "I had to do it! She was gonna turn me in! I had to kill her! Know one will ever know! They won't find her!

He was not pleading. His rambling was vicious. His green eyes were full of hate and he was surrounded by a black, smoky shadow that swirled around him from head to foot. This man was pure evil and a gasping sound tried to escape from within me. He stopped in midsentence as if he heard something, got up off the couch and came to the door. He stared right at me, but couldn't see me.

It's as if I were invisible to him. But he looked right into my eyes; like he could sense my presence. I did not move and the closer he came to me, the louder that irritating humming sound grew until I thought my ears would pop. The woman sat very still on that couch with her head hanging down. I woke up sitting in the rocking chair, jerking and writhing; awakening with a heavy Thud!

Twenty years later, as an adult, I told my mother about the cottage house she used to live in, never mentioning that horrible scene and sure enough, she confirmed that she did indeed live there but assured me that I did not live with her at that time. Yet, I described the square courtyard with the clotheslines and the woman named Ms. Lisette, who used to give my mother candy for me. I even showed her where the building used to be.

There were several of these buildings and behind them was a rectangular-shaped courtyard with those familiar rusted iron poles with wire stretched across and between them. This was the neighborhood clothesline. The courtyard had patches of grass-covered concrete where I saw children playing. I described all of this to my mother, without ever stepping one foot on those grounds all seen from the sanctity of my grandmother's old rocking chair.

Turns out, Ms. Lisette was not just my assigned godmother, she was my mother's stepsister. Poppa, my maternal grandfather, was her daddy. I don't remember meeting Ms. Lisette in person. The only time I remember seeing her was in the dream. One day, my mother took me from my grandmother's house and moved me into an apartment she shared with her new husband. This man was creepy and I felt like he hated me. I also didn't like the way he looked at me and I tried to avoid him as much as possible.

CHAPTER EIGHT

In the apartment house, I was assigned to sleep on an opposite end of the house, near the backdoor, away from the rest of the family. Most nights, I slept there hidden deep beneath the covers, curled up in a corner against the wall, shaking like a leaf because I was always scared. One night someone came into my room. I heard them shuffling. On a rare occasion when I peeked out from beneath the covers, I saw the largest, whitest, scariest eyes ever. This thing was merged with the darkness and had bent down to me. It was staring at me with a penetrating gaze that frightened me all the way to the bone and I curled up in a tight ball wrapped inside the bedcovers so tight, I had to struggle to breathe. Even my mother admits that apartment was haunted. I hated that place. I told my mother of another strange incident that still haunts me to this day.

She confirms most of it, but will not talk about it. My uncle Lyle, a World War II veteran, had brought me a doll from Europe that could walk! He put batteries in that little blonde hair, blue-eyed doll, pushed a button and she waddled across the floor, making the whirring sounds like a modern-day blender. I loved that doll and would wake up asking for it and go to bed assured that she would be on the closet shelf in the morning. One morning, the doll could not be found. My mother turned my room upside down looking for that doll and found nothing. The doll had disappeared. The night before, from beneath the covers, I heard someone going through my closet but did not dare look up to see who it was. The only thing her husband said with a sinister grin on his face was, "I guess she walked out the house."

The doll was never found. However, a few days later, while at home with him, he told me to come and sit on the steps inside the garage. I obeyed. While I am sitting there, this man emerges from behind the apartment house carrying a shovel and a sack that usually has potatoes in it. The sack was dripping with blood. I could not take my eyes off that sack. When he put it down on the ground, it moved slightly and left a bloody stain on the concrete. I did not ask any questions and he probably assumed I was ignorant. I watched him dig a hole in the right hand corner of the garage, put the bloody sack inside the hole and cover it with dirt and concrete.

At that point, I could not take any more. It reminded me too much of the box going into the hole in the ground, beneath that scary tree, listening to desperate poundings from inside the coffin. Something wicked was happening in this garage, in this space, that was closing in on me like a heavy wet blanket and I was struggling to breath. I lost it. I bolted from those steps and hid in a corner of the bathroom. I wrapped my arms around my knees, closed my eyes so tight, they hurt, and rocked back and forth in a trance.

POW! I jumped at the sounds of the gunshots sounding off in my head. "You nasty little black dog!" That voice was mocking me. "I had to kill her!" He keeps repeating this over and over. Visions of that bloody room in the cottage were swirling in my head and that humming sound was hurting my ears. All of this "noise" is going on at the same time and I started mumbling, "Stop it! Stop!" I felt like I was losing my mind.

I heard him yell at me and threaten to whip my butt if I didn't come out of hiding. I did not budge. I just sat in that corner and just rocked back and forth. I don't think he even tried to look for me. For all I know, that could have been a dead dog he was burying. I didn't care. Whatever it was, the whole experience left a profoundly traumatic psychic effect on me to the point that it is the only experience I question. I did not like this man. He was always watching me and trying to touch on me and it made me feel dirty; and I didn't know what to do about it. I don't even remember coming out of that bathroom corner. But after that day I avoided this man as much a possible. A few days after my doll disappeared, I was playing cautiously on the kitchen floor.

There was a knock at the door. When my mom opened the door, a white police officer came in. He looked down at the floor where I was and tipped his hat to me and smiled. I smiled back. I heard him ask my mother if her husband was home. She said no. As they talked, I overheard him say something about a little girl being missing. I had this friend, I think her name was Coreen, who used to come over and play with me. We used to make that doll walk back and forth to each other. One day, she just stopped coming over. She stopped coming over around the same time my walking doll disappeared. I don't remember what I was told about her. The police officer left and my mother went to the stove and started cooking.

After that horrifying scene in the garage, I refused to go out that door. Instead, I would go and sit on either the front steps or the back porch and just daydream. In the backyard, we had a huge pecan tree, pear trees, and honeysuckle and tangerine bushes. The fragrance was intoxicating. There was also a storage shed attached to the apartment house. As a kid, I used to see people, transparent bodies and sad faces, floating past the door window. There was great sadness in this space. I could sense it. I missed my grandmother, the old rocking chair, and my playground. I wanted to go away, just disappear. I was miserable and no one knew I was crying a lot. This world was lonely, ugly and it hurt. I wanted to go home. This was not my home. ·

CHAPTER NINE

One day I was sitting on the front steps, holding my face in my hands, feeling sad and lonely, when a tall, brightly lit man dressed in black appears out of nowhere. I could not see his face because the way he was standing, a bright light blinded my view. This man looked like the sun dressed in a black suit. Where there was supposed to be hands, feet, and a head; all I saw was this brilliant light. He stood in front of me, opened a large glowing hand and offered me candy. I did not feel afraid of him so I took the candy. He never spoke, but with that same hand, he pointed to the sky and motioned for me to leave the steps, come away from the house and look up into the sky.

I walked toward him and then with one hand on my shoulder, he pointed to the sky as if to say "look up." When I looked into the sky, I saw the image of someone in silhouette leaning over a cloud looking down on me. He or She was smiling so brightly, that my grief disappeared and I felt all warm and gooey inside. I smiled back. When I looked down to see who this man in black was, he was gone. He had disappeared. I went back to my steps, propped my face up with my hands on my knees, ate the candy and stayed there until I was called in for supper. Just before going inside, however, I took one last look into the sky to see if my "friend" was still there. There he was, still smiling down on me.

For the first time since being in that creepy house, I slept with my head uncovered. I didn't feel scared anymore. I still refused to sit on the steps inside the garage; but it didn't frighten me anymore. If I ever felt scared, all I had to do was remember my friend in the sky and the fear would disappear.

I never showed much interest in playing with other children, except my cousins. I didn't feel like a normal child. I had always felt strangely different, like I didn't belong here; like I was stuck in the wrong life. So I entertained myself by inventing stuff like a new alphabet or numbering system, paper dolls, strange codes and songs. Watching those strange details unfold whether from the seat of that rocking chair was intriguing and sometimes scary. But I didn't know it was supposed to be abnormal.

For most of my life, I've tried to put these strange experiences into some kind of perspective. The essence of the bayou's mystique had made her presence known long before I recognized her. Secrets of the bayou's mystique started unfolding in dramatic fashion long before I understood what was happening. By the time she defined herself, I was familiar with her essence, because I recognized my reflection in her still waters of time. All I could do was record what she disclosed and her revelations showed me many things.

I observed shades of life overshadowing consciousness with deja vu. Her secrets hovered just inside sanity sometimes unveiling eternity disguised as spiritual realms. She allowed privileged sightings of time beyond the infinite and guarded innocence with mysterious force while displaying the awesome power of a divine providence. Disclosing the delicate alliance between life and death and revealing secrets of prebirth phenomenon were just some of the secrets she revealed.

She presents this life's existence as an intriguing journey of the spirit borrowing a human form. From her view, humans are fascinating entities. For example, the sperm and the egg are testaments to the awesome creative power of the God who designed them. Each cell is an entity unto itself; existing in solitude. Inside each of those millions of cells, whether it is the sperm or the egg, is the material substance of every human quality that is needed to sustain life.

The color of the eyes, hair, hair texture, teeth, bone structure, skin color, the shape of a smile, the digestive system, central nervous system, vascular system, DNA, everything that makes us human is contained inside two tiny cells that can only be seen with the aid of a microscope. Everything that all humans will become is contained within a cellular structure that can sit on a single grain of sand. At the dawning of a physical birth, at the union of a sperm cell and the egg, some scientists say that a flash of light can be seen, suggesting the entrance of the soul.

After birth, this divine entity encased in human flesh sets out to explore a world that exists in shades of gray; discovering and uncovering what it means to live a finite life of deadlines; yet explore with infinite purpose. This divinity must rediscover its own origin; combat and overcome anger, hate, envy, pride, jealousy, maltreatment, and all manner of that which is determined to destroy peace.

And even as divine providence helps guide our commitment to spirituality and the desire to do all that is good, we must still overcome negative energy and grow through trial and error, into the realization that love is the only power that matters. But the mystique knows that living this dual existence can make or break the bond of faith and destroy our link to the magnificent power, which created those particles of matter that is the human being.

It is so easy for wandering souls to lose focus in this land of dazzling lights and fluffy bright colors. Some never find their way back to the peace they knew before conception. Others choose to mold into the ways of evil. Some of us forget that our job, our reason for being, is to work behind the scenes; repairing the damages of evil. Pain is real in this world; there are no barriers against it. Often it is the actions of mean-spirited entities, those predatory personalities, which strive to make this world unlivable.

And it is so easy for even the most resilient soul, to get caught up in the many windstorms of suffering and think about, even attempt, an early exit from what sometimes feels like a Godforsaken world. I was pulled from the brink of self-destruction as the essence of the bayou mystique and all of her wisdom brought me to a crossroad of change. In the face of all that would destroy me, I chose life. But as you will see, it was not easy.

My mother and her husband bought a new house in the suburbs and I settled into childhood. I didn't like the new house because the color was too dark and a subtle, nagging, uncomfortable feeling kept knawing at me. I had seen this house before, but I couldn't remember where. I had this chronic feeling that someone was always watching me. It was eerie. Spending as much time outside as possible, I enjoyed games of hopscotch, tag, hide-and-seek, double dutch, hand-jive and jacks with cousins and a few neighborhood kids. I climbed trees, played football, swam in the summer, raced bicycles, and did all manner of things kids did.

We even had Easter egg hunts at one of my auntie's house every year. I had achieved normalcy, whatever that means. The rocking chair had been retired. Actually I don't know what became of it. But now I was school-age and had no time to sit in the chair anymore. School was exciting. I would make straight A's and used to get teased for being "too smart" and not having an accent. It didn't matter. I was a happy kid again. Life was okay…for a while.

My grandmother's house was just across the street from a huge Catholic Church campus. The priest who lived there used to sit out on his front lawn and watch us play tag and football, running all over the "priest campus;" that's what we called it. We were raised southern Baptist and thought he looked funny in his long black robe with a hood on it. He never tried to convert us, and he even invited us and the neighborhood dog, a German Shepard named Spice, into his home to see his taxonomy collection.

His collection was spooky. He had a bear's head stuck on a wooden plaque hanging on the wall, an owl perched on the fireplace mantle, a whole deer standing near the fireplace, a moose's head with huge antlers above the fireplace, and a real gray wolf, all posed for observation. We were amazed. They looked so real. We didn't see white people that often and all the stories we heard about them were really bad. So we thought this priest was the nicest white man in the world.

Every August, just before the new school year, the priest would sponsor a "bizarre;" our name for the city fair. These funny looking people would arrive on the "priest campus" and set up bright lights around a Ferris wheel, mixers, a roller coaster, a host of other rides, cotton candy, hot dog and candy apple stands, and ticket booths. Electrical chords snaked over the ground in a tangled mess. It's a wonder no one electrocuted themselves, especially when I rained. It was fun to watch them work and even more exciting when opening day arrived. Rides cost 25cents each; candy apple and cotton candy, 10cents. Hot dogs and hamburgers cost 20cents each.

On opening day, my cousins and I would meet at my grandmother's house. We had to go to the fair as a group. Armed with $2.00 each, which was a lot of money, at 6pm, we almost sprinted across the street to the fair huddled together in a group. In my family, grandchildren are ranked according to age. The three older kids were supposed to watch out for the younger ones. I was the third oldest and we did the best we could. As long as we could spot the younger kids among the crowd, it was every man for himself.

To make the 8:30pm curfew, the older kids would start gathering everybody together by 8pm, pool our money together and load up on cotton candy and candy apples and then head back to my grandmother's house to a feast of southern fried chicken, rice and gravy, homemade pies and red kool-aid. This was our last hurrah before school started. When I was almost five, I attended my Nonna's school, which was on the priest campus, housed in a small building right near the priest's house and surrounded by a chain-linked fence. That was the neatest place to be and you didn't have to be "a big person" to go to her school. I loved that school. We didn't have books.

Nonna was a gifted artist who created coloring book pictures; design patterns; and wall-decorations for her classroom. She bought her own school supplies and designed alphabets and number patterns with pictures that, in another time, would have made her a famous designer of children's activity books. My Nona educated an entire generation of little four and five-year-old, Negro children in that small one room building. And except for naptime, and having to pretend to be sleeping on those uncomfortable trifold mats on the floor, I had a great time. I wondered why the girls had to sleep on the red mats and the boys had to sleep on the blue ones. But, wonderment defined me as a child. Everything was so intriguing.

CHAPTER TEN

After I left my Nona's school, I attended kindergarten at the neighborhood "black school," John Stacy Elementary. This time naptime was fun! The teacher used to play these creepy records with sounds of monsters coming out of thumping coffins, going "boooo", creaking and slamming doors, banging windows, rain pelting tin a tin roof, loud, crashing thunder and lightning, thumping casket lids, all narrated by a deep, spooky voice. This was scary in a fun way, but I think some of my classmates passed out from shock and fear. We had blankets and all of us would lay there with that blanket wrapped around our heads, cowering and shaking in fear. The teacher does not realize that she probably traumatized us into having nightmares.

Each holiday spent in school was marked by festive creativity. With pinecones for a body, we made Thanksgiving Day turkey models, complete with a giblet, a beak and plumage of feathers made of multicolored construction paper. At Christmastime, after making wavy trails of Elmer's glue across circular cuts of more colorful construction paper, we dumped mountains of blue, green, yellow, and red square-shaped shards of glitter on top of the glue, waited for half a second and spilled whatever didn't stick to the glue onto a piece of writing paper; instant Christmas ornaments! We saved the excess glitter for our custom designed Christmas trees.

Our proudest moment was when the teacher punched a hole in the top of our ornaments, place a paper clip in it and hang them on the classroom Christmas tree. Our personally designed Christmas trees (everybody's tree was cut out of green construction paper), which glowed with glitter-traced patterns, also had a hole punched in the top so we could hang it on the string in front of the huge storefront style window for everybody in school to see. She even put our names on our artwork. But, of course nothing could top the designer construction paper cutout Easter bunnies complete with a real cotton ball for a tail held in place by a puddle of Elmer's glue. Our personal designs of those ever-present kaleidoscopic Easter eggs which were colored with real crayons and trimmed with thin films of glitter was the talk of the classroom. The scene inside the classroom was orderly and robust. We were happy kids.

But just beyond these walls, across the yard however, once stood the old high school my mother had attended. This was an ominous building was three stories of crumbling debris and broken out windows. The steel staircases were dirty and covered with shards of broken glass and particles of paper. Inside the classrooms were dried up, peeling chalkboards. The walls were painted dark green, the floors were black, and the doors were made of solid steel. This place was depressing and deserted. When I was in there, I wondered where everybody went. My mother says the school was torn down before I was born. I disagreed. I was inside that building, alone…and I saw everything.

Things like this happened a lot when I was a child. After I started school, I didn't need to be in the rocking chair to see things anymore. Sometimes, just like the day I saw my mother's old high school building, I would get caught up in a "zone," a type of daydreaming spin and see things happening. Usually a loud noise or someone calling my name would cause me to shake my head as if I were coming out of a trance; but I would remember everything.

To attend first and second grades, we had to be bused to a white elementary school clear across town. In this school, the playgrounds were separated by gender. The girls played on one side of the playground where the ground solid cement. Scraped knees, stubbed toes and scuffed patent leather shoes were commonplace. For someone who was used to running on the same turf as the boys, this made no sense to me. The boys had the best playground. They had dirt. No concrete ground anywhere! That was so unfair.

They had everything the "girls side" had, including the monkey bars. But they had a merry-go-round. We didn't have one because as a lady teacher explained, it was not "proper" for girls to run or jump up and down around boys, especially if she was wearing a dress. Every little girl I knew who wore a dress had better have a pair of shorts on underneath it, because the boys might try to see your panties. If he succeeded, as a girl you were considered "nasty." The little boy was hailed as a hero by his peers.

Indoctrination of gender roles and behaviors began early in childhood. Girls were "told" their place. The boys were allowed to make mistakes. The boys would come into the classroom covered in dust while the girls were not allowed to get dirty. All we could do was watch them run and chase each other, playing tag or just wrestling. They even had a tree on the "boys' side" but got in trouble if they climbed it. A very significant thing occurred while I was at this school. It is a situation that haunts my memory to this day.

The year was 1971 and I was in the second grade sitting in my desk coloring a Mickey Mouse picture. I asked the teacher if I could go to the bathroom and of course, she said yes. I was walking down the hallway, toward the bathroom and decided to buy a coca-cola from the big machine. I pulled out a shiny coin from my pocket and headed right for the machine in a big hurry; trying not to run down the hallway. Just before I get to the machine, a teacher, skinny, white, and mean looking came around a corner, walking fast. With an angry expression on her face, she headed right toward me. She had a deep scowl on her face, like she was deep in thought. I stepped to the side, getting close to the wall, to get out of her way, but she blocked my path and stepped right in front of me.

Again, this time looking down at the floor, I tried a second time to go around her. And again, she stepped in front of me. As soon as I looked up to say excuse me, WHAM! She slaps me across the face so hard I dropped my coin and nearly pissed on myself. To this day, I don't know where that coin went. I put my hand on my cheek and looked up at her slowly, with begging and confused eyes. I didn't get a chance to say anything. All I remember thinking is "…I'm sorry. I tried to get out of the way. What did I do wrong?" Tears welled up in my eyes and I wasn't sure if it was from the pain or the surprise. But I will never forget her words, because her one spoken sentence, the fixed hate in her eyes, and the venomous tone in her voice taught me all I would ever need to know about racism. "I HATE NIGGERS!" she snarled. And having said that, she rolled her eyes upward and stomped off down the hallway leaving me feeling like forgotten trash. I walked back to my classroom staring down at the floor, without my soda pop, sat at my desk, buried my stinging face inside folded arms and wept.

That day I found out what it meant to be black in the rural south. I never told anyone what happened. Somehow I didn't think anyone would care. I did ask my grandmother what was a "nigger." She said it's what white folks call us black folks as a nickname. And that was both the extent and end of that conversation. But the seed of anger and mistrust of white people had been planted. After that, I was even cautious of the white catholic priest.

After elementary school, I went back to the neighborhood middle school, John Stacey Elementary. By now the kindergarten classrooms with the storefront windows had been sealed. The school had all black students, a few white teachers and a white principal. We didn't like the principal because he was white. In our minds, no other reason was necessary. This was the turbulent 70's, we were only a few generations removed from slavery, and few people in my generation or our community liked white people. They wouldn't admit it openly if they did.

We were angry and the raised fist was everywhere, even on the Afro pick handles most of us had stuck in our hair. If you could wear an afro, it had to look nice, because it was a proud symbol of defiance against a racist America. The afro was so important, the community held annual Afro Ball contests where contestants would model various seventies clothing fashions and their afros and compete for first, second, and third place trophies. Some of us couldn't wear an Afro.

I abused my hair with oils, sponge rollers and braids, trying to make it "nappy" so I could wear an Afro like everybody else at school. But my native-American DNA would not allow it. My hair was too soft. So I abandoned that project and decided to become a rebel for the cause instead, complaining bitterly about the evils of racism. The incident in second grade had made it easy for me to dislike all white people.

The neighborhood was united for a while. There was scant mention of "Martin Luther the King" by some of the elders; and we had to recite the "I Have A Dream" speech to ad nauseum. But outside of school, we preferred to talk about Malcolm X and the Black Panthers because, black folks were tired of turning the other cheek. My beloved fourth grade schoolteacher, Mrs. Patterson, stood in front of the class one day, sporting a really nice afro and made a speech. She demanded that all of us little Negro children should never tolerate being called "colored." "You are black and beautiful," her voice echoes, "and don't let anyone call you anything different! Especially not them white folks!" We all clapped and cheered in agreement.

I wish she and other teachers like her had taught us not tolerate being called "nigger" either; especially not by other black people. Maybe we wouldn't have this horrible slavery-stain of self-degradation and self-hate hovering in our vocabulary today. Ms. Patterson became a role model for us and it was in her classroom I would meet all four of my lifelong childhood friends.

Soul Train was our main entertainment media. It's how we knew when the latest record came out and who the artist was. Soul Train introduced new entertainers, showed the latest dance moves, and gave us a head's up on what songs the high school marching band would be playing that year during football season. It was a time of rapid change. I didn't have time to think about any spiritual episodes. There was too much going on in the world and I didn't want to miss out on anything.

I spent early childhood during a time when lead-based paint was not yet declared unhealthy; there were no child-proof lids on medicine bottles, doors, or cabinets; we rode bicycles without helmets, knee pads or elbow pads and traveled in cars with no seat belts or air bags. We drank water from the garden hose and sometimes shared one bottle of soft drink between five kids. We would spend hours stripping the training wheels off bicycles, scavenging for scraps of wood and taking nails, a hammer and other tools from our uncle's carpenter's bag to build go carts, which we would ride downhill, eventually crashing into a parked car, a tree or low-lying bush because we forgot to add brakes.

We didn't have personal computers, cell phones, video games, or multi-channel cable TV. We played outside, inventing games like cross-country tag, red-rover, red-light/green light, London Bridge, and ring-around-the-rosies. We hit tennis balls with a big stick and no one ever lost an eye; we rode in the back of pickup trucks and no one flipped out; and fist fights ended with two people becoming lifelong buddies. Kids had respect for the law, neighbors looked out for us and were expected to correct any misbehaviors and show of disrespect; and you knew it was time to find some fake tears as soon as you got home because the neighbor had probably tattled on you and that meant a butt-whipping was inevitable.

During middle school, I attended our neighborhood school, but by seventh grade, we were permanently transferred to the "white" high school and we hated it. At first, fights were a daily event. Black people and white people hated each other; students and teachers alike. An imagined slight, a presumed insult, or even a bad grade could provoke accusations of racism and schoolyard fights. By the middle of the school year, everybody had calmed down.

Eventually, apart from the occasional racial slurs and a few schoolyard fights, we learned to tolerate one another. Music, sports, and mascot loyalty became the accepted bond between the races. We learned to get along by rallying around common interests. Sometime between elementary and middle school, the rocking chair vanished. And except for a few deja vu slights, nothing out of the ordinary happened...except for the dreams.

CHAPTER ELEVEN

At age ten, I had three of the most fascinating dreams I had ever encountered. It was the first time I remember feeling like I was literally leaving my body while I was asleep. All three dreams were amazing. In all three dreams, for three nights in a row, soon after laying down and falling asleep, I felt the sensation of coming out of my body. It felt like I was going uphill on a roller coaster in slow motion.

In the first dream, I found myself standing on this street that looked like solid gold. The buildings in this place were enormous and indescribable. I cannot tell you how they were shaped because we don't have anything like this in our world. I know circles, squares, and 3-dimensional objects. I saw nothing that resembled our world, yet I knew they were "buildings" of some sort because I can still see them in my mind; I just can't describe them.

"Welcome!" he says. His voice is masculine and gentle. I looked at him, but could not see his face. But, I feel his smile. He touched my elbow with a hand that peeked from beneath the cuff of his robe and beckons, "Come with me. We have much to talk about and I have something to show you."

I was walking on streets of shining gold, which glistens under the brilliance of light that illuminates this incredible city. This was a place so far removed from the imagination of man that even with my ability to picture the city, its structures and all of its grandeur, it defies human illustration. It is impossible to sketch its quality; spiritual beauty is very difficult to describe.

When I looked away from this beautiful sight, I notice that my greeter and I were not alone. Three others had joined us and are walking with us. With a large open book levitating in front of us, held up by unseen hands, each of them took turns pointing to passages in this book for me to know and remember. The pages of this enormous book flipped forward as if a gentle wind was blowing them forward. As I glance upward for a brief second, I saw others floating in the air.

Some of them stopped just long enough to look at me and smile, while others passed by, offering welcoming smiles. Those in the air would land so softly onto the shining foundation, that their bare feet never touch the ground. As if a magnetic force was preventing contact. Those who passed by did so as if they are on some kind of conveyor belt. They float forwarded, greeting their curious guest with soft eyes and friendly smiles.

They are not intrigued by me, as if they know who I am and I think they sensed my wonderment. So, without noticeable wings, draped in brilliance, they hovered at a distance and watched. "You will soon understand," they whisper into my mind. The four who walk with me, behind the open book continue their teaching.

I remember each of them pointing to certain passages and saying, "Remember this." "Know this." I absorbed their instruction. But then something else captures my attention. As if moving in slow motion, all five of us come to a place located in the middle of this wondrous city.

My companions cease their teachings and I stop and stare. It is the only structure that allows description and I remember every detail. The grand adjoining doors had no fancy carvings or outside closures. The doors were huge, as they hung on hinges unseen, levitating, just above the path of gold that flowed beneath it; as if buoyed by a force of magnetic energy. Those doors were absolutely magnificent!

My companions say nothing as if allowing me time to absorb what I was seeing. I felt myself becoming absorbed by the light that emanated outward from within the chambered borders of the doors. The light that flowed upward also formed walls on each side of the doors. This light radiated with a force and power of energy that would probably make the sun feel like a forty- watt light bulb. I was mesmerized.

"Who lives here?" I whispered, awestruck by what I was seeing.

"God is here," one of them said.

As if he read my thoughts, he said, "You are welcome to enter the doors,…if you choose." And then, silence. I wanted to stay. As I inched closer, the power was becoming overwhelming. I felt that if I moved in a few inches more, the light would absorb me. But there was a conflicting force within me that was just as powerful as the one that tugged at me to enter those doors.

"Make a choice. It is the one power you have," someone whispered gently. "You must choose," one of my companions said. It was impossible to remove my sight from those doors. I did not want to leave, but I chose to do so. And with that choice made, my companions resumed their instruction. I came away from those doors feeling both saddened and empowered. Love is here, I remember thinking.

Peculiar thing about love; its power means great things to all in its presence. To the natives it was all encompassing; to the teachers it was ultimate guidance; and to the tiny speck of humanity that stood awestruck before its veiled presence, it was life-altering. The power from this dream would prove to be more anchoring than anything else in my entire existence.

With my companions in tow, I slowly walked pass the doors, half wanting to stay but realizing that something had taken root in my awareness and was growing. With peaceful surrender, all four take turns issuing words of warning, assurance and encouragement. And their words became more prophetic. There was one with a beard who spoke with dominating authority.

"You have a great work to do," he says. "You will suffer great difficulty. Evil will seek you and find you. It is the way of that world. Do not give up. Your purpose is important for those who will embrace your message. You are part of a remnant. Others have chosen to go on before you. You will find each other. Those who rule in that realm will disturb you greatly and seek to destroy your light. They cannot. Pray always. You should recognize this place. This is your home. You will return here when your purpose is complete. Never fear. You will not be alone."

They said much more than I can remember; teaching; informing; arming me with information and details on things I may have stored deep my subconscious. We walked to the edge of this beautiful city and my companions bid me "Godspeed." That is the first time I had ever heard this word. "We will meet again," they said and wave, saying "farewell."

I woke up with a thud! as if I had been dropped into my body. It could be that latent memories expanded by magnificent stories I was learning about heaven in Sunday school were now being expressed in childhood dreams. I could assign this to the imagination of a happy-go-lucky child. But, it all seemed so real and I would soon discover this was only the beginning.

The next night, another part of the same dream emerges. In this same vivid memory, I am walking alongside the same set of teachers in another part of that magnificent city. This time one of them is holding an open book of some kind and all four take turns pointing to passages for me to know and remember. I am led to a clearing and suddenly realize that I am on top of a mountain.

It was the tallest mountain in an expansive mountainous terrain; below loomed a valley. This time, I am told to sit down. I sit and with my knees drawn up to my chest, chin resting on both knees and both arms wrapped around my legs, I stare down, peering between clouds, into this strange valley. There was a lot of movement down there. One of these instructors points to my left. "Look," he says.

On a mountain, encircled in clouds, across from where I was, transparent figures glide in a rapid downward spiral, descending into this valley and do not return upward. I watch as each one, one at a time, descends into this valley. I don't know where they were going. While there were many transparent figures on the other mountain, there were only four on the mountaintop with me.

These figures were also transparent. They were very tall, had broad shoulders and were dressed in brilliant white robes. One of them has a long white beard and they all have a rope-belt tied loosely around their long robes. As they spoke to me, they pointed down into the valley, telling me things that I can't recall at this time. They also spoke a different language. It is one I understood but also a language I had never heard before. It was not human language. They spoke in a dialect far more sophisticated than anything I had ever heard and they were teaching me something.

I remember looking into the valley with intrigue. As I began to concentrate on figuring out what was down there, I felt myself spiraling downward. I thought I was falling. I landed back in my body so hard, I felt that familiar thud! and it felt like the mattress bounced as if I had jumped into bed.

I had dismissed the first dream as something special and I didn't talk about it to anyone. The second dream got my attention and I started asking questions. Without revealing too much information, I asked someone to tell me what heaven looked like. "It's a very beautiful place," one of the elders said. That was all she said. I didn't ask any more questions.

Then for a third night in a row, before I know it, I feel like I am being lifted and transported somewhere. When I wake up, I find myself sitting in a field of flowers under a large and beautiful tree. Don't ask me to describe the flowers or the colors; they don't exist in this world. But I am here, waiting for someone. I don't know whom; I just know I am supposed to wait for someone to show up.

I saw someone standing off in a distance staring at me. It looked like a man. He came closer without walking. He would disappear and reappear with ease. I don't remember seeing his face. Of all three of those dreams, this one left me dumbfounded. As the person approaches me, disappearing and reappearing in great strides, I rise and stand beneath the tree, watching him get closer. He is not menacing or intimidating. As he gets closer to me, for a brief instance; I catch a glimpse of a beautiful, indescribable face.

He is too beautiful for words. This man GLOWED!!! Before I realized what was happening, I was knelt down before HIM who was draped in a mesmerizing and bewildering white gown. My head was bowed. Then there was a flash of light so bright, I couldn't see anything but white light. When this cleared, I get a full view of an incredible sight. As if I am having an out-of-body experience, in the midst of this dream, I am watching myself go through an incredible scenario.

The entire scene had shifted to the sandy shore of a large body of crystal blue water, which was moving gently behind this incredible figure. I am now an adult, kneeling before this figure, both of my arms are outstretched, my head is leaning all the way back and I am looking up and into the face of this wonderful person. I do remember what he looked like; but you have to see it to believe it. There simply are no words to describe what I saw.

His right arm is fully extended as he holds his hand inches above my forehead. I could see that his left hand was folded across his chest. It looked like an ordination. I regained my senses and woke with a start so jolting, I jumped out of bed and started patting my clothes like they were on fire. I had to look at them to see if I were still wearing that white gown I was kneeling in! I was breathless. All three of these dreams were astounding.

As a ten-year-old child, I never gave any of them much thought. They just felt good. Children who enjoy vacation Bible school, Sunday school and church service have these kinds of dreams all the time, right? I assumed we all did and I summarily dismissed them as just incredible dreams. But for some reason, those dreams left a permanent spiritual impression inside of me and they would prove invaluable when I found myself standing at the crossroads of hope and despair, rage and peace, and life and death.

Around this time, I also had dreams of things that had happened in the little town long before most of its black residents showed up. I sometimes attended vacation bible school in a church that sat on the corner of Barkstone and Hickory, within walking distance from my grandmother's house. But one night, I had a dream that this church sits on a site that used to be somebody's house. The scenery was encased in a thick gray haze and I am dressed in white gliding over the street in front of the church.

Before the church was built, a house used to be in this space. A white family had lived there. "That's strange," I remember thinking. "There are no white people in this neighborhood." Then I saw a small building with two or three air-conditioners sticking out of the windows, propped up by tall two-by-fours. Inside the building, several children, all white, are taping colored pictures to the windows so I assumed it was a school.

Everything was moving in slow motion and there was a faint humming sound coming from somewhere. Before that dream, I never gave any thought to the history of my little town, but it appears that white people had lived in these homes long before we showed up. When I was growing up, there was only one white man living in our neighborhood. Then there were the dreams about my uncle Melton and my grandfather.

In the dream about my grandfather, I saw him laying in a casket on top of a hill. My mom, her sister and two of her brothers were standing around his casket looking at him. The youngest son, Melton, was not present. I knew the dream meant my grandfather was going to die soon; but it also meant my uncle was already dead. I had this dream before either of them passed away.

CHAPTER TWELVE

It was a sticky summer day at dusk and time for supper when I see my uncle Jay running across the yard toward our house. Our house was right next door to his. He was screaming!

"Flo! Flo! Come, Flo! Let's go to mom! Melton is dead!"

"What!?" My mother acted as if she did not hear him correctly. "Melton is de..." she dropped to her knees, "Did you say Melton is dead?!" "Oh God, no! No! No!" "What happened?

"He drowned, Flo." "He just drowned." "Come, we have to go to mom." The scene was chaotic.

My aunt Nona who was visiting us at the time let out a scream so loud, I had to cover my ears. She fell to her knees, beating her fists on the ground. My uncle Jay, stopped resisting his pain; too weak to stand, he laid sprawled out on the ground, sobbing loudly. All the adults were crying inconsolably. All us kids could do was stand by and watch. It was heartbreaking.

I watched my grandmother suffer; she cried for months. Uncle Melton's twin had died at two months old from, according to the symptoms, dehydration. Tears from the kids began to flow when we realized what we had lost. Uncle Melton used to chase us out of my grandmother's willow tree with a switch. He would take the time to play hopscotch and jacks with the girls and marbles or cops-and-robbers with the boys. He was Santa Claus at Christmastime and a prankster during storytelling time. Uncle Jerome, Uncle Melton's brother was a gifted storyteller. He could hold the attention of us kids with some of the scariest stories I ever heard. Sometimes they teamed up on us.

One rainy night, mixed in with the sound of thunder and lightning, and a hard rain beating against the tin roof, Uncle Jerome said he wanted to tell us a story. He turned off the kitchen lights, turned on some flashlights and began telling us the story of a boy named John that went something like this. John's mother sent him to the store to buy some liver for her to cook for dinner. On the way to the store, John had to walk through a cemetery. As he approached the center of the cemetery, John saw a man leaning against a crypt. The man stopped him and asked where he was going. John told him he was on his way to the store to buy some liver for his mother to cook.

The mysterious man said to John, "I have some liver. Give me the money and I'll give you this liver and you won't have to walk all the way to the store." So, John gave the man the money and took the brown package with the liver inside and went home. Bad move. What John did not know is the man was the devil in disguise that had just robbed a grave and stolen a dead man's liver. That night, the dead man came back to John to get his liver back.

Uncle Jerome used many voice inflections. When the dead man called out to John in the middle of the night in a slow and menacing tone saying, "John, John, I'm in the backyard, John," his voice got low and ominous. When he described John's fearful responses, his voice got high-pitched. He was exciting to listen to. At the climax of the story, while all of us watched our uncle's face, wide-eyed and spellbound, hanging on every voice inflection, every word of that story, he said "John, John, I'm right behind you John! I GOT YOU!" Uncle Melton jumped out from the shadows of a dark hallway with white perfume powder covering his face and a flashlight under his chin and yelled, "I GOT YOU!"

All of us screamed at the same time; high-pitched, ear-piercing screams of fright as we abandoned the close-knit bundle we sat in and scurried around on hand and knees trying to find a place to hide. We found hiding places all over the house. I ended up inside a kitchen cabinet competing with pots and pans for space. My cousins hid underneath furniture, beneath beds, everywhere but that creepy room with the vanity in it. Both of my uncles laughed themselves to tears. They got us good that night. Unfortunately, this would be our last story time with Uncle Melton.

Uncle Melton had decided to go to Tennessee one summer to spend time with cousins. While there, the boys went swimming in a lake not far from home. I don't know if Uncle Melton could swim but he was a prankster, at times pretending he was drowning while standing in shallow water. They warned him to stop playing. But, he did this once too often. They saw him beating on the water, pleading for help. Tragically, he had ventured out too far and none of the other boys could swim.

They watched helplessly as my uncle slipped beneath the waters and never resurfaced. He was only twenty years old. The kids were allowed to attend the wake. My aunt Toni took me by the hand and brought me up to the casket where his body lay. He looked like he was sleeping. "Wake up, Uncle Melton," I started whispering to him. "Come on!" "Get out of this box!" "We don't want you to go!" "Come on, wake up!" When he didn't move, I started to cry and through the tears I continued to beg.

"Wake up, Uncle Melton." "Please, tell him to wake up, aunt Toni." I wanted my uncle back. "He's gone, Sue," she said as she began pulling me away from the casket. "He's in heaven. You'll see him again someday," she said. As I am pulled away from his casket, I look at his body one more time and see a tear flowing down the side of his face.

"Don't cry, Uncle Melton. I'll see you again." And with that, I turned away, took my seat and held my head down, sobbing, for the rest of the service. Funerals are the saddest events in the world. All of my cousins, aunts, uncles, friends and especially my grandmother were crying. Uncle Melton was a special person and it hurt to lose him. He is still greatly missed.

He wasn't crying; he was starting to defrost and fluid was leaking from his eye socket. But in my innocent mind, he was crying. I felt guilty for a long time because I knew when he was the only one not present at the site of my grandfather's casket, that he was already dead. How does a child explain something like this to anyone? I didn't tell my mom that poppa was going to die, either. No one would have believed me.

My grandmother had kicked poppa, my grandfather, out of her house many years earlier. She chased him away with a double-barreled shotgun because he always wanted to beat her up and he gambled too much. Poppa became a wandering alcoholic when my grandmother kicked him out. He suffered with chronic health problems but refused medical attention. He lived in near poverty status, in a one-room row house not far from the store. My mother patronized him with free groceries from the store; but that was more to heal her own conscious. She didn't like him either. He was not a nice man. To me poppa was fun. He was almost seven feet tall and the few times I did see him, he would pick me up and sit me on his shoulder.

With my arm wrapped around his head, sometimes covering his eyes, I held on tight, feeling like I could touch the sky. He had a deep baritone voice that made his chest rattle when he spoke. I wasn't close to him, but I liked him. My grandfather's body was not found until several days after he died. I was told that he suffered both a stroke and a heart attack at the same time and he was found after another resident complained about the bad smell coming from his room. My uncle and my aunt Nona found his body his barber's chair, in a grotesque and contoured position. We couldn't attend his funeral, because the minister was concerned about the smell from decomposition.

My grandmother held a closed casket funeral for the family at the burial site and the kids were not allowed to attend. I didn't need to be there; I had already seen him in his casket. I didn't know him well and he never spoke much. But I was curious to know why I was named after his mother. I never got to ask him. In another strange dream, I was standing in a carpeted room, somewhere in a place I had never visited. A young man of about age 20 or 21 comes around a corner, wearing a blue shirt, blue jeans and glasses. This dream did not last long; more like a flash. I just remember he was a black man with a nice smile. He didn't look like anyone I had ever seen in my little town. I didn't think much of it until I saw him again, eleven years later. He was my husband.

All these dreams occurred before the age of eleven. Any traumatic turmoil of my early years was quickly smoothed over under the watchful eye of my grandmother. Apart from the bloody sack, that stupid white teacher, and the mean old woman, I was fine. When my grandmother won a floor model black-and-white television set at the annual fair, I would stand in front of the screen and dance to the tunes of Captain Kangaroo and Sesame Street the way our kids danced to Barney and Lamb Chops.

My cousins and I would draw hopscotch blocks so large you had to make a running start just to jump into the third block, landing on one foot. During my years in elementary and middle school I learned to play musical instruments. By the age of twelve, I had almost mastered the clarinet and tenor saxophone. I was playing the alto saxophone in concert band and had taught myself how to play the keyboard. I was writing my own music, singing in the church choir, winning talent shows and singing as a lead with a local band headed by the high school band director. Life was great…but that would soon change for the worse.

CHAPTER THIRTEEN

In the summer of 1975, six months before my twelfth birthday, my mother's husband lured me into his bedroom and raped me. He threatened to hurt my mother if I told anyone. This would mark the beginning of a life lived in hell on earth and how I would come to understand what it means to hate. His disgusting actions would break the bond of maternal instinct and stress the spirit of resilience to its breaking point. Before this happened, I didn't even know what sex was. I was too busy being a kid. But he was a predator; one of those nemesis personalities that feeds off innocence as a source of power. At the moment that he stole my purity, I stopped living. A light went out inside me and the bayou mystique sealed shut. My grades went from straight A's the previous year to all F's.

My memory stopped working because thinking forced me to relive the incident. Subsequently, I had a hard time remembering. My short-term memory was horrible. After he did this, my personal sense of cleanliness turned into feelings of abject filth. I had never felt such self-hate, so dirty, so nasty, so much like him in all of my life. In his own obscenity, in his act of grimy selfishness, he had managed to pull me into a world known only to his kind of evil. His way of gaining power was to devour the innocence and vulnerability of those least able to defend themselves. He was a coward in every meaning of the word. I had never liked him anyway and this was the ultimate insult.

In my eyes, from that day on, he became a vile creature and a worthless form of human flesh with no self-respect or pride. I hated every breath he took, but my mother took his side, treating me, an eleven-year-old child, like I was her competition. Since I could not get back at either of them, I turned on myself and spiraled into darkness so deep, it took divine intervention to pull me out. For the first ten years of my life, barring a few tense moments, memories from the old rocking chair, visuals from strange dreams, endless school activities, vacation bible school, and numerous joyous times spent playing with cousins made for a blissful existence.

My mind was on chasing the ice-cream truck with a dime in my hand; running barefoot behind the mosquito truck that drove down my grandmother's street spraying pesticides all over the road; and climbing trees with my cousins. I knew evil existed but not this kind. For years I blamed myself for what happened to me. I was incensed because I had underestimated the depth and persistence of evil. Given my level of spiritual sensitivity, I was furious that I didn't see this coming.

I was an eleven-year-old child when this monster raped me. He took something from me that did not belong to him and engaged on a seven-year campaign of terror and manipulation against me to avoid getting caught. He showed me the nature of evil. By watching his behavior, I was able to figure stuff out for myself. I realized that people like my mother's husband, who choose to do such things, hide their real intentions until they succeed in deceiving anyone who is not a target for their filth. He is and always will be a sexual predator.

People with this kind of predatory personality are, generally speaking, the nemesis of all that is good in the world. Their pattern is sinister and their profile reads like a villainous character movie script. With haughty eyes; a lying tongue; hands that shed innocent blood; a heart that devises wicked plans; feet that run rapidly to evil; false witnesses who utter lies; and one who spreads strife among people; there are those who, like my mother's husband, practice such things without a conscious.

There is a flip side to this personality. Common characteristics include low self-esteem replaced with delusions of self-importance; extreme arrogance; deep-seated narcissism; an intoxicating hoarding of power; and severe emotional stagnation. All of them have been abandoned by a trusted support system in some significant way and they let everyone know it. Letting people know this is vital to their wicked behavior.

These people wield their pathetic stories of lost innocence like a chiseling tool, targeting and manipulating weak-minded people to set up a support base. They wrap themselves in self-pity and use the contents of their history as a barrier against feeling empathy and an excuse to avoid change. They love to play the victim and subsequently seal themselves inside a bubble of self-importance, while viewing the rest of the world as either opportunities or barriers to gaining power. We call their opportunities "victims." Child abusers and sexual predators are the serial killers of innocence and vulnerability is their weapon of choice.

They routinely hurt others with no regard for the victim's pain. You see, in their eyes, there are no victims. And if you try to show them the damages they cause, they are quick to point out not only that life has not been fair to them, but also that the person they hurt probably deserved it. In their minds, the people they damage did something to cause their own pain. The predator would also have you believe that they are actually the victims of the people they hurt. That's the garbage they try to feed everyone.

In actuality, all sexual predators adopt a philosophy of entitlement and act as if they have a right to violate another person's body anytime they want to and with no respect for the word "no." They go through great lengths to prevent anyone from showing them the pain they've caused in the lives of others and resist any suggestion that their behavior is demeaning, despicable and evil. While their filthy actions inspire shame and rage in the victims, the sexual predator actually feels empowered. Rarely, if ever, does the sexual predator express empathy or regret.

Violation of a victim is not personal. I could have been any child in the community and my mother's husband would still have attacked me. Monsters like him don't care about the people they hurt or preserving the humanity of another person. They enjoy watching people suffer. Some mental health professionals say that these people cannot be cured. I believe that to be true. Given my own experience, observations and research, I have concluded that for child abusers and sexual predators to acknowledge their damage, forces them to feel, one of the things they avoid.

By the time there is intervention, usually after they get caught, they have done so much evil, empathy is an unwanted burden and they resist change on purpose. Sexual predators try to act like God is not watching what they do, especially people who are in positions in the church. It is woeful displeasure for these to face the madness in their own soul, which is why they dismiss the suffering and pain they inflict on their victims. But someday, they will have to face God and answer to their offense.

Repentance to the sexual predator, is repulsive and not an option. They don't fear repentance; they avoid it. To highlight the suffering they've caused forces the conscious to take stock of restitution. They don't want a conscious. It reminds them that someday they will have to pay for their crimes. These people have no desire to restore their victims' credibility because it diminishes their own source of power. To make them acknowledge the suffering and pain they've caused; to force them to listen to reason and adopt a philosophy of empathy is to deny them access to a victim and the equivalent of pulling the plug of life support on their reason for living. Hunting for victims is not just what the do; it's what they live for.

They would be nothing without a broken person to gloat over. They cling to their victims' pain and suffering with sinister control and rage against anyone who tries to intervene. The suffering of others keeps them happy. Keep in mind, this is not personal. Sexual predators like my mother's husband don't care who the child is or who the child's family is. Their offense is not about a particular child; it's about gaining power.

Everyone has suffered some level of heartache. But most do not adopt a philosophy of destruction. These people simply choose to be the way they are. No responsibility; zero accountability is how they choose to live. It is also critical for them to manipulate and deceive the enablers, those who make excuses for their behavior, because this is their support base. Predators are classic manipulators who control everyone in their sick world who is willing to do as they're told.

Tragically, in many cases of child sexual abuse, the predator's strongest supporter is the child's mother. These are women who at some time or another may have experienced extreme loss of support from a significant caretaker and were frightened into self-isolation. A manipulative predator comes along and notices the mother has a small child or small children, especially girls. He lures the mother in with promises of money, companionship, a lifetime without loneliness, and creative dreams of a false sense of security. He convinces the mother to abandon everything meaningful in her world, including her own child, for the opportunity to feel secure. There is a sinister method to their madness.

As soon as he knows he has manipulated the mother's heart in his favor, he begins to devour her children. I believe that the cries of her child initially get the mother's attention. But when the child complains, he denies everything, putting the mother in position to make a choice. Either heed the cries of a wounded child and do what you must to protect him or her or lose the lifestyle and security the predator has set up.

He makes matters worse on purpose by calling the child a liar, threatening to leave, beating the mother into submission or playing on her emotions by showering her with gifts and empty promises. All the while his focus is on regaining access to the child. But maternal instinct is the most difficult bond to break and the predator knows it. So he interferes with that bond by discrediting the child making special efforts to paint the child as a liar and purposely gets in the way of a mother interacting with her child.

He feeds her pathetic stories of his own childhood that are laced with extreme claims of his own victimization, isolation, abandonment, and lack of love. He repeats this story over and over, even producing phony tears periodically, until the mother's emotions shifts from the cries of her wounded child to this monster's manipulation and she now reacts to his life's story with greater importance and sincerity than the pain of her wounded child.

The child may still be reeling from an initial attack, wondering why his mother will not come to his aid. But help is not coming. In all of the predator's ramblings of pathetic victimization, the child is never mentioned. That's part of the strategy. The predator now has complete control of the mother's thoughts and emotions. He showers her with phony praise and offers promises of lifelong companionship and security and she believes him. The child is now vulnerable, unprotected and in grave danger.

The sexual predator's successful manipulation is what these mothers call "love." They think this is a relationship. It is not. He has set his sights on her child because the child is his source of power. In order to feel in control he has to physically break someone, and he goes after the child. But, now he has a silent partner. The child's own mother deliberately turns away from the cries of her child, because this monster has succeeded in destroying a maternal bond, the most powerful bond in the animal kingdom.

I believe that eventually, the cries of the child become loud and irritating to its mother and threaten to disrupt the mother's secure world. She does not want this to happen. So to protect her false sense of security, she turns on her own child by becoming a partner with the predator. They both engage in a horrifying and disingenuous behavioral pattern of keeping the child silent through isolation, neglect, forced submission, and abuse of parental authority. And whether they are aware of it or not they have forged an unwritten alliance and agreement that as long as neither of them feels empathy and compassion for the child, the sexual predator can keep his power and the mother can keep her secure little world.

They enforce this inhumane reign of terror by proclaiming to God and the rest of the world "what happens in the family, stays in the family." This statement is designed to keep the child and anyone else from seeking help. All inquiries by concerned members outside of their secret family world are met with hostile objections and warnings for everyone to "mind their own business." The child has now become the family's dirty little secret. Sexual predators like my mother's husband deliberately hunt for women with small children for the sole purpose of sexually abusing the child. It is the equivalent of a hungry lion stalking its prey. The mother is incidental; the child is the prey.

Some mothers go so far as to blame the victim for the actions of the predator. When my brothers inquired about my hostility toward her husband, my mother told them "I was still mad about the way he treated me." She avoided telling them *how* he treated me or *why* I was mad. So, of course, in their minds, I am the problem. That's exactly what she wanted them and their families to believe and that's how they treat me.

She goes so far as to have grandchildren staying alone in and around his presence as if to prove to everyone else that I have always been the problem. What she does not tell them, however, is that I threatened to come after him if I hear that he has molested any of my nieces, nephews, or any other child ...and I meant it. As long as the family believes whatever half-truths she tells them, she never has to explain why she chose to support and stay with a man who raped her child. She addresses all my feelings of anger and resentment toward her husband as "a problem with me." She has probably also told her husband what he did to me is not a problem, that I probably asked for it; or I caused him to do this grotesque thing. She supports him to the point of them both believing that he did nothing wrong.

I don't know about anybody else, but as a victim, this leaves me feeling empty. It is incomprehensible to believe that any mother would actually step aside and allow her child to be victimized and feel satisfied with her own life. These mothers have to feel the immense void they've created within the hearts of their children because of abandoning them in such an evil way. They have to, at some point in their own shallow lives, look at themselves in the mirror and ask themselves, "What have I done?"

It is hard to believe that any mother can totally abandon a life she brought into this world to such evil, without sinking into a level of denial so deep that even trying to live a virtuous life after the child is grown or dead, is overshadowed by reflections of a dastardly past brought on by such an egregious decision. In other words, she purposely avoids the self-analytical question, "How can I live with myself?" Mothers who support these monsters to the demise of their own children probably seal themselves inside a bubble of narcissism. They may feel entitled to material possessions, companionship and anything else these monsters promise them and will sacrifice God and child to keep it.

There is no excuse for adults to behave this way. It's wrong and evil to do such things to children. I've seen several sets of statistics on the issue of incest and sexual abuse and all the numbers are staggering. At least three out of every four women and four out of every six men in America have been sexually violated, exploited, or abused either as a child or an adult. I don't know what the stats are on mothers who support these monsters, but I will find out.

I think I understand what most victims of incest and rape go through. When a predator forces himself onto a child, he succeeds in defiling the most sacred countenance of the human existence, life itself. What this monster does is create an internal void by violating all that a man or woman treasures about being human, her dignity. The natural consistency of internal self-love and self-respect is either ripped out or interrupted with traumatizing force. Like a deflated balloon, what is left in the wake of this vicious attack is a decompressed shell of human flesh. While languishing in this hollowed-out existence, this predatory evil force a victim to redefine what is sacred about the human existence.

All that exists in the world that these monsters create is filth and to this monster, nothing is sacred. Some victims implode in order to survive and regain some sense of cleanliness and dignity; refilling this void with self-prescribed virtues and defenses designed to protect a fragile self-esteem. Healthy compassion and self-empathy sometimes becomes loathing self-pity and general happiness often turns into depression as he or she tries to make sense of this forced transformation. Victims go through many changes in attempts to stay connected to humanity without feeling indecent. But a child's transformation from light into the darkness they are forced into is a sentence of perpetual disintegration.

These monsters and their enablers watch, as the victim becomes a mere shell of their former self, sometimes lying motionless in an eerie silence, blinking and staring into an empty and hopeless future. They watch the light dim inside of a once vibrant child and feel empowered by that child's broken soul. They see the child reaching out for help and deliberately block all avenues of hope by isolating her from the rest of the world.

They isolate the young soul and purposely ignore all of the child's cries for mercy, because doing so requires empathy; something the predator and his enabler have agreed not to extend. And they watch as the child puts a fist through her heart to try and fill a void of immense loneliness. They mock the child's desperate cries to God and become more ruthless in their horrible treatment of the child each time she prays as if to prove to her, no one is listening and no one cares. And they mock adolescent attempts at forming meaningful relationships and friendships with ominous verbal warnings that "no one can be trusted."

The predator and his enablers become partners allied against a helpless child, the closest thing to God's heart, and take turns making sure he remains silent. I became my mother and her husband's sick little secret.

He was an evil predator when she met him and she didn't know it. But after she became aware of what he was doing, nothing was done to stop him. Any mother who would allow a predator to ravage her children is a disturbed woman. And it is my opinion that any mother who stays with a man that rapes her child needs serious psychiatric help.

CHAPTER FOURTEEN

My mother is married to a psychopath, a person who likes to absorb the effects of power at the expense of others, particularly those weaker than himself, and he ignores the pain he inflicts to gain that power. She has tried to make me feel sorry for him with regurgitations of his pathetic stories of childhood pains and problems, but I refuse to buy into any excuse he or any other predator offers as justification for raping a child.

Although they love to play the victim, no matter how bad their past was, monsters like my mother's husband choose to live their lives without moral boundaries. The abuser makes a conscious choice to abuse his victim. Such a person is an evil coward; whether this is a parent, grandparent, stepparent, uncle, cousin, aunt, the minister, a schoolteacher, a catholic priest, an entertainer, sports figure or a superstar. I don't care who it is.

These monsters need to step outside their cowardly narcissistic bubble they hide themselves in and grow some self-esteem and a conscious. Each time a predator violates innocence, it appears he (or she) feels an increase in personal power. They seem to feed off vulnerability the way fire responds oxygen. I applaud the professionals who work with the child sex-offender because the most diabolical transformation for any victim is becoming a clone of the predator who abused them.

Sometimes the child victim will repeat the abuse that was done to them, by abusing other children. But I believe there is hope for these children. They can still relearn that personal pain is never an excuse to violate others. I believe we can heal these children and their victims. But the adults, in my opinion, are hopelessly evil. Most of society cannot understand how anyone can abuse a child. We often expect the answers to come from the abusers themselves. Most child abusers will not answer this question with any measure of sincerity, because the attention focuses on the well being of the child. Child abusers don't care about the children. When they abuse children, they don't even see a child. I believe they see a mirror.

In that mirror is a reflection of envy; their own narcissism and all that is hopeless about themselves; all that was lost; all that is painful, hated, pathetic, mutilated, agitating, denigrating, debased, destructive, and disgusting about their own personal childhood experience. I believe all predators and child abusers have experienced some level of arrested development; they get stuck in a "bullying stage."

I've seen and heard the rage. Feelings of revenge seem to dominate over virtue and they engage in spouting out nasty combinations of critiques and criticisms designed to destroy a child's self-esteem. They unleash pent-up and intense anger laced with envy on someone who cannot fight back. They don't want boundaries because of a sick need to feel powerful over someone perceived weaker than themselves. They prey on vulnerability and innocence, paths of least resistance.

What child abusers and predators do to children is beyond comprehension and I believe they do such things because for them to look at a child is to feel disgust; first for themselves and then for the child. They live in their own self-hate, mulling over their own life experience, resenting the beauty and peace that children bring into this world, believing that the carefree nature of any child somehow means that child has it better than they did. They force their neediness onto the shoulders of a child ill equipped to handle adult pain...just like the environment they probably grew up in. Children shed too much light on emotional pain; the kind of pain the abuser does not want to deal with.

It is easier to attack the light that reflects it; put it out; beat it out of commission; destroy the smile and the happiness; make the abused children replicas of themselves; destroy a child's sense of dignity and force innocence to live in darkness. They break the child, this metaphorical mirror that reflects to them all that is missing inside and end up seeing only distorted images of themselves in the reflection of a broken mirror, a broken child; ...their past. Only then, through the broken spirit of an innocent child, can they see a true reflection of themselves.

Child abusers and sexual predators dehumanize children, creating for themselves an avenue for preserving personal power. I make no apologies for my disgust. I don't owe these people anything. Neither the courts nor society owes them anything. Nobody owes child abusers or sexual predators anything except a hard way to go. Mental health professionals are here to intervene, if these people seek help at all. Most don't believe there is anything wrong with them.

If you have been victimized, I strongly encourage you to seek the professional help of a psychologist, counselors, or therapist, but I'd like to comment on a consistent theme I hear far too often; *"you have to forgive (him) in order to move on."* I sought counseling for my abuse. One counselor tried to convince me that most child sex offenders feel remorse for what they've done, especially in cases of incest.

She went on and on about how I should try and understand what it's like for the person to admit to committing such an offense, suggesting that I should feel sorry for him in some way. She claimed that predators feel embarrassed, ashamed, and angry with themselves for having done something so horrible and that some wish they could undo the offense. As a responsible person, I don't doubt that this occasionally does happen; but, as a victim, I don't care.

Another counselor, a male, even suggested that I sit down and talk with this predator to find out why he did this to me. This kind of bullshit rhetoric makes my blood boil. This kind of talk reminds me of my mother and countless other family members, friends, and relatives who make it a personal crusade to protect these monsters as if their religion depended on it. It amazed me that a counselor expected me to extend virtues of empathy, compassion and vulnerability to an asshole that has proven that he does not care about boundaries or anyone else's sense of dignity and well-being. I couldn't understand why anyone, particularly a mental health professional, would advocate or encourage a victim to become vulnerable and extend compassion to a sexual predator who used those very virtues as tools to violate innocence in the first place.

These therapists made me feel like I didn't matter. They acted just like the families who protect these predators, by putting on blinders and convincing themselves that incest is an isolated taboo that does not need to be publicized or dealt with exclusively from a victim's perspective. Just like the families who protect these monsters, I feel like these counselors purposely close their eyes to the victim's nightmare, in order to either explain or justify the predator's sinister behavior.

In the process of doing so, they ignore a very specific and disgusting truth. Everyone must remember this one very important fact. This predator *pre-meditated* his assault. Sexual predators watch their victims with the stealth of a hungry snake. They plot, prepare, and execute a filthy plan of attack on a child like the sexual cannibals that they are. What part of this diabolical maneuvering should I or anyone else in society take time to understand?

I spent several years in therapy trying to undo the traumatic evils of rape and child abuse. I attempted to digest this version of forgiveness. But, the only thing it did was make me mad because what several therapists tried to do was get me to forget about what happened and try to understand the offense from the predator's and my mother's point of view. This was unacceptable, and I believe these counselors were either incompetent or insensitive to the point of avoiding my pain…on purpose.

I believe they preached this mantra of forgiveness because it kept them from having to feel empathy for a violation that is truly disturbing to empathize with. If I had been just beaten or abandoned or ridiculed into shame, I believe any counselor could have extended some level of empathy because they could identify with the dynamics of physical and emotional pain. But a victim of rape, incest or sexual violation carries an aura of physical indecency within the dynamics of their pain and their story. Empathy requires some level of visual and physical self-identification with a victim, but for those who have never been violated, identifying with the dynamics of a sexual abuse victim, particularly on these two levels, feels bad; it feels dirty; it feels disgusting. No one wants to own or envision these uncomfortable feelings…ever. Not even counselors. It's so much easier for counselors to focus on forgiving the behavior of the perpetrator and their enablers and let the victim figure out the rest or learns to "get over it."

Let me tell you something about forgiveness and how I learned to deal with it. When someone physically attacks us, we have every right to defend ourselves or retaliate. And we are not in the mood to feel sorry or compassion for someone who has no problem beating the hell out of a child; stripping someone of their dignity; preying on vulnerability; or destroying innocence. Forgiveness only means that we've decided to build a barrier between the pain and the right to retaliate; choosing instead to voluntarily set aside our right to beat the hell out of that son-of-a-bitch for complicating our life. This menace is not worth going to prison.

Forgiveness is not an emotion; it's an action that requires you to make a decision to *do something* that will eventually lead to a desired effect or change. It can represent making a decision to put up a temporary barrier against the onslaught of pain these people cause. For some of us, it is choosing to let God or someone else deal with the evil while we concentrate on healing. Think of it this way. As a victim, if you were in a car accident and suffered injuries, you must leave the scene of the accident and heal before you can come back and deal with the carnage. There is very little you can do if your injuries are two broken legs and a shattered collarbone. You must leave and heal before you can deal with the after effects of the trauma. Forgiveness in situations such as this is a lot like walking away from a bad accident that was not your fault.

Leave that mess right where it is and choose a path away from the pain. Heal first. Then come back and deal with the issues. This is only one version of forgiveness and I'm sure there are many others. My intention is to stress that forgiveness in this context, is the decision to hold all things constant, freezing your past and your pain in time, until you are ready to assess the damages and deal with the effects. It allows you to turn away from the memory until you are healthy enough to deal with the pain. Choose to create a path away from the pain and work on vindicating your honor and restoring your faith in God and humanity.

There is only one power, in addition to God, that can overcome this evil and that is love. You must learn to reestablish, rather than redefine, what is pure and wholesome about your existence, using the one thing no monster, predator or evil can touch; your own soul. Learn to love yourself from the inside. I do realize that some attacks are more vicious than others and I don't want to minimize the enormous amount of courage it takes to overcome and survive in spite of the attack. But, I do believe that the power to heal is in us of all.

As hard as it will be in the beginning, focus on the positives of what you want to create, rather than on what you want to change, because creativity comes from within. And no matter what has happened to you, nothing can take away the powers of love and creativity. Cry as much as you need to; tears can be cleansing. But embrace the fact that it's okay to love yourself; create within yourself a personal space of purity; hold on to the power of prayer and your life will find its light again.

If this evil menace is already dead or no longer in your space, in the words of a wise psychologist, remember he or she cannot hurt you anymore. Seek the help of a professional on how to choose or create a path away from the pain. When somebody ravages your dignity with such evil narcissism, they force you to discover extraordinary strength. That strength abides in the potential power of the spirit. When you rely on the spirit for strength, you can stand down evil and overcome anything it can throw at you. I went through many changes because of what happened to me. All victims of abuse go through changes. Abuse forces change. The predator and the enabler ignore the opportunity to change. Victims of abuse should always embrace the opportunity to change because it may be the bidding of the spirit's power that it is time to heal.

To these counselors and family members, relatives, or whoever you are who support these freaks and work overtime to protect them, I have this to say. Until you've been victimized by these monsters and understand what it's like to have your dignity violated; until you can look a victim in the eyes and say "I would gladly trade places with you if I thought it would stop your pain;" until enablers can look these predators in the eyes and say to them that living a respectable life does not mean prowling for sexual victims with the mindset of a vibrating sex toy; until these counselors are willing to support legislation to mandate that all convicted sex offenders serve the life sentence it sometimes takes their victims to heal; until you can convince these monsters that a child's body is not their personal property; and until you can inspire a Godly conscious in these predators who molest children; if their only purpose for living is to use human beings as sexual property, they will be regarded as a disgusting waste of human life.

All that I just spoke of, I had to learn. Getting through this was not easy and achieving healing was a struggle. Most of the characteristics I described about the child abuser, the sex-offender and the enablers are based on my own life experience. The strange little child who loved her great-grandmother's old rocking chair was caught off guard by the depths of evil. I suffered greatly, but I was not destroyed.

I relied heavily on pearls of wisdom acquired by following the guidance and wisdom of the elders and the bayou's mystique. There was also a spiritual perspective to my observations that gave me something extra to hope in. And if you believe in a spiritual afterlife, I would encourage all silent sufferers not to worry; neither the abusers nor their enablers will get away with any offense.

CHAPTER FIFTEEN

I had recorded all of my childhood dreams and other visions in a diary when I was growing up. But my mother's husband poured gasoline on my diary and set it on fire. He burned it right in front of me. I guess he figured I had written down details of how he tortured, raped and molested me and didn't want anybody to find out. But, that wasn't enough. He took away my music, my instruments, my writings and my freedom. Life became a prison.

This man was a deacon in the church. He carried the communion tray during the Sunday service ritual of the Lord's Supper. On the Sundays that he carried the tray, I would refuse to accept communion, because, I felt like he had defiled the purity of the service. On occasion, he prayed for himself, never mentioning his filthy indiscretions and offenses against me and perhaps, others. But his prayers were baseless. According to scripture, "he who turns away his ear from listening to the law, even his prayer is an abomination." That explains for me, why he has found only sickness and ill health rather than the peace he prayed for.

He has sealed his own fate. They all do. Trust me when I say this. No one gets away with anything. And for those of you who have done such horrific deeds and thought no one was watching, I have disturbing news. I saw a bumper sticker once that said, "If you have been living like there is no God, you'd better be right!" As I mentioned earlier, my mother and her husband owned one of only two grocery stores in the black part of town. I worked there all of my adolescent life. I was a lonely little person. Friends were afraid of my mother's husband, so I only saw them at school. By the end of middle school, I was isolated, a common tactic of child molesters and abusers.

I was not allowed to talk on the phone, go to parties, or watch television. I used to sneak and watch TV when he wasn't around. The store, church, school and, visits to relatives' homes became my only outlets. Sometimes, when I got a break from the store, which was rare, I would steal away to my Aunt Toni's house. No one knew I was going over there. Uncle Lyle, the one who had given me the walking doll, had passed away years ago and I would go to visit my aunt just to stay close to family. Besides, she made the best homemade cakes in the world and had the patience of Job. She taught me how to make "popcorn balls," a favorite childhood snack. I would sit in Great-Aunt Toni's T.V. area, in uncle Lyle's big easy recliner that had cotton stuffing sticking out of holes in the seat and listen for hours, as she talked about her life as a child.

"I was bon skinny an black as tar; but momma died the day I was bon," she would say. "I nevva knew ma momma." I *loved* listening to the elders speak. There was so much wisdom in their words. But there was also revealing truth mixed with immense sadness. Their words were spoken with magnificent strength; yet, mixed in the stories were moments of pain and regret. Most days she would pour us both a cup of coffee milk and start every conversation with "I don know why de white people tret us so bad; it din mek no sense for dem to tret us so bad. We was good peopous." She (and her siblings) spoke with a thick Creole accent and I do no justice to the beauty of the dialect.

But as this conversation took a more serious, personal turn, the air in the room became thick and heavy with emotion; an ominous feeling crept over me. Today would be different. "We came from a plantation in Virginie; Anna walked all de way from Virginie with a lot of oder black and Injun folk; come wid a lil' boy name Richard. Anna don bon in Geech I'lan; brought to dat Virginie plantation to work in de white folk kitchen. A'ter slav'ry stop, she and dat boy come yere and set down. Dat's whad de tole me."

By word of mouth, someone had kept track of the family ancestry which was traced all the way back to a plantation in Virginia and a place called "Geechie Island." Great-aunt Toni, my grandmother, and their two surviving older brothers all had shiny, dark black skin and piercing *"sky blue"* eyes. No one knows "how" they got those blue eyes; but today, while I stared intensely into the windows of her soul, she would tell me a story about her life that pierced me so deeply, I wept alone, in silence for days.

"Yo granmoder, yo daddy's momma; dey's some evil folk. Her sista, dead, dat's what we call her, she married ma daddy when ma momma died. Dat woman was mean as a snake." Tears began drop from the distant stare in her eyes, onto her face, but her voice never cracked and she spoke without hesitation. "You know wat she use to do? She would cook fo ha'sef an poppa; dey wood eat first. Den she wood bring some food out in a pan when poppa was not around and put it on de ground or on de poach. Here, Lil' black dog; dat's wat she call me, a lil' black dog; here yo food." "Lil' black dogs don eat on my plate," she say; an den jes thro de pan down so hard sometime de food wood fall on de ground or all ova de poach. I had ta drank wader out da faucet outside.

She was mean, dat one. Poppa nevva sed nothin. I don tink he knew. Sometime when poppa wen huntin, she mek me sleep on de front step outside cause, lil' black dogs don sleep in her house. I din let no hate set in ma hart. When I turn sixteen, I ran away an got marry to a military man an travel to Europe wid him. I nevva come back to dat house again."

I could not believe what I was hearing. My great-aunt Toni was treated the same way I was by the same family and I started to cry. "Don cry, sha. It be awright. God don lack ugly. He tek care of dem soon 'nuff." Another long pause; the tears don't stop flowing. But, she continued. "You know, Nan-Lee, (my grandmother) did not lack dis fam'ly; special when yo momma marry Dead nephew. She din lack it one bit! Special when dey took you from Nan-Lee house an med you stay wid Dead sista. Oooh! Nan was fightin' mad. Nan-Lee nevva lacked yo step-daddy.

Dat whole fam'ly; dey's some mean folk. You be careful, Suzaunna. I don lack dat man eeder." That would be the last conversation I would have with Aunt-Toni. My mother's husband found out I was going over there and stopped me from visiting unless the whole family was there. I cried for my aunt for a long time after that. And I didn't realize it at the time, but I was also crying for myself.

Those tears, both hers and mine, would provide the cleansing I needed to keep my heart from growing cold. My aunt Toni was one of the quiet, humble members of the church community who taught me to pray with sincerity. I learned that day, to be compassionate. But I held strong contempt for this man and his family. After they stopped me from going to my aunt's house, I started sneaking away to a different hideaway.

Behind the now torn down rubble of the dilapidated John Stacy High School building across the street, sitting on the football field, stood an old, run down, yellow building, in desperate need of painting. This was the school/town library. It sat high off the ground on concrete blocks. The rear end of an old air-conditioning unit was always sticking out of its only window; running full blast in the hot, sticky, summers.

Inside were two small kindergarten-sized tables with four chairs each, which provided support for exploring an author's work. The books and the building smelled like mildew mixed with Crayola crayons and Elmer's paste glue. The aroma is nostalgic now. I could go inside the library, sit under the window-mounted air-conditioner and read anything I wanted to.

Most of the time, the librarian and I were the only ones in there. This was my hideaway from a world of torment. When I needed to exhale, this was my space. This is where I first met Curious George, Dr. Sues and the Hobbit. When I arrived one day to find the door permanently locked and the windows boarded up, I sat on those concrete steps and cried. *But, …I have books to return…*was all my bleeding heart could spit out.

I walked away from that little building in tears, with a lump in my throat and my face dragging the ground, looking back over my shoulder several times, hoping the door would open by itself. I *needed* that space. My world was ugly again. My friend in the sky had disappeared. I needed something to hold on to. I had clung to this space, and now my little corner of peace, my safe haven, the little library had shut me out. "Where do I go now?" I wondered.

As I was walking slowly away from that building, it started to rain. My thoughts drifted to a time when I was about six, when life was simple. Before age ten, my mother used to send me to vacation bible school at my grandmother's church, during the summer. The school was held in a little red brick building across the churchyard. I sent my pain to a time when we were taught to memorize bible verses.

We would sit outside and eat cookies and milk for lunch and then prance around the church campus playing ring-around-the-roses with other little girls. I didn't have a care in the world. I used to bring home treasured bible verses and colored picture cutouts for mom and grandmother to feel proud of me.

Vacation bible school was fun. Twenty elementary school kids, six and seven year olds would sit on church pews, girls in white dresses and boys in black pants and tucked-in white shirts and listen to the bible teacher, usually a fat lady wearing a white hat and a white dress, tell us about the "greatest story ever told." She told us about this man who died because some mean people nailed him to a cross. "He let them kill him," she told us. "He died to save everybody in the world from sin."

"What's a sin?" we would ask each other during break.

We didn't know what sin was; just that it was really, really bad. The class would always end with a song every little southern child grows up singing, and today, in this painful moment, the words rang loudly in my ear: "Jesus loves me this I know; for the bible tells me so; little ones to him belong; they are weak but he is strong. Yes, Jesus loves me; Yes, Jesus loves me; Yes, Jesus loves me; the bible tells me so." As tears fell down my face and started I shaking from the chill of wet clothing, walking in the rain, I wondered as I began feeling sorry for myself, "Where is Jesus now?"

CHAPTER SIXTEEN

My aunt Toni was taken from me, the little library had locked me out and I had grown weary of living. The year was 1976 and it was a hot, sticky, humid July summer day. The air was so thick it felt like he was pressing down on my face with a pillow again, smothering me, trying to muffle my screams. My life was in chaos and I had become a deeply troubled child. I wanted to die. It's all I thought about and I was consumed by the finality of death.

In my confusion, I rejected all hope and it was moot to try and reason with my irrational thoughts. At age twelve and a half, I hated my life; the sparkle of innocence was gone, the old rocking chair was gone, my dreams had stopped and I no longer believed in hope. The time had come for me to force the inevitable. I don't know how the concept of suicide entered my mind, but it did.

Soon, suicide was the only choice I wanted to make. It was the only rationale I allowed. I had planned this for at least six months, ever since "it" happened. There was no way I was going to live in this evil world; not like this. I had to die and get away from this place and today was the day. I pulled out the large bottle of Bayer aspirin I had taken out of our grocery store, went into the bathroom, emptied all 100 pills into my mouth and washed them down with water. Then I went into the den where my mother's husband was sitting, passing right by my mother who busied herself in the kitchen, and in absolute defiance, filled with rage, and wanting to punish both of them, I sat down on the couch and waited to die… right in front of them. "Look at him," I remember thinking, "I don't know why he's holding the newspaper open. The son-of-a-bitch can't even read!"

Neither of them even acknowledged that I had walked into the room. It didn't matter. Living in this family was a curse. I didn't know who put me there, but I was determined to leave. Death was my only exit. I waited; pretending to watch some kind of sport show on television. Pretense had kept me alive. That's how I survived since the day he hurt me. I pretended that life had swallowed me whole, making me obsolete and unimportant. I pretended to live, even though I was already dead inside. I barely spoke a word to anyone, even in school. Soon, life would be over and I wouldn't have to pretend anymore; I wouldn't have to cry anymore.

I could rest the weary soul of a once vibrant, weird little girl whose life had now been unfairly broken. Once this is over, I reasoned, I wouldn't have to feel angry, enraged, miserable or even hopeful anymore. I did not even THINK about God and praying never crossed my mind. I remember those moments so clearly. In a few minutes, after starting to feel lightheaded, I waited to just go to sleep. I assumed I would just die and everything would be good for me again.

Maybe I could start my life over with a new family that cared about me. I was already living in a coffin; all they had to do now was burry me. Suddenly, the room became a blur; I started hearing muffled moans coming from somewhere and there was a strange ringing in my ears. My head started to feel very heavy and I actually breathed a sigh of relief. "Finally!" I thought. "I am dying. It will all be over soon." I slumped over... to the right...and blacked out.

"Stop it! Leave me alone!" These were thoughts that suddenly popped into my head, because halfway down, my body jerks back up into the sitting position, pushed up by an unseen force. As my body begins to lean sideways again, under deadweight, someone pushes me on my shoulder again; shoving me with tremendous force. It was forcing me to sit upright and wake up! In my mind, I started screaming, "LEAVE ME ALONE! STOP IT!" The second time my body slumps over and I'm shoved back into a sitting position, my head, feeling like a ton of bricks on my shoulders, turns to the right seemingly under its own power. In a drug-induced stupor; I am trying to see who keeps disturbing my death. I was consumed by anger and learned that day that even in death, anger follows.

I was dying in the same emotional state I presently lived. Did I think it would be any different? The thought had never crossed my mind. I thought the pain was going to stop; it didn't. At first, I thought the culprit was one of my little brothers. The oldest one, a vibrant nine year old, was famous for jumping off church pews during Sunday School when he was seven, so I just knew he was the one sitting there irritating me. I glanced to my right with blurred vision and when my eyes began to water, I fought back the tears with rage. "NO!" I mumbled. "NO TEARS!" "CRYING IS NOT ALLOWED!"

I felt like my soul was already dead. There was no part of me left to feel anything. I had long since learned to avoid any offerings of love because it frightened me. There would be no crying on this day. I had cried enough. I had planned for this day; and it was my time to finally remember what it felt like to smile. I glanced over my right shoulder to see who kept pushing me on my shoulder. *No one was sitting next to me.* "Who keeps shoving me?" I asked angrily. "STOP IT!" "LEAVE ME ALONE!" This time I heard myself spit out these words, but I was too weak to yell and my tongue felt like a brick.

Off in a distance, muffled by the ringing in my ears, I heard the distinct sound of a rattling newspaper and clanging dishes; but neither of them said a word to me. I didn't care anymore. I was dying right there in front of them; barely breathing, gasping for air and feeling like my lungs were on fire. I was losing my hearing and getting weaker by the moment. I stayed calm with a bizarre self-assurance and enough satisfaction in knowing that soon they would have to suffer the inconvenience of burying me.

I slumped to my right one last time and everything faded to black. But then suddenly a massive light appeared in front of me; first as a huge ball and then it takes on a human form. This light reaches inside my body and lifts me off the couch, *right out of my body*, leaving it lifeless and slumped over on the couch. Too weak to stand on my own, this light, this very powerful being, cradles an embrace around and beneath my shoulders and hoists me up while both arms dangled at my side. There was absolute silence.

Everything was so still. And without a body, I was keenly aware of everything; I "felt" like I still had a body, but I could see it slumped over on the couch as I struggled to stay conscious. I started fighting to stay alive because I needed to see who this was. The anger, the rage, the pain, had all disappeared. All was silent, but I was not at peace.

While I am being held up, my head is bobbing back and forth and feeling very, very heavy. *"Who is this?"* That question dominated my thoughts. It was neither my mother nor her stupid husband. Although my peripheral vision was a complete blur, I could "see" them as clear as day, ignoring me. They probably saw my body slumped over on the couch and thought I was sleeping.

My awareness was so sharp that I felt like a spectator, watching this whole thing unfold; and yet I could feel everything that was happening to me. At one point, my head rocked back so hard, I thought it would fall off my shoulders. I glanced over my shoulder. My vision was a blur; so I don't know how I saw this but, just over my shoulders loomed an ominous darkness. I saw human silhouetted forms shifting around in a smoky haze. It was creepy. These people were just wandering. I felt absolutely dumbfounded.

But there was an awareness about me, a form of consciousness that was recording everything. A brilliant light surrounded me. This person who snatched me off that couch, out of my body, glowed and something was happening to me that I cannot explain. I felt warm all over but I had no physical power. As this person continues to carry me, my head jerked forward, and I glanced at the floor. The tips of my toes were *dragging* against the floor. I don't know if I were already dead or still dying.

But someone was carrying me; holding me up; and walking me in circles around the dinner table. I was hanging there on this powerful arm like a wet towel. I focused my vision on the unusual bright light that surrounded this strange being and all I saw were rays of a brilliant light. This is how I stayed awake. This person, a large human form, glowed with an unearthly brilliance that is hard to describe. My body was lifeless; but this light would not let me die. That strange light seemed to penetrate, almost replace my soul.

Something was happening to me; like I was being transformed from the inside. I felt no pain and no pressure. My body was lifeless; my soul was out; but this person would not let me die; not like this. This someone who was keeping me stuck somewhere between here and there, was changing me and carried me as if it were his mission. I remember looking once more into the brilliance of this light; then my head jerked forward, violently, and everything faded to black again.

I woke up laying on my bed, with my stomach feeling like I had just swallowed sour pickles and salted ice. Nauseated, dripping with sweat, and fighting this annoying ringing in my ears, I ran to the bathroom and started vomiting until green stuff came up. That was so disgusting. But, then I got angry. "WHY AM I STILL HERE?" "I WAS SUPPOSED TO DIE!" Indeed, I wanted to die. "I HATE THIS PLACE!" I was yelling into the air. I didn't want the light to leave me and I felt abandoned again. Now, I was angry at the light that had saved my life.

CHAPTER SEVENTEEN

Saying "I want to die" was a daily mantra for me. I became excited at the possibility that I might die at any moment. I craved death because the abuse had gotten worse. I refused think about what happened. I was too angry. I didn't want hope; it was too dangerous and only led to more pain and disappointment. Life in this world was ugly. I blocked out everything from that first experience with alcohol. I couldn't deal with this the pain in this life.

But I would soon find out in dramatic fashion that the experience had left an indelible imprint on my life and allowed me to see and experience things far more spiritual than anything I had ever learned in my Southern Baptist church service. It seems the "bayou mystique" was coming back to life, needing to disclose more of her secrets. But the rules had changed. Now her revelations and disclosures would become a means for survival. For a while, after the suicide attempt, the abuse stopped. I woke up this particular morning angry and muted.

In early August that same summer, just before the start of school, I was outside half-heartedly playing cross-country tag with some cousins. One of them fell and twisted his ankle. Without hesitation, I ran over to him, touched his ankle, and got more than I bargained for. In a flash, I saw his parents fighting, while he cowered in a corner, frightened, shaking and sobbing uncontrollably. Immediately, I jerked my hand away from him like a snake had just bitten me, ran into the house, into a corner of my own room and started pacing back and forth. "What the hell just happened?" I questioned. "How could I have seen this?"

I grabbed my head in my hands and started trembling, screaming in my own mind, "No! No! No!, I don't want this! I don't want this!" After that, except for accepting a rare hug, I touched no one. But then something strange started to happen which made me realize I didn't need to touch anyone to see into other things. The daydreaming thing I used to do when I was a little kid started coming back stronger than ever. But they were filled with distortions of torture. I think I was becoming psychotic and didn't realize it. I started drinking heavily to avoid the dreams, the visions and to numb the pain, but all this did was make things worse.

Now I couldn't tell if I were really dreaming or if the alcohol was causing me to hallucinate. Whatever happened to me the day my life collided with the light was profound. Something was different about me. I was not sure what that "something" was, but I felt like I had been flipped inside out. There was something else. I realized that the daydreaming visuals appeared distorted because I was starting to remember things about the failed suicide attempt.

One day while I was sober and sitting in a lonely corner of my room, my mind wandered back to the day my death collided with the light. And I started to remember everything; a revelation of just how much I had changed. While I was dying, with just that chance glance over my shoulder, I saw into another realm. Let me tell you what I saw. This place looked like some kind of park or holding place.

I saw people who had passed on, "living" in that space in the same emotional condition in which they had died. They looked despondent and defeated. They were crying, wandering, sitting, or moving about slowly, but going nowhere. Although there were many people there, they did not talk to each other. Each person seemed too wrapped up in their own suffering to realize they were not alone. There was no peace here.

In another area, I saw several people who looked like ministers dressed in fancy robes. They each held a mask in front of their faces. They appeared to be preaching to an audience of people, dancing and performing like minstrels in a dramatic stage play, putting on a show for spellbound followers. People were gathered around jumping up and down, crying, screaming, yelling, dancing around, and praising this strange messenger, all the while ignoring the stream of light which shone in their midst. I couldn't hear them, but I read their body language. I saw people who looked alike, gathered together. They shared the same features; like they were clones of each other. This whole place was surrounded by a wall of darkness.

There were overwhelming feelings of bitterness, hostility, anger, resentment and rage just lingering in a smoky swirling haze that surrounded this park. In my hour of death, I probably should have been sentenced to this realm. I don't know why the light rescued me. Perhaps, even after crossing over into this realm of darkness, there is hope. Perhaps the light was still available to everyone in this realm and they must go into the light...by choice. I don't know what it meant. All I know is I didn't speak to anyone; no one seemed to notice I was there. And I don't even know how I made it back into my bedroom.

But after that incident with my cousin, I did not want anyone to touch me. I could see into the lives of certain people when they touched me and not all of it was pleasant, especially the man who continued to rape me. There was so much hate coming from this man, that I would get nauseated at the smell of his presence. And most times, after losing yet another desperate fight against him, with a shirt, towel or a pillow pressed against my face to muffle my screams, I would dissociate and mentally leave my body; disappearing into a field of beautiful flowers, the same field of flowers I saw in a dream when I was ten years old.

My dreams returned; but, now they had turned into nightmares and for several months after the suicide attempt, I couldn't distinguish between fantasy and reality. My concentration deteriorated. I started having horrifying nightmares of being attacked by huge snakes, finding my mother's head in the clothes dryer, and seeing my brothers chopped into pieces and strewn all over the house. When the dreams became too disturbing to sleep, insomnia took over. Sometimes I stayed awake for days at a time, hallucinating, hearing and speaking to imaginary voices and holding conversations with my stuffed animals. I had become a psychological mess.

But I had two dreams one after the other that saved my sanity. They made such an impression on me that the nightmares and hallucinations stopped immediately. The first one occurred at night on a rare occasion when I was able to sleep and had not been drinking. I felt that familiar sensation of feeling like I was going slowly uphill on a roller coaster and POP! I am out of my body and sort of half-floating, half-walking down the hallway in my mother's house.

The kitchen had a strange orange glow to it. There was a glass storm door attached to doorframe of the kitchen and the main door was open, allowing me to see the van we owned parked inside the garage. All of a sudden I see something come to the door and shake it violently like it's trying to get in. Someone chases it away. Then I hear a loud bombing sound, BOOM! I jumped as if someone was shooting at me. I heard commotion outside and watched four men, dressed in white robes put something in the luggage rack, on top of the van. They had wrapped it in a white sheet. A portion of the sheet fell away from what appeared to be the outline of a body and what I saw horrified me.

This thing looked like a burned and charred gargoyle. It was ugly and stared right at me. It had slanted eyes, pinpoint pupils, fang-like teeth, claws or extra-long nails and a sarcastic grin on its face. This thing, if it had been shot, was not dead. Its gaze followed me and warned that it was coming for me and it was going to kill me. I backed out of the kitchen, went back to my room, jumped back in bed and covered my head; trembling in fear. I woke up startled and stayed awake the whole night, afraid to go back to sleep.

The next day I swore off alcohol, fearing that monster might make good on his promise if I continued to drink. The next night, the other dream occurred. The same thing happened. I was about to go to sleep when I felt like I was traveling uphill on a roller coaster and Pop! in the dream, I am out of my body again. This time I find myself crossing over into another realm, literally stepping across a line drawn in the sand.

CHAPTER EIGHTEEN

I stepped through a veil of smoke and found myself standing at the entrance of a cave. I leaned forward and looked inside. Suddenly, I heard commotion coming toward me; so I moved to the left side, ducking beside the cave's entrance, attempting to get out of sight. As the noise got closer and an interesting sight goes pass me. I saw several large, charred, dark centinnal-like creatures surrounding and walking alongside transparent people who looked like ghosts, as if they were escorting them into the cave. These people kept their heads bowed and they did not look happy.

I remembered thinking, "I've seen this creature before." This felt creepy but I was not afraid. After they went pass me, I peered into the cave again and began walking a path inside. When I look to my left, I notice the walls were charred. The floor of the cave was covered with what looked like ashes and swirling smoke. And I also noticed a faint orange glow off in a distance and walked toward it. The glow turned into dancing flickers and subtle hollow moaning sounds began to emerge from deep inside this cave. It was ominous. Something compelled me to continue.

An opening appeared at the end of this corridor and the distinct features of a large circle began to form in the center of this chamber of charred walls. Standing in a hollowed out opening of the corridor, I saw a sight that is forever burned into my conscious. Many people, hundreds of them, male and female, transparent ghostly figures, were immobilized and stuck against the charred walls of this enormous circle, in rows and layers.

Some of them flailed transparent arms and legs all over the place as if trying to free themselves; others moved their heads in odd contortions; and some just wrung the hands. All of them had something to say. Some moaned loudly as if in agony and intermittently those moans quickly turned into deep, penetrating sobs; uncontrollable weeping; and cries for help. Some were apologizing. "I am soooo sorry." "Please, help me." "How do I get out of here?" Others shouted obscenities and threats. "I hate you!" "Get me off this @#!%* wall!" You @#$%* make me sick! "I'm glad I #@$!%* did it!" "Die!"

The noise was deafening and their cries were indescribable. I remember thinking, "These people are in serious trouble." The venomous tones of rage were incredulous. This was more than just agonizing confinement; these people appeared to be condemned. It was clear that all hope was gone. No one came to their rescue. There was no light here; just that strange flicker dancing and bouncing shadows off the charred walls. I thought I also heard the faint sound of menacing laughter. Someone thought this was amusing.

At first, I could not understand why these poor souls didn't just get off the wall and leave this place. It soon became clear to me why they would NEVER leave this place. They were escorted here, but not against their will. They had earned this space. Quick flashes of movement caught my gaze and when I realize what it was, I knew I would never again doubt the existence of hell. With just a subtle gaze toward a space just within sight of any one of these people, right on the charred walls, for their own personal viewing, scenes of heinous acts of violence played over and over again, like movie highlights. They were watching every scene of their own lives in review; their hands committing evil against humanity.

The offenses of the condemned were on display for their own personal viewing. But, what was most intriguing is the scenes would shift and show the turmoil of the victims after the crime was committed and the condemned was forced to live through their victims' suffering. Lives in review were everywhere; too disgusting and too horrifying for words. Even as I tried to ignore the replays, I could not get away from the hopeless sense of finality of this place.

While standing completely inside this chamber I noticed a huge pit in its center. That's where that strange flickering light was coming from. There were other transparent people standing around the edge of this pit. "Why are they just standing there?" I remembered thinking this. I moved in for a closer look. It looked like fire but it didn't "feel" hot. I inched closer to get a look inside this pit and became transfixed and frozen with terror by what I saw. There were people's souls in this pit.

Transparent, ghostlike figures were inside this strange burning pit. This fire was not normal; the flames looked like invisible rays from the sun. But these souls were burning! This strange fire would consume them completely, revealing grotesque and distorted grimaces; facial images of unrelenting pain. They burned, in slow motion, unmercifully, and non-stop. I wondered how did they get in there and soon I got my answer. They just *appeared in there.*

I watched a bizarre scenario unfold. First the figure would come away from the wall, disappearing from the wall and reappearing at the edge of the pit, with their reviews following them. While standing on the crest of this pit and then as if on command, they would just appear inside of it, screaming in extremely high pitch voices. Some were completely consumed and never reappeared, reviews and all. Others, as soon as the flames consumed them, their souls would reappear, as would their reviews and they would burn up all over again, as if this person had more than one victim.

The moaning, deep, heart wrenching sobs, and desperate cries mingled with that menacing laughter and were non-stop. As they burned, scenes of their lives played over and over again, but some of them seemed focused and transfixed toward the ceiling of this chamber as if they were staring at both the scenes of their lives and *someone*. I wondered who they were looking at, but this time I didn't want to know. The thought of asking that question was enough to jolt me back into focus.

I didn't look up to see nor did I wait for an answer. This place housed too much suffering for me. The scene was ghastly and I wanted out! I began to slowly back my way out of the chamber, to get out of this horrible place when I was startled by the sound of movement to my left. Oh…my…God! A scream stuck in my throat. I will never forget what I saw. There on the wall of the cave, my mother's husband hung upside down by one leg, stuck to the charred wall; not as a ghostly figure, but in the flesh. He had a look of absolute terror in his eyes. Every other being was right side up; he hung upside down.

He stretched out his right arm, reaching his hand toward me, as if signaling me to help him down. "No, I cannot help you," was all remember thinking. I don't know if I could have helped him or not. I didn't want to and I didn't try. As I am backing out of this horrible place, my last sight was of him holding out his hand in the entrance of that cave still beckoning me to help him; the shadow of his outstretched arm dancing on the charred walls of the corridor; a shadow cast by the flickering glow of radiating, wavy, energy coming from the pit.

I woke up with that familiar Thud! and a bad headache with that image in my head, hoping he was really dead and the evil was finally gone. He was not. But that day, I accepted that this was his final destination. The moment that dream ended, the nightmares, the visual hallucinations, hearing voices, even the habit of talking with my stuffed animals, all stopped. My mind became clear and I felt a strange sense of peace that is hard to explain.

This happened in the Spring of 1978. The dramatic events and significance of both dreams halted psychiatric symptoms that had interfered with normal functioning on every level. My concentration and grades improved; church functions were tolerable; and I made new friends at school. He stopped attacking me, and for a while, I could breathe. I was allowed to visit my grandmother more often. The old rocking chair, however, was gone and the house was being remodeled.

That summer, his niece and her nine kids came to live with us. All nine of her children were for nine different men. And she was no different from the rest of his violent family. They came to live in our little town because the department of family and children services had threatened to take her children away because she was a drug addict and was neglecting them. I was already burdened with caring for two pre-adolescent stepbrothers and an infant stepbrother; but he took them in and I was told to take care of her nine kids as well.

There were eight girls and one boy. While their mother stood outside smoking marijuana with other drug heads, I was forced to comb the girls hair, wash all the childrens' clothes and cook for the entire family while my mother worked at the family grocery store. At age fifteen, I was expected to care for the needs of a crack-head and her nine children, my own three brothers and two adults pretending to be my parents. There were no visits from friends, cousins or relatives and I was almost completely restricted from talking on the telephone or watching television.

One night the youngest of his niece's kids, a nine-month old, started crying and no one could make her stop. She cried all night, non-stop. At around 7am, my mother told me she would take the three of us to the store with her. From there, I was to take the child and her mother to see con-Gwin. When we arrived at the faith-healer's home, we were greeted by the same mysterious woman who was there when I was four; only her hair had turned gray just like con-Gwin's. The child was still crying when we got there.

When we stepped inside, the child's mother, holding the screaming child in her arms, stayed close to the screened door and looked around the house very nervously. When I saw her begin to push the door open, I intervened. "No!" I said. "Wait." She inched slightly away from the door but was clearly frightened. "Give me the child," con-Gwin instructed. I reached for the crying infant and the mother held her tighter. "It's okay." I assured her. "Con-Gwin is going to help her get better."

When she loosened her grip on the child, I grabbed her and placed the crying child in the faith healer's lap. Then Con-Gwin did something amazing. She took her right hand, waved it over the child's face and the infant not only stopped crying immediately, she looked at everyone else in the room and smiled. The innocent smile of an infant could melt an iceberg and her silence was golden. But the mother was not impressed.

"What the f..." she almost got that word out.

"No! Don't say that!" I warned. "Just watch."

Con-Gwin ignored both of us and had already started praying for the infant. I watched as she touched the top of the head and her tummy and pulled her hand back as if a snake has bitten her. "She has the fever and sour milk on her stomach," she said. With that she motioned for her assistant to hand her the ball of string. Just like before, she broke off a piece of string with her teeth, pressed segments of the string against the child's stomach, and prayed while we watched knots form in the string.

After twisting three knots in the string, she tied it around the child's right wrist and told her mother not to remove it. She said the child was healed but the string should stay in place to make sure the fever did not return. She also said the string would fall off in three days by itself. With that, she handed the child back to her mother, I put the money in the crystal ashtray and we walked out the door. "That was some weird sh.." the mother began. But before she could finish, I raised my hand as if to say, "I don't want to hear this." We walked back to the store in silence.

That was a rough summer. In whatever spare time I could find, I stole away to the city library, clear across town and read a lot, especially science books and non-fiction. There was no emotion in science; no reminders of my personal pain. I hated my life; so I looked outside myself for ways to feel good about living. My grandmother could not read or write. She would make me cry with stories of how she had to quit school in the third grade because the teacher frightened her so much. "All of ma life, she said, white people told me dat black peopous was stupid and dat we would never 'mount to nothin'."

So when some educational books showed up at her house one day, I don't know where they came from, I made it my purpose to help her learn to read and write. One of my proudest moments was watching my grandmother write her name for the first time, especially since I had helped her do this. She called me to her home one day and said, "I have something for you."

She gave me a small, but heavy wooden box and said, "Dr. Silverstone gave me this and said maybe one of my grandchildren could use it." Inside that box was a microscope with several slides. A scientist was born. I looked at everything I could find underneath that microscope. I used to sneak and watch television and tried not to miss one episode of Quincy, M.D., my favorite television show. But I left the microscope at my grandmother's house because I knew my mother's husband would find it and destroy it.

That microscope ignited a passion for science in me that lives on today. At that moment, I had found something to live for. Trying to feel normal again, and believing I was out of harm's way, I also became involved in band, track, and talent shows. I absorbed anything that took me away from the hell at home. But it would not be long before the desire to die crept back into consciousness like a recurring addiction. Although he was not attacking me anymore, he watched me constantly.

If I got something he didn't personally give me, he took it from me or he made me give it to my stepbrothers. Everything he could take from me, anything that made me happy, he took and destroyed; my diary, my music, my life. Eventually he isolated me again, from everything and everyone as much as possible. When his niece finally cursed him out, he sent all of them back to their hometown, and I became a prisoner in this life again. Except for not allowing him to hit me in her presence, my mother did not intervene.

CHAPTER NINETEEN

If you were to ask me why I did not tell someone what was happening to me; I have only this to say. I did tell someone. I told a school classmate, who in turn told her mother, who then called my mother's sister. My aunt Nona called my mother and told her that I had confided to a school friend that her husband was beating me down and raping me. That evening, my mother called me into the laundry room of the house, did not ask any questions, but said these words: "if someone has been doing something to you, I am going to hurt them for doing it and I am going to hurt you for telling me."

"What?" I was confused. "But I didn't do anything wrong," I said. "I don't care," her tone was hostile. Do you have something to tell me?" and with that, I said, "no." I put my head down, feeling like I had been put in an impossible situation, and kept my mouth shut. The last thing I needed was both of them beating up on me. It became painfully obvious at that time that my mother did not want to do anything to help me. I was trapped in a no-win situation. My mother's husband was abusing me and she *wanted* to ignore it. Now everything was starting to make sense. That's why she ignored me when I begged her not to leave me alone with her husband. She knew what he was doing to me.

White police officers rarely came to our part of town. As a matter of fact, the police officer assigned to our corner of the world was his brother, a violent spouse abuser who had himself been arrested for breaking his wife's jaw and giving her two black eyes. My mother's sister-in-law, aunt Martha, eventually became the Sheriff assigned to our district. Our homes were separated by about 50 yards of real estate; we were neighbors. One summer, I suffered a serious eye injury while playing "war" with my cousins on mounds of concrete, dirt and rocks. One of my cousins fired a piece of dirt at me and struck me right in the eye, cutting into my pupil. I still see a floating scar to this day.

After suffering four days, when the infection and the swelling in my eye got so bad I couldn't open it, I was taken to the health clinic for treatment. The doctor prescribed a special antibiotic eye drop to help me heal from the injury. My mother had to work during the day, so Aunt Martha volunteered to come over and put the eye drops in my injured eye. At night when mom put the drops in, three of them, it felt cool and soothing; when Aunt Martha put the drops in, it felt like my eye was on fire. When my mother looked into my complaint, she discovered that my aunt was putting "toe cone remover" in my eye, instead of the antibiotic.

This stuff was acidic, designed to dissolve hardened dead skin. My eye was being destroyed and worse, she wanted to put this stuff in the other eye too, saying they both needed to be treated. According to my mother, she didn't even know how the cone remover got in the house. Aunt Martha never helped me again after that. She was the town Sheriff; keeper of the law.

And as for the church minister, well, he was at the house almost every other Sunday evening for supper and acted like my mother's husband walked on water. He thought we were the "perfect family." In the minister's eyes, we were "well-behaved." When he came over, mom always put on a "happy face" and served a good meal. Her husband was all too eager to discuss bible stuff; and the minister (and sometimes his wife) was served as much food as he could eat. No one wanted to see the down-turned smile plastered on my face, so I stayed out of view as much as possible.

That monster could pretend all he wanted to, but the minister didn't know that this man cursed him with venomous and hateful words as soon as he left our home. He complained about how fat and greedy the minister was and how he hated wasting his food on him and anybody in his family. The minister did not know about the magazines I found while cleaning my mother's bedroom. I saw one of them sitting on top of the dresser one day.

The cover had pictures of "little girls" on it. At least I *thought* they were little girls until I decided to open the cover. "Yuck!" I got nauseous. These were not little girls; they were grown women. I saw pictures of grown white women dressed in little girl dresses, socks and shoes with their hair in pigtails, tied with ribbons. They posed with their legs gaped wide open and none of them had on panties. It was disgusting.

They were grown women with fully developed breasts posing as little girls. A glance over the side of the dresser revealed a huge stack of these magazines in a messy pile on the floor. The pictures told the story. He was perverted and coveted pornography, with a particular fondness for little girls. I felt dirty and trapped after that discovery and there was no one I could turn to. This monster told me constantly, no one would believe me. He also said if I tried to run away, someone would turn up dead and it would be my fault.

We were one of the town's wealthiest families. He pursued public office and managed two female baseball teams. I was forbidden to become a team member. And worse, he often criticized me in front of the teams. I was being crushed under the weight of his evil. The only freedom I had left was to die. Soon, I would try again. But this time, the experience would be much more ominous. Praying made things worse, so I stopped praying, gave up on hope and gave up on God. It seemed nothing could save me. Going to church was just a way to get out of that hell-house.

The abuse started up again the following summer, but this time he was beating me into submission. Blocking all images of the 1st attempt, at age 15, I tried again. This time I took about 20 Valium pills, turning the bottle up into my mouth and washed it down with water. I remember laying down on the bed, waiting to die. As I the medication started to take effect and I began to lose consciousness, my right hand jerked as if a nerve had misfired and the bottle I was holding rattled.

I was awakened and confused by the rattling sound because I had turned the bottle up and emptied the contents into my mouth. I made sure there was nothing left in that bottle. In that moment of confusion, extreme nausea seeped in and I ran to the bathroom, vomiting until the only thing coming up was this pucky green stuff. Again, I emerged angry at the world. "Why couldn't I get this right?" I wondered in between a dizzy feeling. At least two other kids in my neighborhood had successfully committed suicide. I couldn't understand what was I doing wrong.

After coming out of the bathroom, wiping that familiar green stuff off the corner of my mouth, I sat in a corner of my bedroom feeling sick, weak, and absolutely miserable. I was angry about the things I could see in other people; the abuse that would not stop, despite pleadings; and the fact that neither my mother nor death seemed to want me. The room started spinning and pulsating and I felt like I was losing my mind. Then, I felt a subtle shift in consciousness, a slight "pop" and I was outside my body! I came out of my body, right through my head.

I levitated and floated in front of this pathetic heap of flesh sitting in that corner, hating what I had become. I stood there for a while and stared at this thing, this body I hated so much, this shell of myself sitting in that corner, with my knees drawn up; my arms wrapped around my legs and my head leaning hard on my knees. The feelings of misery were so heavy, I turned away in disgust. I had simply given up on life. I remember thinking, it's time for me to leave this place and instantly! I was somewhere else and found myself facing a most intriguing situation.

I was standing in the center of a "Y-shaped" crossroad; a single path that divided in two; feeling so much confusion about what to do next. The place was empty; no trees, no grass, no light; just a strange, unimpressionable gray hue and a deep, abiding loneliness. I was completely alone and not at peace. As I stood there wondering what to do next, I looked back to find my body still in that same folded position. I could see myself, my room, and its contents. I could see right through the walls, inside the bathroom; down the hallway; inside my brothers' room; and clear into the carport. I could even see the yard outside.

When I looked away from my home and surveyed where I was I noticed that I was in some type of enclosure. A deep chasm, with no bridges loomed between where I was and where my body was. There was no barrier wall on the side where my body sat in that pathetic heap. I could have gotten up and walked off the edge of life and fallen into an abyss. But another strange barrier separated me from my body. I was behind what looked like a wall of liquid glass, very thin in appearance and transparent. I got the impression I could just step right through the thin wall and be on both sides at the same time. I could see everything with such clarity and worse, I could still feel my own pain.

The chasm between life and death was wide; the edge of reality was laced and jagged. The side from within where I stood was as smooth as the liquid wall. But I gazed inside the abyss. It was some type of valley, and I could see movement. Someone was in there. The crevice or valley was not empty. I was witnessing life after death, something I had never learned in Sunday school. And although I was extremely lonely in this place, the sight of my body sitting in that pathetic heap was enough to convince me that I did not want to go back.

I had been flipped inside out and my broken soul wanted to stay free. Even though I was not at peace and feeling frightened by my own confusion, I did not care. I had no desire to go back to there because there was too much pain. I turned to look in front of me. I remember thinking, "Where is this place? Where am I?" Then out of nowhere, two people appeared. On the left, was one draped in a dreary gray robe. He felt bad. On the right was one draped in brilliant white. He felt safe. Both wore hoods and I could not make out a face on either of them. They kept their hands folded over their chests and tucked inside the sleeves of their robes.

I didn't know what to make of this strange sight until someone else, a person unseen, spoke to me, in my mind, and said "choose." The one in gray spoke first. "Look at yourself," he said. "You're pathetic. You don't have to stay like this. Just let go; go ahead and lose your mind; let them take care of you. You will never have to worry about life again." The one in brilliant white spoke next. "No," he said. "You can get through this. You do not have to give up. You are stronger than you know. Don't give up. You are not alone."

It must have been the message from the one in brilliant light who made more sense, and besides, I remember thinking, …he feels familiar. Before I knew it, I felt a thud! I was stretching out my legs and wiping my face that was wet with tears. I stood up, feeling drugged and weak, stretched again, and laid down on my bed, forcing myself not to think.

Trapped in a deep depression, I laid down and went to sleep. I never spoke of this to anyone. But for the next six months, I would try once again to drown my pain in alcohol and food. I didn't care if that monster came back to kill me. Any place was better than staying here. I became an overweight, teenage alcoholic, who stood 5'0" and weighed 225 lbs. I was isolated, pitiful, suicidal, needy and severely depressed.

CHAPTER TWENTY

I tried to ignore the visions but they would not go away. They would appear like camera flashes. Thinking it was the effects of the alcohol, I decided to stop drinking, so I could analyze what I was seeing. When I was not drinking, I was able to focus on the flashes I kept seeing. Images of people I didn't know were going about life, doing normal things; visuals of people and places standing beneath road signs, next to mailboxes, and working in their yards. I convinced myself that they were hallucinations. I avoided people as much as possible.

I tried not to let anyone touch me because I would see things about them I didn't want to know. Sometimes, I would enter daydreams, in a type of semi-trance state, stay fully aware of everything, mentally put myself behind that liquid wall, and see the lives of other people as an observer. I could see two realities, observing people's soul apart from themselves, inching dangerously close to those same jagged edges of reality I saw in my own suicide attempt. It was unnerving.

Socializing after the second suicide attempt, was a challenge. If I knew things about people they didn't think anyone else knew and I commented on it, they avoided me. I became known as the "weird" one. Sometimes I felt like I was losing my mind because those dreams and visions felt more real than reality. And I held all of it inside.

One day I was walking through a thrift store with my mother and came across a little red book with a lock and key attached. It was a diary. It cost me 25cents. I wrote everything in that diary. Pretty soon writing became my voice; my way out of loneliness. All of my thoughts either went into that diary or on paper. My short- term memory was horrible and cognitively, I struggled. The only time I could form coherent thoughts was when I put them on paper. And my diary, my writing became a lifesaver for me.

One particular night, about a week after the crossroads suicide experience, I was in a sound sleep when I bolted straight up in bed, as if someone had hoisted me up with a pulley. My eyes were bulging so wide they hurt, I was breathing heavily and I was drenched in sweat. An overwhelming feeling of fear, dread and doom consumed me. I was mortified. Something was terribly wrong. Confused and terrified, I began to look around the room starting to my right, in the darkest part of the room.

All I saw was darkness; nothing unusual. Everything was so still. The foot of my bed faced the door and hallway of the house. When my eyes met the doorway of my bedroom, my soul froze into a petrified state. I could not speak and my body began to shake violently. I was petrified with fear by what I was seeing. It emerged from my mother's bedroom. This is the only way I can describe this situation. There, standing in the doorway, glaring at me with slanted eyes, was this super-sized, broad shouldered, extremely tall, form that carried so much darkness, that shadows bounced off it.

It swayed back and forth looking at me with piercing eyes. I could not make out a face. I sat absolutely still; afraid to breathe and a scream stuck in my throat. This thing had a low, piercing, growling voice that I could hear with my mind. "I WILL destroy you." It stated this with ease and assurance. This is what I saw each time that monster touched me; that's why I dissociated into the field of flowers. I watched this thing hover in the doorway. As I looked closer at the entrance, I could see, almost in silhouette, a bright, thin white haze began to form and rise from the floor upward; finally covering the entire entrance of the door.

In the seventies, all television stations went off at midnight. The thin film across the doorway looked like the haze on the television screen, after television went off. The light was barely visible, almost transparent. I felt like this thing was attempting to enter my bedroom. At first, the light did not look strong enough to keep this menacing evil out of my room. But, as big and as powerful as this thing appeared, each time it pushed against the hazy film, it could not enter. The light was unyielding. That thing could not get pass the light. I looked at this nightmare that was trying to get to me shaking like a leaf, and those piercing eyes held its stare. As far as I know, it never looked away from me.

It made one last attempt to break past the lighted haze. It bumped against the light and bounce right off of it. At this point, the slanted eyes squinted, this thing let out a high-pitched sound that I cannot describe, turned to its right and with great speed, vanished down the hallway. The bright haze slowly disappeared and I sank back into my bed feeling totally exhausted like I had just been in a fight for my soul. Squeezing my eyes shut, I moaned over and over again, "It's not real." "It's not real." I pleaded with myself not to believe what just happened. "Momma," I called out and whispered into the darkness. "Nona, Aunt Toni, Somebody, please, help me," I whispered between tears. "Somebody, please make it stop!"

These were the muted screams of a life in torment, spiraling into a mental meltdown. I couldn't take much more of this. At age 16, I swore off alcohol completely, and that is when the migraines started. One of this predator's self-amusing habits was to hit me in the head while I was suffering from a migraine. He also never missed an opportunity to say ugly things to me and about me. "Look at you!," he would say, "Who do you think you are?! You're nobody! You make me sick! Get out of my face, nigger! I hate looking at you! You are so stupid; you'll never amount to anything! I disown you, so get out of my face!"

This venom was spewed at me almost daily, along with constant slaps to the side of my head. He would laugh at my nakedness and call me disgusting names. Then in the same breath, apologize and beg for sex, while wrestling or beating me down; raping me with a pillow pressed hard against my face to smother any screams; or he would wrap his shirt so tight around my head and neck, I would be choked to near unconsciousness; all the while asking me "how does it feel?" Sadistic; evil; these don't even begin to describe this monster. I *hated* him. The rage and feelings of helplessness were so intense I would sink into a deep, muted depression and stare into space for hours.

I felt like he wanted to kill me and probably would have, if he could get away with it. I would plead and beg my mother not to leave me alone with her husband or send me home with him. She would simply turn her eyes away from me, never questioning why I never wanted to be alone with her husband.

He used to play this sadistic cat-and-mouse game with me, especially when he was mad about something else. It went something like this: I had to pass by a counter in the kitchen and enter a hallway to get to my room. He would lean against the counter at the entrance of the hallway, glaring at me. As soon as I would try to walk pass him, WHAM! He would slap me on the side of the head. "WHY ARE WALKIN' 'ROUND ME LIKE YOU SCARED?!" I was never scared of him; I hated him too much to be afraid.

"GO BACK!," he would screech. "DO IT AGAIN! AND STOP WALKIN 'ROUND ME LIKE YOU SCARED! He would do this most of the time knowing I was suffering from painful migraine. "GO! AND DON'T ROLL YOUR EYES AT ME! WALK, NIGGER! GET AWAY FROM ME!" Dazed and often in excruciating pain, my eyes burning and tearing up from the bright lights, my focus was on getting away from this monster and laying down; so I would try again.

Because the migraines were so painful and unpredictable, if I held my head a certain way, I could lessen the pounding. But again, WHAM! He would slap me on the side of the head, screaming at me, "DON'T TURN YOUR HEAD LIKE THAT! LOOK AT ME! If I looked at him, "WHAM!" I would get hit again. "DON'T LOOK AT ME LIKE THAT!" he would scream. The pain was unbearable and his screeching was absolutely unnerving.

I don't know if it was the pain or the constant hits to the head, but I swear his eyes would change colors, from green to yellow to hazel and back to green while I was looking at him! He would repeat this sadistic behavior four or five times before shoving me down the hallway, telling me to "get out of his face because he couldn't stand to look at me no more." But I believe the only reason he would give up is because he couldn't break me. With all the pain I was in and him beating up on me, I never cried.

CHAPTER TWENTY-ONE

Complaining to my mother was useless. She claimed she never saw him do anything to me. When I complained, he denied everything. He had cart blanche' to treat me any way he wanted to. The abuse became more violent and unpredictable, because by now I had become more aggressive in fighting back. But now, I was being attacked in the shower and he would break the locks on doors to get at me. He told me if I tried to run away, someone would die. Life was a living hell and I was enraged at God for forcing me to live. Despite desperate begging and pleading with my mother to not leave me alone with her husband, she ignored me.

I withdrew from life and cowered in a coffin; that is what my body had become. I was not a human being. I felt like an animal; a freakish play toy; and a thing to be used for entertainment purposes only. Depression and constant thoughts of suicide kept me going. The only thing that kept me smiling was knowing that eventually, I was going to die. I became obsessed with suicide. I knew eventually I was going to take my own life, I just wasn't sure how. Someone kept interfering.

I had seen hell and I didn't think I was going to end up there. I believed I would end up in a lonely place somewhere outside of heaven and that was fine with me. As long as I was out of this world, I would be safe. I dismissed the visuals of the second attempt and disregarded everything that had kept me alive thus far. I was in tremendous emotional pain and I wanted it to stop. Emotional pain creates a life of its own and forces you to ignore all signs of hope. Despite having been wrestled from death twice, I had grown weary of fighting this evil. I also wanted to get away from those tormenting visions and dreams.

School was a safe haven, but I had grown fearful of letting anyone get close to me. One young man tried to talk to me in the 10th grade. He thought I was cute and wanted to be my boyfriend. I felt both shy and sadness toward Langston. He was such a gentleman. He was a momma's boy, but a kindhearted, respectful young man. His stepmother, a proper-speaking woman from up north, was an English teacher who taught at our school. I loved listening to her speak. His father was the kindest man in the world.

His parents liked me. My mother's husband hated Langston. He called him lazy and sneaky. He tried to convince me that Langston was only after one thing. He lied to me. Langston never asked me for sex. When I could get alone with him, all he talked about was how he was going to design and build a big house for me someday. His dream was to become a famous architect and a builder.

While still in high school, he sketched a drawing of our dream home. He asked to take me to a movie once, but that predator told him no. My heart ached all the time because I wanted to be with him. But, that monster used an exceptionally sinister tactic to interfere with our relationship. When he knew I would be spending time with Langston, he would force himself on me and mock my feelings by saying, "Now, you can go."

He was always talking about hurting Langston. He threatened to provoke fights with him and bragged that "no one would find him." To protect Langston from what I believed was imminent danger, I turned on him. I became mean and hostile so he would go away. I didn't want him to get hurt. Eventually he agreed to stop seeing me, but only if I agreed to never forget about him. Other painful situations compounded by this one were difficult to the extent that I convinced myself that no would be able to help me.

For instance, I never knew my father's side of the family. Mother's response to my inquiries reflected more of her hatred of my father than her willingness to introduce me to his family. She kept me away from them for purely selfish reasons. "Your daddy is so ugly, I don't even know why I slept with him," she used to say. She left out one vital piece of information. Someone on his side of the family was looking for me.

One Friday afternoon, a Jr. High schoolteacher called me into her classroom and told me I had a half sister. She would know; my sister was her niece. It seems my father was a player. My mother was pregnant for me at the same time Mrs. Hewitt's sister was pregnant for my father. Mrs. Hewitt called me over to her one day and said, "You have a sister."

"I have a what?" I asked. I could not believe what I was hearing.

"You have a sister," she continued. I was stunned.

"Who is she?" I asked. "What's her name?"

"Her name is Lacey. You and your sister were born two months apart, but you are the oldest. It's a shame. You live in the same town and she lives right across the street from your grandmother's house. You go to the same school and both of you are in the band. It's wrong that you've never met. Y'all need to meet each other and get closer. You are sisters; you're family. Ask your mother about this. She knows."

Mrs. Hewitt was right. My mother knew everything and she never told me. She had hidden that information from me on purpose. She must have discussed it with aunt Nona because my aunt felt sorry for me. Over very hostile objections from my mother, aunt Nona told me everything. "Your mom told me to mind my own business, Sue, but I don't think it's right that you don't know your daddy's family," aunt Nona said. I still have great respect for my aunt for listening to her conscious and telling me the truth. When the information about my sister was confirmed, I became ecstatic. A sister! "Finally," I thought. "She would be someone I could talk to! I felt so much excitement at the thought of connecting with a real sister that I could hardly think of anything else.

I made plans for Monday to find my sister and introduce myself to her at school. I couldn't wait for the weekend to be over and I spent the weekend fantasizing about spending time with her. This was especially exciting because I was so isolated and lonely. I wanted to be close to someone. Her aunt told me what homeroom she was in.

When Monday arrived, I rushed to her homeroom class, eager to talk with my sister for the first time. When I found her, I started walking toward her, eager to hear her speak. My heart was pounding in anticipation. But, someone stepped in front of me and intervened. I do not remember who this person was but, what I was told was more than I could bear. I don't remember every word verbatim, but they said something like this: "Your step dad stopped by your sister's aunt's house on Saturday. He told her aunt to mind her own business and threatened to kill her if she came near you again. So you can't talk to Lacey. You can't ever get to know each other or someone might get hurt. You have to stay away from her."

I was devastated. My emotions went numb. That monster got in the way again and all my mother said when I complained was, "You need to stay away from that family." I remember taking a deep breath and just glared at this woman who was pretending to be my mother thinking, "Who is this woman?" I ran into my room, closed the door, sat on the bed and cried. And while painful questions swirled in my head, I started praying.

"God, why are they doing this to me?" I said, choking through tears. "What have I done that is so bad and so wrong to deserve this kind of treatment? I've never hurt anyone. I make good grades. I take care of my little brothers. I cook; I clean; I try to do everything I'm told to do and still they treat me so bad. I don't understand. What did I do wrong? Where are you? This is not supposed to happen to children. You're supposed to protect us. I just don't understand."

I was in so much pain, I don't even remember everything I said. But I ended the prayer with this request. "God, if you're listening, please take me away from this place." This happened in the fall of 1979. After that horrible situation, something snapped inside me. I stopped caring about everything. I would sit in class and stare into empty space. I don't know how I kept my grades up. I hated my life and I wanted to die. I convinced myself that no one was ever going to take me seriously, or help me.

Death was my only option.

In the late summer of 1981, on a Wednesday morning, at 2:40 am, after another surprise rape attack, I called it quits. I had had enough. I put my diary and other writings in a shoebox and stored it in a corner of my closet. I made peace with myself and decided once and for all that this was not the life I wanted to live. I decided he had won. The only way to get away from this monster and his wife, was to die. And this time, I would not fail.

I finally resolved within myself that he was not going to do bad things to me anymore. I was going to die today and no one, not even God would save me from myself...not this time. It was time to curse God and die. I realized that day that sometimes a human soul in torment cannot see hope because despair causes blinding pain. It is in the immediacy of the moment, when the culmination of evil clashes with the bitterness of chronic and severe pain that the boundary between what is right and what is wrong becomes indistinguishable. There was nothing anyone could say to make me change my mind.

The pain was so intense, I felt like I had to do something to make it stop, permanently. There is no voice of reason in this state of mind, when pain is the only voice speaking. I calmly walked to the corner of the kitchen where my mother kept a loaded .38 caliber handgun she carried for protection in the store and pulled it out of the money bag. A classmate of mine had just successfully committed suicide by shooting himself because of relentless beatings from his father. That's what his note said.

I figured it was the best way to finally end this horrible existence I had found myself in, but there would be no note. As I stood in that corner of the kitchen, I looked at the telephone and started to pick it up and call my grandmother. "No," I reasoned, she'll just call someone to come see about me." I did not want to be rescued. I looked down the hallway; half hoping one of my little brothers would wake up and need to go to the bathroom.

That would give me a reason to put the gun away. "No," I reasoned again, they'll just go tell mom or their dad."

I started feeling sorry for them. "What are they going to do," I thought, when they see me laying dead on the floor with a bullet hole in my head?" But I justified my action. "They would be better off without me," I told myself. Then I looked toward my mother's bedroom and remembered why it was necessary for me to die. I could not take another moment of this evil. I pulled the hammer back, put the gun to my right temple and squeezed slightly before a voice out of nowhere interrupted. "Put the gun down," it said.

I looked down the hallway; there was no one in sight. "It's not real!" I told myself. I was not insomniac and had quit drinking eighteen months ago. I dismissed the voice as hallucination. I repositioned the gun, with the hammer still pulled back and squeezed again. Before I could squeeze with enough force to release a bullet into my temple, the voice sounded off again, this time louder than the first time. "PUT THE GUN DOWN!" it said, this time with authority.

I started to cry. But, I had learned to hate tears. They felt weak. "NO!" "NO TEARS!" My mind was screaming. "STOP IT!" "STOP SPEAKING TO ME!" "YOU'RE NOT REAL!" I whispered angrily between clenched teeth. I started wiping away that icky wet feeling with the empty hand, using masochistic force, rocking my head back and forth, slapping and beating myself in the face until my face was dry, but in a lot of pain. My face was stinging from slapping myself like a lunatic but I refused to put the gun down. I held it against my temple hoping it would go off by itself because of all the activity of me slapping myself.

The gun was pressed so hard against my temple that sweat sealed the barrel against my skin. But for all the commotion and movement, the gun, which had no safety, did not fire. I did not see any bright lights and no good spirits. The room had an eerie stillness that gave me chills. I was the only one in that room. I could not understand why I kept hearing this very authoritative voice commanding me to stop trying to kill myself.

"No! I'm not putting it down!," I whispered between clenched teeth. "I want to die!" "Leave me alone!" "You're not real!" I had no idea who I was talking to, but I was enraged and defiant. The whole scene was surreal. Almost like an out-of-body experience, here I am standing in the kitchen with a gun pressed up against my skull trying to find the courage to pull the trigger; arguing with a disembodied voice. "LEAVE ME ALONE!" was all I could find the strength to scream.

I was sure those would be my last words, because in the heat of that angry outburst, I pulled the trigger. CLICK! Nothing happened! I was still standing. I touched my head; it was not bleeding. No angel, no crossroads, no sound of that irritating voice. And worse, I was not dead. With the gun in my hand and too weak to do anything else, my knees buckled and I dropped down to the floor and started sobbing out of control, screaming into the darkness.

"WHY ARE YOU DOING THIS TO ME?!" "JUST LEAVE ME ALONE!" "LET ME DIE!" "Please,…just let me die." By this time, I am a sobbing mess, crying uncontrollably in an ominous stillness. "Why can't I get this right?" "Why am I still alive?" No answer. "Okay, fine," I said getting back on my feet in haste. "I'll just try again." I stood up, flipped on the kitchen light to reposition the gun and make sure there were bullets in it. I pointed the nose of the gun toward my face and looked inside the barrel. My intention was to prepare the gun for a second attempt. But what I saw changed my life forever.

I am not a gun expert and I didn't even know this was possible. But the bullet had lodged outside the chamber and was hanging precariously in the balance between the edge of an open chamber and a partially closed hammer. The gun had misfired. During the commotion and movement of me slapping myself like a lunatic, the bullet must have slipped out of the chamber. My life had been spared again.

I remember feeling a surge of energy; a strange kind of strength that I had never felt before; like I had won a major victory. And like the movie review-style dreams I used to see when I sat in my great-grandmother's old rocking chair, memories I had recorded in my diary came flooding back. I thought about the first suicide attempt, the light that carried me and the abysmal realm of wandering souls. I thought about the second attempt, standing behind the wall of liquid glass and those two people at the crossroads. Remembering the features of that burning pit and those condemned souls watching replays of their crimes against their victims made me shudder.

I thought about my grandmother's house; the old rocking chair and the dreams I used to have when I sat in it; and I thought about the three child's fantasy dreams of heaven. As if I were reviewing my life on screen, the memories came flooding back and with them the desire to live. On that fateful Wednesday morning, I surveyed my life and realized, I had one more year in high school. Once I leave this hell house, I promised myself that I would never return.

I was determined that from that moment on, that monster would never abuse me again, not if he wanted to live. This happened in July of 1981. In that same month, at a church revival, I heeded an alter call and dedicated my life to God, although I was still very angry with Him. But, holding on to the heavenly dreams of a ten-year-old child, I hoped to someday be where God was.

CHAPTER TWENTY-TWO

That year I lost over 90lbs and in February of 1982, I signed myself into the United States Air Force, and left for basic training six weeks after graduation. But after that fateful night, that monster never touched me again. As a matter of fact, he avoided me. But he still hated me. We had one final confrontation before I left that house. On a cool night in April, three weeks before graduation, I attended a sleepover to study for final exams with several friends from school; all girls. After dinner, we settled down and started studying when someone knocked at the door around 7pm.

My friend's parents had stepped out and we were not expecting anyone, so she cautiously went to the door. Peeking through a small window, she saw one of the high school basketball seniors waiting at the door. We knew, so she let him in. "Can I borrow some notes for the final on Monday?" he asked. "No," one of said, "but you're welcome to study with us. But, you have leave by 9pm. Call home and let your mom know where you are cause we don't want to get in trouble for having you here." So, he called home, told his mom where he was and we settled down in the living room to study.

A few minutes later, the doorbell rang. "I hope it's not the rest of the basketball team," someone joked. The rest of us stayed back while my friend answered her door. I heard her say, "hello" to him. Did I hear her correctly? Then I heard, "WHERE IS SHE?" "She's in the living room; we're studying." He barged in, saw the male basketball player, and exploded. "WHAT ARE YOU DOING HERE?!" He half-shouted and half-whispered through clenched teeth.

"Nothing sir, the frightened teenager said, just studying. My mom knows where I am." "DON'T TALK BACK TO ME!"

"YOU!" he screamed, pointing at me, "GET YOUR STUFF! LET'S GO!"

Nobody could understand why he was so upset. I knew what it was. He thought I was trying to have sex with the basketball player. He was always accusing me of having sex with all the boys in the neighborhood. I was, in his words, nasty and disgusting. Filthy minds like his never think about decent things.

"But she's supposed to spend the night," my friend was almost in tears.

"SHE'S COMING HOME! RIGHT NOW! LET'S GO!" He would not be reasoned with.

To avoid any further embarrassment, I looked my friend in the eyes and whispered, "It's okay, Claire. I'll see y'all at school."

I gathered my belongings and walked out the door without saying a word. But, rage was boiling within me. I had reached the boiling point of frustration. All the way home, sitting in that speeding truck, barely avoiding accidents, he ranted and raged about me being easy; nasty; a whore; filthy; disgusting; sneaky; a lying, stupid nigger; and a good-for-nothing piece of shit. I sat there in a tense silence. "DO YOU HEAR ME TALKING TO YOU?! he yelled. Again, all he got was silence.

He screamed at me for the entire 20 minutes it took to get home. I never answered him. He sped into the driveway, jumped out of the truck and almost broke the glass storm door off its hinges, storming into the house. "What are you doing home?" my mother asked when she saw me walk into the house. "TELL HER!" "TELL HER WHY YOU'RE HOME!" He never stopped screaming. "I don't know why I'm home," I said. "He just showed up at Claire's house, told me to get my stuff, and brought me back home." "YOU LYING BITCH!" He came at me with closed fists and for the first time, my mother jumped between us. "No!" she said to him. "Go outside, Suzaunna," she commanded.

I walked out, shoving the door, infuriated. He pushed past her and came after me again. I guess he thought I was going to run. He was wrong. I turned to face him with enraged, hate-filled eyes that begged him to hit me. He stood there frozen with amazement that I did not even flinch when he raised his fist to strike me. Before his punch landed, my mother jumped in front of him again and tried to push him away.

He pushed her aside, and WHAM! his fist caught me on the right side temple and I fell. As I was getting up, he came up from behind me and kicked me back down. I heard my mother say, "That's enough!" and saw her run next door to her brother's house to get help. "STAY DOWN!" "IF

YOU GET UP AGAIN, I SWEAR, I'LL TRY MY BEST TO KNOCK YOUR HEAD OFF!" "STAY DOWN!" His words raged with venom.

I was on my feet so fast, I don't even remember getting up. "Go back to hell, you fucking monster!" I stood straight up glaring at him and dared him to knock me down again. I refused to stay down. "It's going to take more than that to keep me down." I knew he was trying to kill me, but I didn't care. I had made up my mind that one of us was not going to live through this night. "You stupid bitch!" he growled at me again. "I'm gonna knock your head off!"

I glared at him without blinking and stood my ground, shaking my head at him. "No, asshole," I whispered to him. "I'm not going down anymore; you're gonna have to kill me." This was a grown man and I was a seventeen year-old female. I was no match for him and yet that coward made it his purpose to beat up on a female adolescent just because he could. All I had the strength to do was stand.

Here is where the true image of a sexual predator emerges. He was a sexual predator who was losing his power because his victim was now willing to die rather than stay broken and the rage that all sexual predators hide from the rest of world was coming out. He was now being forced to face his own shame, his own weakness, his own loss of power. And the only way to restore his sick sense of dignity was to try and force the inevitable, he needed to find a way to blame me, the victim for him having to kill me. As long as I fought back, if I died, he could always claim self-defense.

When he charged at me again and got right up on me to where I could look into his angry green eyes, a childhood memory flashed back like the light bulb of an old-fashioned camera. Those eyes,...a distant voice whispered a hollow memory into consciousness and I froze in place for a moment, "There is no light in him-only darkness." I had seen this monster before in one of those dreams from the seat of the rocking chair. I didn't have time to wonder about it. He raised a closed fist into the air, above his head. But before he could land another blow, a white police officer drove up and that coward did what all cowards do-he pretended to be the victim.

He was pathetic and predictable, claiming to the police officer that he was jumped by my mother and I and was just trying to defend himself. My mother and uncle, who had also arrived on the scene, stood there in silence with that *"negro, please"* look on their faces. I just glared at him the whole time. The police officer must have seen right through his lie and told him he could either go to jail or leave for the night and let things cool off. He got in his truck and left. My friends at Claire's house called and talked with me all night. I didn't know they cared and that gave me hope. He never hit me again after that night. I spent the rest of my time in that hell-house wishing he would drop dead and biding my time until graduation.

One thing sexual predators will do is try to bribe their victims by showering them with gifts so if they complain, everybody would call the victim ungrateful. My mother's husband tried to do this. I had four bicycles. The only one I rode on was the one my mother gave me. I had three radio/eight track tape players. Two of them stayed unopened in the box stuck in the closet. I played the one my mother handed me. My mother bought my clarinet and she gave me a keyboard. I borrowed a tenor saxophone, an oboe, and an alto saxophone from the school music room. I didn't want to touch anything he gave me because I hated him. When he realized I was not going to let him rape me anymore without a violent struggle, his behavior changed from abusing me to confiscating my possessions.

He took the bicycles, radios/eight track players, my clarinet and the keyboard and put them in storage. I returned the borrowed musical instruments to the school because I didn't want his ignorant ass to take something that didn't belong to me. If it was mine, he destroyed it or took it. He found my diary and other writings, wrapped them in thick electrical tape, put them on top of some garbage in a large metal drum, poured gasoline on them, and set them on fire. When he clicked his cigarette lighter, before setting the diary on fire, he looked at me with a smirk on his face and said, "I guess you won't be needin' this no more." He burned everything and glared at me as if looking for some kind of reaction. I didn't even blink. "Get used to the flames, asshole, I whispered to him. "You will see them again." I watched my diary and my papers burn to ashes and then walked away.

This man had no idea how insignificant he became in my eyes that day. He was not human; he was a despicable creature. When I was muted and isolated, my diary and my writings became my voice. I had recorded the dreams from the rocking chair, the visions, and the prebirth memories in there. I had written about Sunday school and vacation bible school; the details of those three dreams I had when I was ten; the death of my grandfather and my uncle; the microscope my grandmother had given me and even commented on episodes of the television show, Quincy, M.D. I had written about how good it felt when I watched my grandmother write her name for the first time and how hard it was to watch her cry when my uncle drowned..

I wrote about the little library and how it had abandoned me, the tears I shed for aunt Toni, the nice young man who wanted to be my boyfriend, the anguish I felt when I was denied the love and companionship of my sister, and the devastating disappointment I felt when no one showed up for my birthday party. I had written down daily events of things that happened at school and band practice because my concentration was so bad, most times writing things down was the only way I could remember anything.

I had recorded dreams and nightmares, visions and predictions, and other unexplained events that seemed to happen almost daily. I recorded the most significant parts of my life in that diary and in times of exceptional loneliness, I would pull it out and re-read each entry so I could feel human and less isolated. He burned my diary, my voice, my only hold on freedom without realizing that neither the diary nor the writings contained one single word about him or what he had done to me.

I crossed a threshold that day. Something inside me snapped and I breached a point of no return. I knew from that moment on, no matter what he did or said; no matter what my mother said about him, I would never see him as a decent human being. I fixed in my mind from that day forward that at the core of his existence, there was nothing salvageable about him. He was a waste to humanity and I would never truly forgive him for what he had done to my diary and to me.

He made one final move and found out in no uncertain terms, how much I hated him. My mother was giving me her car for traveling purposes; so, I stopped in to that hell-house after basic training to pick it up. While I was there, he got angry because I refused to speak to him. So the day I was leaving, he started his sinister gestures. "YOU THINK YOU'RE BETTER THAN ME, DON'T YOU?!" "God, he is so stupid," I remember thinking. I ignored him and walked outside; he followed me. "DON'T IGNORE ME!" "HEY! I'M TALKING TO YOU!" "LOOK AT ME WHEN I'M TALKING TO YOU!" Again, I ignored him.

My mother had stepped out and I was waiting for her to return before leaving. I stood outside, with the car between us, my back to him, staring into empty space, feeling weary, exhausted, and mentally drained. I wished he would go away. But he continued ranting. "TURN AROUND AND LOOK AT ME!" he yelled. I sighed heavily, but I didn't look at him. I took a deep breath and stood very still. I heard him coming around the car. He came and stood right in front of me.

I gave him a look that said, "Go away," shook my head and rolled my eyes away from him. I just wanted to get in the car and leave. He raised his fist as if he was going to hit me and I looked him deep into his eyes and said very calmly, "Go ahead." Do it. But, I promise you, it WILL be the last time. Because the next time you see me, you'll be looking up from hell."

He stepped back, slowly lowered his fist, looked me up and down, made some insulting comment I don't remember, and stormed off toward the front door of the house. Suddenly, I heard CRASH! And turned around very slowly to see what it was. He had brought his fist down on the windshield of the car on the driver's side and shattered the glass. It was still intact, but looked like a mangled spider's web.

With a half-grin on his face, he growled, "Now you can go." I walked slowly, right up to him, getting right in his face and looked him in the eyes. Feeling all the rage and disgust of having to look at his hideous face, I looked into those sadistic eyes with the unblinking intensity of a madman said very calmly, "You're lucky your fist didn't go right through the glass and cut your arm; because, I would have stood right over you and watched you bleed to death. Nothing would make me happier than to watch you die." He backed away from me slowly with a look of surprise like I had never seen and kept eye contact with me the whole time. I was so angry that day, I don't even remember how the windshield got fixed. But when I finally drove away from that shadowy-colored house, I felt at peace. We wouldn't speak again for almost twenty years.

I started changing after the third suicide attempt. From the moment I put the gun down, I knew there was a purpose for me being here and I was determined to find out what it was. The dreams did not stop. As a matter of fact, they became more vivid. I just let them linger and set off on a life journey of self-discovery, seeking to understand the purpose of my life in this world and the next. What I discovered was more shocking than anything I could have ever imagined.

CHAPTER TWENTY-THREE

Getting out of that house was a breath of fresh air. Eventually, I learned to forgive all of the people who harmed me. I needed a powerful barrier against the rage and forgiveness became the metaphor I used. Forgiveness is a peculiar double-edged sword. In my situation, forgiveness became essential because holding on to the pain meant lingering in an endless, wretched anger. If I held on to the rage, I was doomed to self-destruct. That doesn't mean he all of a sudden became my best friend as my mother has been trying to manipulate. I still don't like him and I never will.

My forgiveness just meant that I had to make a choice between the menacing darkness of perpetual self-hate he had forced me into and the hope of divine providence, meaning travel a path away from the pain and let God deal with these people, his way. I would come back and deal with the pain later, when I was stronger. But at this time it was essential that I start to heal.

Some important lesson learned during this chapter of my life, suicide is not an option. When I "died" from my attempts, where I ended up was never a good place. I was completely isolated and cut off from communication or contact with everyone, good and bad. I was alone with my feelings of anger, loneliness, and despair. The feelings did not go away because my memory and my emotions survived the journey.

I can't speak for everyone else; but I would encourage anyone considering suicide to please, find another way to deal with your problems. Suicide should never be an option. I had to learn this the hard way. For years, I struggled with finding a path that could lead to something meaningful in life and eventually I found it. More than twenty years had gone by and I was sitting in my kitchen having a conversation with my baby brother.

It started out as a beautiful springtime Saturday morning. The aroma of freshly brewed coffee mingled with the conversation.

"Sue, you've always been kinda "strange" huh? My brother asked me with a mixture of fear and suspicion. He probably had been thinking about this ever since he was a little boy. When I left home, he was only seven years old; but he had heard stories about how weird I was as a kid. I don't remember the conversation verbatim, but it went something like this.

"Sue, do you still have those dreams?" he asked.

I sighed and said, "Yes."

"Have you gone to see one of them, you know "head people?" He seemed concerned for me.

"You mean a psychiatrist or a psychologist?" I corrected him. Yes, Mike, I've seen several different therapists over the last twenty years and they all say the same thing. I'm a little weird, but not crazy. I was in therapy for seven years. If I was crazy, it would have been discovered during that time."

"But what about…, he started and I didn't let him finish.

"I don't need medication!, I shouted."

He looked hurt and started to apologize. "Don't apologize, Mike. "I know this sounds crazy. Sometimes I wonder if all those "shrinks" could be wrong about me."

Dark clouds were showing up; rain was on the way.

"Perhaps they see the degrees," I continued, the numerous years of successful employment, lack of stress, and good social skills as evidence of psychological stability. I am the classic over-achiever, four degrees, including a doctorate, with specialties in medicine, education, forensics and psychology. I feel like I was in school forever."

"Maybe THAT'S what's wrong with you. You have too much stuff in your head stopping your brain from working right," he said, trying to be a wise guy.

"Ha Ha, very funny, big guy. Education is the key to success. Of course, I think I kinda overdid it," I surrendered.

"But, you've seen things ever since you were little, right?", there was a hint of intrigue in his tone.

"Yes!" A subtle confusion rises in my heart. "I don't know why, just that I've always been this way. It's been strange living this way, to say the least. It's kind of weird."

I gave a heavy sigh that made him flash me one of those I-feel-sorry-for-you looks. I sensed it in his eyes.

"Don't even go there," I demanded. "DO NOT feel sorry for me."

"I'm a little confused, but I don't want your pity. Someday, this will all make sense. In the meantime, I just need to get past my own frustration. We don't serve a God of confusion; in due time, I will understand what this all means...and you'll be the first one to hear about it!"

"Okay!, he said with excitement, but just don't tell me when it's time for me to,...well, you know."

"Mike, I hear your wife calling you!" I started messing with him. "Go home, before I tell you what I DO know about you!"

And with that, he hurried out of my house and made the 10-minute drive to his own. Pouring myself a cup of coffee, staring out into my backyard, waiting for the rain to start, my thoughts drifted back in time. This whole experience has been intriguing. I still feel like an observer of my own life; just like when I was a child. All of the static I endured in my mother's house could not erase the deep-seated longingness, a craving inside to give meaning to these unusual circumstances. You know, sometimes, I wish I were crazy; at least then everything would make sense in a "make believe" kind of way. No one has been able to explain to me what it is I am dealing with.

Gray clouds show up and off in a distance, I hear the soft rumble of thunder. With my hands embracing the warm coffee-filled cup, my thoughts continue to drift. "He was too young to remember," I thought. I am twelve years older than he is. He does not know about the hell I went through. He doesn't know how I used to jump in front of crowbars, two-by-fours and stiff, swinging snakeskin belts that tore the flesh out the tender skin of his two older brothers; trying to protect them from vicious beatings. He was too young to remember me getting between his father and our mother, who was cowering in a corner of the hallway, with a loaded double-barreled rifle his father had pointed at her head.

He would never know that I used to take him everywhere with me, away from that house, making sure he was out of harm's way. He doesn't even realize how important he was to me; how clinging to him replaced my impulse to cut on myself and self-mutilate; how his innocence helped me stay connected to love. I felt like his protector during annual visits to Angola State Prison, where we were forced to visit his father's brother, a burlesque, towering, bald, scary, muscular, convicted murderer who spent seven years of his adolescent life on death row and was now enjoying a commuted life sentence.

I hated going to those stupid annual prison rodeos where this man was the "featured hero." He was famous in the prison for jumping between the horns of angry Brahma bulls and claiming the $100 dollar bill that was attached to one of its horns. No, my little brother did not know that his smile, his laughter, his thick curly hair, his innocence, his need to be nurtured and protected; he was one of the reasons I chose not to pull the trigger a second time on that dark and fateful Wednesday morning.

My mother is still married to the man who abused me. She knows the whole story, but claims she doesn't remember stuff, like the night she flipped on my bedroom light, caught him in my room, fully erect and standing over me, fighting with me because I refused to let him rape me. I'll never forget that night, because I watched her creep up behind him, assured that she was coming to help me. I don't know what she saw, but she didn't chase him out of my room. What happened next sealed my fate as an unwanted child. Rather than interfere, burned in my memory is the image of her stupid husband standing between my mother and I glaring at me with a sinister look on his face as if he was daring either of us to say something.

My mother looks at me, calls me a bad name, flips off the light and left him standing in my room. She closed herself inside her own bedroom and locked her door. Shocked, mortified, and paralyzed in spirit, I wrapped myself into a tight cocoon inside the bed covers, sheets, and anything else I could find, from head to foot, and determined that this monster was not going to violate me. That night, I cried myself to sleep. From that moment on, I knew and accepted that I was completely alone in this world.

If someone were to ask me if I believe my mother loves me, I would have to say no. I think in her own heart, she believes she loves me but it's conditional. To win my mother's complete affection, I would have to enter into an agreement of denial. I would have to live as if her husband never violated me or hurt me in any way. I would have to live in world wrapped in a false sense of security and pretend that her husband is a decent man and a loving father. I would be required to erase all memory, surrender my dignity, compromise my self-respect and agree to accept that what he did to me was my own fault. I would have to enter a partnership with the two of them that as long as I agree to live as if nothing ever happened, he gets to keep the power he took from me, she gets to keep her secure world.

To protect this man as fiercely as she has even after he confessed and confirmed his crimes to her, she has probably had to avoid feeling empathy, compassion and any other emotional connection to me. Sometimes, I don't feel like my mother ever wanted me in the first place, like I was a mistake she made with a really ugly man (that's how she refers to my father). Instead she is constantly trying to convince me of what a "good man" her husband is. I know better.

She refuses to accept that her husband treated me in the horrifying ways I described to her; she has never acknowledged that what he did to me was wrong; she has never said to me, "I'm sorry for what he did to you; I wish I could have stopped him," even after he admitted to her that everything I said about him was true. My mother has never offered any emotional support or compassion for the hell her husband put me through. And I am looked upon with disdain because I refuse to act like nothing ever happened.

But that's what happens when any mother buys into the manipulation of a madman and ignores the cries of her own child. She compromises and subsequently, loses the instinct of maternal bond with the child she sacrifices. And years later, when material possessions have withered, disintegrated or lost its glitter all she has left is a deep longing to right the wrongs of that shattered maternal bond and a desire to clear her conscious before she has to face God.

I have a daughter and if someone abused her, I would not hesitate to go after him or her. It is my God-appointed duty to protect my child from predators at all costs; not make excuses for abusive behavior and I certainly would not demand, insist, or try to convince my daughter to make friends with her abuser. To not come to her defense would be saying to my child that I don't have the courage to confront your abuser, I'm not responsible for what someone else does to you, and/or I don't really care about what has happens to you. I don't know that I'll ever fully understand why my mother made the choices she did. But, this legacy will be a painful reality for me for the rest of my life.

As a kid, on rainy days, I took comfort in the sounds of thunder and lightning; they reminded me that God was still out there,…somewhere. Sometimes, I felt hopeful that maybe I wasn't so alone after all. As long as I could hear thunder, see lighting, and smell the rain, I could feel the power of his presence. There were some lonely times. Thunder, lightning, the changing sky all represented hope for me. I clung desperately to nature during some very dark hours, opening my diary, reading and re-reading the entries. The words soothed me. The sounds of the bayou, a hard rain with thunder and lightning, and my diary were all the faith I had that God was still listening.

CHAPTER TWENTY-FOUR

Listening to the sound of the rain on this day, soon after my brother left, I reminisced. My times in basic training and military school were uninteresting. Except for a few stressful moments with someone yelling in my ear every ten minutes, nothing unusual happened. Life was disciplined and routine; but I would soon discover that a life of child abuse creates open wounds in the life of an adult. That monster had left me psychologically damaged, spiritually wounded, extremely bitter and physically self-conscious and I didn't realize it until it was time negotiate my chosen path in life.

When I stepped into the great big world, against hostile, controlling, and smothering objections, I was ill prepared for the challenge. I had spent so much of the last several years trying to die; I did not know how to live. Just before I left, some of my cousins hurled insults at me, calling me a traitor to the community, a sell-out, a white girl wannabe, and at one point, I thought the elders were gonna "break my plate."

Tradition dictates that everyone has a place at the dinner table, sometimes each with his or her own special plate. If an elder disowns you for any reason, your plate is crushed to the floor and broken, meaning you are no longer welcomed at the table; you are no longer a part of the family or the community. You have been ostracized; officially disowned.

They didn't break my plate, but I felt like it was coming. I had to get out of that little town; out of that hell-house; far away from the "bayou's mystique." Her mystery, her secrets, my birthright, had become a burden to me. I needed to get away from her-I didn't get far. On my first plane ride ever, headed for basic training, my thoughts drifted back to more nostalgic times. With my head pressed hard against the cool window, looking out on the patchwork landscape of fields, I went way back.

Band rehearsal was a time of escape and release. Every summer, during the week day, we had to be in the band room by 7:30am. At 7am, some of us early birds would walk to the local bakery. It was the only bakery in town, a family owned operation that had been in business since 1859. It had huge storefront windows so we could see the huge mixing bowls kneading dough; watch the owner roll the dough into classic doughnut shapes; and stick them in a large pot.

It always smelled so fresh in this bakery. By 7:20am, we were ready to get our instruments out of the locked storage room and sit in assigned chairs. Chairs were assigned according to skill level. I started playing clarinet in fourth grade. By the seventh grade, I was a skill level one. By 8am, in the cool of the morning, we would be out on the football field, before the players showed up for practice, learning the new marching moves and dance steps for the season.

By 1pm, it was time to go inside and learn the music. As a band member in an all-black band, you were expected to dance while playing an instrument and no one carried music sheets. You had better memorize it. High school football half time shows was a time of crowd entertainment, disco dancing, blowing musical notes to deafening tones and showing off. There was no place to hold a sheet of music.

Every year, the band went to Mardi gras in New Orleans. We participated in half-time performance shows at a local university, and marched in holiday parades in our hometown. Those were fleeting moments of peace and fun.

"Please fasten your seat belts and prepare for take-off," I heard someone say.

What the…? The flight attendant startled me.

"Ma'am, she repeated, please fasten your seat belt."

"What seat belt?" I inquired. The flight attendant gave me a sarcastic look and pointed.

"I'm sorry, maam." I apologized, "I didn't even know there were seat belts on airplanes."

After I locked myself in, I drifted back into my thoughts. In rare moments in high school, I enjoyed the company of my friends. As far as I know, all four of my high school friends were virgins. We gossiped about certain boys, but all of us were deathly afraid of getting pregnant. Besides, none of the "cute" boys would talk to us unless we agreed to help them pass a test. I leaned on them for academic support. We were the "smart" group. Grades, not boys, were important. Getting an "A" was natural; B's were tolerable; and C's were unthinkable. Anything below a "C" meant life support.

The five of us had met in Mrs. Patterson's fourth grade class and have remained friends to this day. We graduated at the top of our high school class with multiple titles and honors. Most of the time, I pretended to be happy around them. But there were many moments of immense sadness especially when they talked about waiting until marriage to have sex. I used to feel so unclean around them. I wanted to wait, too.

The English teacher liked my writing skills so much I was voted the senior class Secretary and newspaper editor. My most celebrated accomplishment was attending school for twelve years straight without missing one day. My friends came over to my house only once. None of them liked my mother's husband and they were afraid of him. When I think about my childhood friends, one especially painful event stands out in memory as one of the cruelest things anyone can do to a child.

It was my fifteenth birthday and I had permission to plan for a birthday party. I made a list of everybody I wanted to invite, filled out invitations and invited my four friends and all of my cousins. I gave the invitations to my mother to deliver for me. She, in turn, gave them to her husband. The party was supposed to start at 3pm on a Saturday. By 6pm, no one had showed up, not even my cousins. There was no cake, no decorations, and no presents. It's as if no one knew about the party.

I was so devastated that by 7pm, I went to bed and tried to cry myself to sleep. Both of them came into my room together and pretended to console me, by telling me the guests may have forgotten about the party. "But, where's the cake?" I asked with tears rolling down my face. Neither of them answered. As a matter of fact, my mother's husband was grinning. The next day I found all the invitations sitting on the seat of his pickup truck. He had never delivered them.

"Maam, can I get you something to drink?" the flight attendant asked with a look of concern.

"No, thank you," I stated politely leaning my head against a tear-stained window.

"Where did these tears come from?" I wondered.

I didn't realize I was crying. No wonder the flight attendant gave me a concerned look. My heart was aching as I longed for peace. "I just wish this pain would stop," I whispered and went to sleep.

CHAPTER TWENTY-FIVE

Basic training was like attending a "strict" Girl Scout camp. Most of my years in the military were uneventful, except for day I got married, the birth of my children, deployment during Operation Desert Storm, and the Christian retreats. My husband was a Godsend. I leaned on him so hard during the first three turbulent years of our marriage, I'm amazed that he didn't leave me. He endured countless hours of illogical rantings of how men could not be trusted; spent many miserable days and nights shouldering insecurities and fielding false accusations of infidelities; sat in silence, watching cautiously, as I tried to piece my broken soul back together. We've been married now for over twenty years.

Before the birth of our daughter, I became anorexic and weighed only 95 lbs. When she was born full-term weighing only 4lbs and 5ozs, I cried more than she did. I felt responsible for her low birth weight. During the second trimester of pregnancy with my son, the doctor discovered cancerous tumor cells lining the outside my uterus and demanded that I abort the pregnancy to begin chemotherapy treatment. I refused. "Find another way to treat the cancer," I pleaded, "but I am not killing my child; I don't believe in abortion."

She warned me that I could die without treatment. "As long as my child survives, I don't care," I insisted. She decided to treat the tumors with a powerful chemotherapy cream for the duration of the pregnancy and nine and one-half months later, my son was born weighing in at 8lbs and 9ozs. But my reproductive system had suffered irreparable damage. At age twenty-eight, I enter full-stage menopause. During my own research of early cancer and premature menopause, I discovered that sexual abuse can lead to both. This intensified my rage toward this monster whom I now blamed for me being unable to bare any more children.

During my first year in the service, the poison of child abuse began seeping through. I was a psychological mess. I had lived so much of my life in chaos; peace had become a threat to my existence. I found reasons to stay angry. By recommendation, I was sent to speak with a chaplain, to deal with my anger. He was a nice man, but I didn't trust him.

He was a *man*. How could he possibly understand what I was going through? On my first visit, he welcomed me in, wrote down some demographics, and asked only one question that revealed in grave detail just how severely damaged I was. The only thing he said was, "Tell me what happened." It started from the inside; an internal implosion; a feeling like someone was crumbling together every part of my insides, first my heart, then my soul; I started gasping for air and before I could utter a sound, I became muted, unable to speak and was beginning to curl up into a fetal position right before his eyes. I felt like I was disintegrating. When the tears began to fall and he realized I was in serious psychological trouble, he spoke words that I will never forget.

"It's OK, he said very gently, "Whatever it is, whatever has happened to you, build a brick wall around it; put steel doors in front of the brick wall; put chains across the locks of the doors; pour a concrete wall in front of the doors with no openings and seal everything shut. You never have to open that door again until your are ready." Looking back on this event, it is obvious he was not prepared to deal with the extent of the damage to my broken soul. I was not ready to deal with my pain; so he helped me "put it away" until I could. And for years, I left that pain entombed behind those walls, unwilling and unable to deal with it…for a time. I decided to pursue another passion and chose to chart a path away from the pain.

I wanted to keep my commitment to get to know God, so I joined church at the Base Chapel for Baptist services and got involved with church activities, such as bible study and youth groups. I also did my own research into other religions. The one I grew up knowing had too many hypocrites. I needed to find something I could depend on otherwise I considered becoming agnostic. I was still mad at God; but my early life experiences with the rocking chair, the strange dreams, deja vu savvy, and unusual knowledge kept me from abandoning Him.

One evening, during a bible study meeting, a chaplain, introduced me to several of Josh McDowell's books, including Evidence that Demands a Verdict, More Than a Carpenter, and He Walked Among Us. I read C. S. Lewis' discourse, Lord, Liar, or Lunatic and I found what I was searching for. In the pages of these books, I found both the scientific evidence and spiritual confirmations I needed to feel renewed in my faith. As I read these books, and those of other great Christian writers, such as Watchman

Nee, Hannah Hunnard, and Dr. James Kennedy, a light grew brighter inside of me.

Everything I had learned in vacation bible school, connected. The teachings of the elders in my community were confirmed and I was able to reconnect with my childhood spirit. I didn't want a religion; I wanted hope. I needed my faith restored in love, life, humanity, in myself and most importantly, in God. I needed to believe in the power of prayer again. Everything I read restored my hope. The stronger my confidence grew in the existence of God, the more I learned to trust in a power I could connect to.

I also gained insight into what was keeping me stuck. I had held on to a fantasy of healing that went something like this: If I could just get back to the feeling of a time when this ugly thing never happened, then I could be happy again. For years, I had longed for a return to the feeling of innocence where none of this pain was real and sex was what adults did. I wanted things back the way they were when I could sit in the old rocking chair and see those bizarre dreams.

I wanted to get back to the excitement of playing marbles with the boys and hopscotch with the girls where nothing mattered except who won and who lost. I longed to feel again, the fun times when my cousins and I used to run to the fairgrounds on the priest campus, clutching our $2.00 loot and getting dizzy on the Ferris wheel ride. I wanted to get back to the time I would play dress up in my grandmother's jewelry and hats, stare at a mirror and remember how good it felt to smile and say "I like what I see."

I had been changed by the trauma; and it was a sudden change. I became a different person the moment I was violated. The innocence I had known was gone…instantly! and all I had time to do was react and cry. Trying to live as if this ugly trauma had never happened only made me more vulnerable to depression. It was so hard to accept the truth and reality of my situation. There was no going back to innocence; there was no getting around the trauma; there was no denying my pain or my past. I had been raped, my innocence stolen by a vicious predatory mindset and there was no way I could get it back, reason this ugly truth away or pretend it didn't happen.

In order to begin healing, I had to move beyond mourning the loss of my innocence. I had to stop trying to live each moment with the frustrating, illogical wish that this horrible situation had never happened. It did happen and it had changed how I behaved, how I dealt with people, my thought processes, my logic and my life. The rules of engagement governing daily living were dramatically altered the moment I was violated and if I was going to survive, I would have to change my focus.

In a moment of insight, I concluded that I could either linger in my pain and self-destruct or I could find my passion and a purpose for living, overcome my pain, and move beyond the effects of the trauma. Unfortunately, I had already tried to change my reality by attempting to end my life. That didn't work. So, I did the next best thing. I prayed for help and God answered. I understand now that my spirit is part of a divine source and since I am an extension of this omnipotent spirit we call God, there was nothing I could not overcome. His spirit is stronger than any problem I have and I leaned on him for guidance. I also learned to renew my trust in the power of prayer.

Over time, the depression lifted and the walls I had built and formed around my bleeding heart fell, one layer at a time, on their own. I didn't need the defenses anymore. I had found the path I was looking for. It was time to heal. Before I could embrace his promise, however, I had to let go of the pain. So, I sought psychological counseling to rebuild a firm foundation of mental stability and learn to love myself. I entered a college program and pursued a graduate degree in psychology to study scientific rationale for psychological processes and looked forward to a future of helping others deal with issues similar to my own.

For a brief period, a series of nagging question started creeping into my conscious like a sinister sabotaging spirit. Where was God when you were raped? Or when your mother turned her back on you? Why didn't she stop that monster from hurting you? Even when you prayed for him to stop, God did nothing. If God is so powerful, how could he let this happen to you in the first place? My heart ached at the realization that these questions threatened to destroy my newly found peace. I didn't have any answers. Negative thoughts can be influential, but it is an influence of options. I had the option of accepting them or embracing a greater truth. I had to remember something very important. Each time I tried to murder myself, God stepped in. Three times I was spared from death. I don't know why. But, rather than blame God, I set my sights and the blame on the people who had hurt me. I am certain that God will deal with them properly, in due time.

CHAPTER TWENTY-SIX

California was a state I had dreamed of visiting. An aunt used to bring me special gifts from that state almost every summer. Because of my isolation, her visits and the gifts were especially meaningful. So of course, when I received military orders to get stationed in California, my soul started singing. California was everything I had dreamed of and more. The wineries, groves, the ocean, the picturesque Bay Area, Golden Gate Bridge, just the magnificence and beauty of the entire state took my breath away. My soul was free to explore. Both of my children were born here. I was reborn here. Soon after completing my research into different religions and deciding to walk by faith, I joined a Christian women's group. Every spring, we spent weekend worship retreats in tree-lined mountainous areas that were highlighted by breathtaking views of waterfalls, still waters, and reticent lakes.

We could sit atop man-made perches built into the trees and watch the deer feed just below us; watch the sun rise in the morning or set in the evening; or just sit and watch the birds fly to and fro in a peaceful, hyaline blue sky. There was peace here. One spring, for some reason, we could not go to the resort for retreat, so we decided to have a smaller version of the worship service in a small building in a nearby town. Everyone had to put on nametags so we could greet each other by name, especially if a new member was among us.

I decided to use my middle name; it's what everyone called me. As we were about to begin services, a white woman burst into the building, excusing her intrusion, by explaining that she had just flown in from South Africa, on break from missionary service to poverty-stricken regions. She and the lead speaker were friends. The usual opening prayer initiated the beginning of the worship service through bible discussions and life applications of scripture readings. At the end of service, it was tradition to form a circle and join hands which provided closure to the service with prayer.

Going around the circle, everyone had the opportunity to say something, if they desired. This time, things would be a little different. The missionary from South Africa stood in the middle of the circle and began to tell us of the miracles she had witnessed among the natives, especially during prayer. "Oh boy, here we go," I remember whispering sarcastically. I thought to myself, "We don't need anyone coming in here bringing tall tales of demon possessions and miraculous healings. It's just going to mess up the great spiritual atmosphere we already have." As if she heard my thoughts, my friend, Konnie squeezed my hand as if to say, "Stop it!" "Okay!" "Okay! I'm sorry!" I shook back with an apologetic look.

Before she began, the missionary said, "If it's okay with you, I would like to lay a hand on your shoulder. It's how I know there is a message for you." Well, now I had a problem. I didn't like anyone touching me. By now I had learned how to control any visions I received when someone touched me, especially during prayer circles. I'd simply shut them out. But now someone wanted to touch me and worse, she was a spiritual person. I did not want her to see all the things I had experienced, the visions, the premonitions, the weird experiences; she didn't need to know any of those things about me. I started to get nervous and almost broke the circle. "Not a good idea," I thought, "If I did that, everyone would get suspicious."

She had looked everyone right into the eyes and touched their right shoulder. But, when she got to me, she placed her right hand on the top of my head, looked me in the eyes, and said, "Cameron," she spoke slowly and deliberately, "You have been anointed." "You have a purpose for being here. God has a great work for you to do." And that was it. We exchanged smiles and she moved on to the next person.

At the end of her contribution to the Aglow meeting, the leader provided closure with prayer and we headed for the refreshments table lined with sandwiches, cookies, punch, crackers, dip, potato chips and mixed nuts. Where's Konnie? I wandered around the room looking for my friend. I found her mingling in the crowd. "Hey!" Konnie said, When did you change your nametag to your first name?

"I didn't." I said. "When I came in, I wrote "Suzaunna" on it. See?"
I peeled off the nametag to show it to her.
"Yeah, I see that," she said looking confused.

"Then why did the missionary call you by your *first* name?" she asked sounding concerned.

"What?" I looked down at my nametag, which still read, in bold black marker, "Suzaunna."

But Konnie was right. The missionary had called me by my first name, Cameron, but my name tag clearly said, "Suzaunna."

"How did she know my name?" I was confused. "I don't know this woman and I rarely use my first name except in formal setting." I had never seen her before and I was too shaken up to go up to her and ask how she knew my first name. I left it alone, sticking in the back of my mind like the words of a popular song.

Every time I think about the missionary and her message, those words shake me to the core. The memories take me all the way back to my last failed suicide attempt, when I had decided to live and find out what my purpose in life was. I thought about the dreams I had when I was ten, of that beautiful, glowing man holding his right hand over my head. All I could do was sigh. If nothing else, the experience left me with the impression that I was at least on the right path.

CHAPTER TWENTY-SEVEN

After that incident, my retreats, Aglow meeting, and education were interrupted by indefinite orders to Operation Desert Storm. "Indefinite" meant I had no idea when I was coming back home, to my husband and two small children, ages 18 months and three. After all, I was active duty military and it was time for me to honor my commitment and protect my country. We were deployed to a "classified" location, so I can't say much about that.

However, I can say that this was a difficult time to be a soldier. As a transfusion medicine specialist, I saw the worse damages and ravages of war. As a volunteer counselor in chaplain services, the mental injuries were just as severe as the loss of limbs witnessed in the intensive care unit. Between the brief relief sessions of watching movies in the makeshift hospital theater, dancing at the base nightclub or occasional visits from four-star generals, we wept. There was so much suffering.

Directly across the street, alongside a concrete sidewalk, just to the right of the mess hall, stood a bunker, stacked floor to ceiling with black, rubber, body bags; a chilling reminder of the ugly side of humanity. War is Hell. At the end of this tour of duty, the war had convinced me to surrender. My unit was headed for Somalia and I decided I had seen enough bloodshed for one lifetime. I was honorably discharged after ten years of service and moved my family back to the south where the cost of living was easier to deal with. The drive across the countryside provided a lot of time for reflection. I had become a new person. Suicide never crossed my mind once in my ten years service; but reflections of my past did. Some things still hurt; but now they didn't hinder.

After a year living in an apartment, my husband and I bought a home and our family settled into a routine life of school, work, church, family vacations and visits. Nothing out of the ordinary had happened since the incident with the missionary. But the dreams continued. One summer morning, I was awakened by a gentle voice whispering my name. My eyes popped wide open and I could sense a presence near my side of the bed. When I turned my head, my eyes met the transparent presence of an old woman. She had very dark, brown skin, looked like an African slave, wore a kerchief on her head, and was dressed in an old slave dress with a white apron tied around her waist. She stood there holding her hands in front of her body. I just stared at her for a few seconds and she did not move as if she wanted me to be sure I was not hallucinating.

Without moving her lips, through thoughts only, she said very gently, "I need to get to church. Can you help me get to church?" "Sure, I'll help you," I said. So I reached over, shook my husband awake and told him, "this lady needs to get to church; we need to help her." He opened one eye, looked at me and said, "Sue, it's 3am; go back to sleep." I didn't catch the logic of what he was saying. I shook him again. "But she's right here, look! And she has no way to get to church. We need to help her." He turned over and said, with a hint of frustration in his voice, "Sue, go back to sleep." Next thing I hear is snoring. "Fine! I'll take her myself," I protested and got out of bed.

I remember two things; getting out of bed and coming back to myself standing in the middle of my bathroom floor, which was adjacent to my bedroom. The old woman was gone, but there I was, standing in the bathroom feeling confused. "Who was that?" was all I remember thinking. "She looked familiar." When my husband got up later that morning, he said, in his typical sarcastic manner, "Well, did you get her there?"

"Ha-Ha, you are such the comedian," I countered. "No! We didn't get there. She disappeared and I ended up standing in the middle of the bathroom floor. I don't even remember how I got there."

"You're weird, you know that. You are weird." He said that a lot.

"Yeah!" "Yeah!" I countered, defensively. "Whatever!" "But I know her from somewhere."

"Probably somebody from your past," he said.

"Wait a minute," I whispered. The kerchief on her head, that dress, the apron…oh my God! It was her! "It was the old woman from that mean woman's house."

"Who?!" He looked spooked.

"You know, the one who told me to bring pecans so I would have something to eat, because that mean old lady wouldn't feed me! The one who used to turn on the bathroom light for me because I was too short to reach it myself! That was her! I think she came to say good-bye."

"Maybe," he said, looking at me out of the corner of his eyes. "Now can we talk about something else," he was getting a little nervous.

"Okay, I'll change the subject," I promised.

By this time I was seeing a psychologist to help me move past lingering effects of child abuse and incest. I told her about the visit from the old woman. She believed me, but didn't have any answers for me either. My speculation stands; I hope the old woman walked into the light. The psychologist was a phenomenal therapist and a wonderful person. She was also an avid physical fitness fanatic. I needed to get back into exercising, so she introduced me to her trainer. He seemed like a nice enough man who was polite, attentive, and patient. I agreed to let him train me for a week as a trial run. One day, I showed up at his gym, which was in his home, for a scheduled appointment.

He escorted me to the area where all the exercise equipment was and asked me have a seat, which I did. He had a few questions for me before we began the session. I expected to hear questions about height, weight, and training expectations. Instead, I experienced something so bizarre, I'm still not sure what to make of it.

He said to me, "I am a medium."

"A what?" I said. I didn't know what that was.

"You know, he continued, "a person who allows spirits to speak through them."

"You mean like *dead people*?" I was getting nervous.

"Yes," he stated, "I allow dead people to speak through me. I am also clairvoyant."

"So what does any of that have to do with me?" I asked.

"Well," he said, "When you first came in I noticed that there is a powerful aura surrounding you, so I know you are sensitive to spirits. Would you mind if I contact the spirits surrounding you?"

"What the…, I thought I was here for a training session," I said with a hint of indignation.

"You are", he continued, "It's just that you have such a strong presence, I HAVE to know where this power is coming from. I can't work with you unless I make friends with your source of power. Please, would you mind?"

This was strange to me but I was intrigued and I agreed with certain conditions.

"Okay, I said with caution, but DO NOT TOUCH ME!" I was firm about that. "AND I AM NOT CLOSING MY EYES!"

"Okay, he agreed, "I won't touch you and you can keep your eyes opened."

He didn't push. I was already leaning slightly forward sitting in a chair to his right. He leaned in towards me, closed his eyes, and in a trance-like state, began waving his hands slowly in front of me, and belted out this howling noise that sounded like wind whistling through cracks in a tool shed. It was loud, ear piercing and unearthly. I had never heard a human make this kind of sound before. This went on for at least five minutes. Then he stopped, slumped backwards deep into his chair, with his eyes closed and fell still and silent. He didn't move for at least 30 seconds. Then, with a swiftness that startled me out of my skin, he sat straight up and just stared at me, almost like he was looking through me.

"What?" I had to ask. The look on his face was weird and expressionless. "Well, what did you see?" trying to be humorous. None of this frightened me.

"WOW!" was the first word he uttered. After a long pause, he said, "You are surrounded by four of the most powerful spirits I have ever encountered. Two of them cautiously acknowledged me; one of them stood still and watched as I approached. But the fourth one was an awesome powerful force, the strongest of the four. This one not only denied my request, but after doing so, refused to respond to me at all. The others immediately resumed their positions around you and totally ignored my requests and my presence.

You are protected on all sides and no one can get to you. You are protected by the most powerful beings of light I have ever seen. You've been through this world many times, living different lives, each time creating enormous change. You don't even realize how powerful you are. There is something really important you have been assigned to do to need such powerful protection. Your protectors won't tell me what it is."

"Well, I don't know either," I said sarcastically. *"Living different lives?...please. That is the biggest crock of crap I've ever heard" I scoffed and echoed these words to myself.* "This is the first time anyone has said anything like that to me" I said politely. He didn't need to know about the missionary.

"Now, can we..." I started to speak. But now he was on his feet.

"I'm going to pour myself some hot tea." "Would you like some?"

"No," I said, I don't drink hot tea." "But, thanks for the offer. I would like to get on with the...," he interrupted me again.

"Would you like anything to drink?", he persisted.

"No, I'm Okay," I snapped. "I am just eager to get the training session started. Fifteen minutes of my one-hour appointment has gone by. "Can we please get started? I'm not paying full price for this," I said out loud as he rushed into the kitchen. He was stalling and I didn't know why. I thought about walking out but I didn't want to be rude. So I sat back on the couch and waited for him to return.

CHAPTER TWENTY-EIGHT

At first it was a feeling; a pressure coming out of nowhere, like the walls were closing in on me. I swear the walls in the hallway vibrated. THUMP! THUMP! What the hell is that? THUMP! THUMP! It was coming from the hallway; I could see the walls vibrate. My eyes became fixated on an empty hallway, but the walls clearly showed movement. I squinted, blinked, and shut my eyes at least twice to make sure I was not hallucinating; and there it was again. The walls ARE vibrating! I watched something that looked like heat waves emerge from the hallway. I watched its movements until it had gone past the walls and momentarily disappear inside the exercise room, which was directly in front of me. I lost sight of it for a while.

"Martin," I called out, "come in here please." I got no response.

Something emerged in the exercise room and looked like a rippling mass of heat waves. I blinked again, hoping I was hallucinating. I was not. It moved closer toward me.

"What?" I thought, "No, this can't be happening." "What the hell is **that**?"

My heart was beating fifty miles per minute and almost skipped a beat when the first ripple crossed over the slant bench. I had to lean forward to stop myself from running.

"Martin, you need to come in here," I called out a second time. Again, I got no response.

When the second ripple crept over the leg extension bench, I sat straight up and scooted my butt closer to the edge of the couch, ready to run. Then the movement stopped, but something resembling heat waves radiating off hot asphalt on a scorching summer day, was in this room. I watched as this rippling mass of energy position itself right in front of me and just vibrate with a menacing continuity. The air was heavy and still. I did not move...not at first; because I was paralyzed with fear. This felt bad.

The rippling stillness of this creature took me way back to the feeling I had when I dreamed about the cave and the pit of burning souls. The ripples reminded me of the strange fire in that burning pit. It was eerie and I was scared...but only for a moment. Sensing my fear, it moved with an unearthly swiftness and lunged at me and I jumped to my feet as if someone had jerked me up by the back of my neck. That's when I realized what I was dealing with. My faith took over.

"DO NOT MOVE AGAIN!" I warned holding my hand out in front of me. The fear disappeared. I pointed a finger at him and spoke with my mind. "I COMMAND YOU IN THE NAME OF MY LORD AND SAVIOR, JESUS CHRIST, DO NOT COME NEAR ME! STAY WHERE YOU ARE!" This thing froze in place only a few feet away; but the feeling that it wanted to rip me to shreds, lingered. It was time for me to leave but I dared not take my sight or my mind off this thing. The trainer reappeared and I was not happy to see him. He apologized for being gone so long. I sat down, keeping this thing in my sight.

As he was sitting down, I said to him, very calmly, "We have company."

He looked right in the direction of this thing and said, "Oh, that's just your great-grandmother." I was not fooled.

"No, it's not," I said. "I know what she feels like and she likes me. This thing is not my great-grandmother and whatever it is, it HATES me." "What is this?!" I demanded to know.

"Okay," he began, "Now I understand why your angels would not talk to me or let me near you. They know this guy. He wants to get to know you. Relax, close your eyes. He's harmless."

He was underestimating me and I was tired of his patronage. I got up close to him and looked him deep in the eyes. My voice took on a calmer, deeper tone than usual and I said to him very patiently, "Do you take me for a fool?" "Did you not hear what I just said?! This thing HATES me! And I want to know who this is. I will ask you one more time, "Who is this?"

He must have sensed the seriousness in my voice because he started talking. "I don't know who he is," Martin said. There was fear in his eyes; this thing scared him.

"What do you mean you don't know?" I countered. "Martin, this thing is dangerous. "Where did he come from?" "How did he get here?"

"You need to get rid of this thing." I was getting upset and starting to feel afraid for him.

"He doesn't like you," Martin surrendered.

"Wow, now there's a revelation." I answered in anger. "I already know that; the feeling is mutual." "Martin, who is this? You must know something about it."

"I don't know who this is," he said looking down at the floor. He raised his head slightly and asked, "How did you get him to be still?"

"Well, this may sound strange to you," I said, "but I commanded him to stay where he is." He looked at me with a sarcastic grin. He didn't believe me.

'It's a Jesus-thing, Martin. You wouldn't understand. But, I need to know how he got here."

He finally surrendered the truth. "Cameron," he began, "I'll be honest with you. I dabble in witchcraft and satanism. One evening a group of us were playing with a Quija board and we contacted somebody. After everybody left, I called out to the spirit that had identified himself. He said he was the spirit of a friend of mine who died several years ago and asked if he could enter."

"Enter what?" I interrupted.

"He asked if he could enter my world." Martin said.

"And then what?" I asked.

"I told him yes," Martin answered. He was visibly upset. "He tricked me. This was not my deceased friend; he was something scary. He is violent and destructive. He gets angry when I ignore him. He busted up my television for the third time and has broken windows in the house. Sometimes he throws things at me. I haven't been able to get rid of him and I don't know what to do."

I had not even noticed before but about two feet away from the chair I was sitting in was a shattered television set scattered all over the fireplace mantle and the floor. It looked like it had been thrown against the fireplace. I saw broken picture frames on the floor; shards of glass everywhere; the sliding door screen had been shredded, like a vicious dog had clawed into it; and books were all over the floor in disarray.

"Well," I continued, "This may sound stupid to you, but I've commanded him to stay away from me, so he won't be coming home with me. But, you need to get rid of this thing. It's time for me to leave. This place is not for me." You are one evil son-of-a-bitch, I whispered under my breath. "I don't think I'll be returning," I said out loud. "Thank you for your time."

Martin stuck out his hand. "No, I am not going to shake your hand." I flashed him a "look." He got the hint, because he quickly withdrew his offer of a handshake and I walked past that vibrating menace, through the hallway, and out the front door. It felt so good being outside.

"One more thing," he said. I faced him impatiently. "That thing inside…his mission is probably to destroy you. Each time you reincarnate into this life, he follows because every time you come back, you do great things."

"I don't believe in reincarnation, Martin" I shot back in anger. He ignored that statement.

"You are a major threat to evil spirits. They can't get to you because they are no match for your power," he stated.

"I told you, I don't believe in reincarnation," I repeated in anger, nor do I posses any "special powers" to fight off evil spirits. I think you're crazy, Martin," I snapped. Again, he ignored me like I hadn't said a word and continued his speech.

"Your guardian angels are fierce protectors. You don't have to worry about evil spirits harming you, because these protectors cover you on all sides. There is something you must do. Find your purpose." And with that he closed his door.

"Good-bye, Martin," I yelled…and good riddance."

I was so happy to leave that house that I played my radio really loud, singing out loud to old school R&B, dancing in my head to the tunes; anything to get what just happened out of my mind and my conscious. I wanted to erase the memory of that terrifying experience. I had no idea that this experience would open a gateway to dreams so far-fetched, even my family confirmed that something strange and irreversible was happening to me.

CHAPTER TWENTY-NINE

I started studying for a doctorate a few months after completing my master's degree. That was an exciting time for me. I was finally going to uphold my grandmother's honor and prove to her and every mean white person in her life that all black people were not stupid. This doctorate was in honor of my grandmother. The school was in another state. The program was unique in that you had to spend five days a week and nine hours a day in class, at least twice a month. I worked weekends, so it was easy for me to keep this schedule. Spending seven hours on the road every two weeks, driving back and forth, housed in a local hotel was grueling and expensive.

I was tired a lot, but determined to finish. For four years, I maintained this schedule. On my second trip to school, I had an experience that was described by one of my professors as "harrowing." I arrived at the Holiday Inn Express hotel at around sunset; unpacked; freshened up from the long trip; and settled in for the evening. Soon the television was watching me and I dozed off laying on my back. In the dream, I am wearing a sundress, driving south down T. Trail looking for a bookstore. There it was in the center corner of a "strip mall."

I parked my automobile facing the highway, right near the blue post office mailbox and walked inside the bookstore, greeted by a tall African-American man. "Hello," he said. "Can I help you find something?" "Yes, I am looking for the psychology section," I said and he waved and signaled that I should follow him. As we get to a small clearing in the store that had a descending staircase, I saw the "Ladies" room and decided to detour and catch up with him later.

As soon as I made a turn to my right, he grabbed me from behind, put a huge hand over my mouth and half-carried/half-dragged me kicking and screaming down the stairs. At the bottom of the stairs, he kicked open a door where two other men, another black man and a white guy were sitting down on a carpeted floor, smoking cigarettes and playing cards. "I got one," that monster who held his nasty hand over my mouth barked out. "Here! Shut her up!" as he throws me in the middle of the cards, sending them flying all over the place. "No! Let me out!"

These guys ignored me. One of them tied my hands behind my back; another one tied my feet together; and the other one slapped a piece of large black tape over my mouth. Then they carried me to a corner of the room that had some weird equipment sitting on a small table. "Electrical chords! What the hell…? One of them started putting out lit cigarettes on my legs. "No! Stop it! You sadistic bastards! Let me go! Let me go!" They just laughed at me. I woke up kicking and struggling against the wind. My heart was pounding!…hard. "Wow! I'm staying in for the evening," I decided. The next morning, I attended class without incident or thought of that nightmare from the night before.

When classes ended, I returned to the hotel room to freshen up. Since I still had car food, I didn't need to go out to eat; so I turned on the T.V. and reviewed my notes. At 8pm, the phone rang. "What the…who knows I'm here?" I had not yet spoken to my husband; no one knew my room number. I figured it was the hotel concierge.

` "Hello?" I answered cautiously.

"Hello, Ms. Tennessee." His voice was deep, silky and sneaky. He sounded like a bad imitation of Vincent Price.

"Who is this and how did you get this number?"

"Never mind who I am. I was calling to see if the three of us can come down and have a little "party" with you.

"Hell NO! And don't call my room anymore!" CLICK!

I slammed the phone down; it rang again.

"Now, that wasn't very nice; we won't hurt you. We just want to have some fun." Scenes from the nightmare crept in and I started asking questions.

"How do you know me?"

"I noticed your license plate. Oh, we've been watching you since you got here. You didn't realize it, but I walked right past you when you were returning to your room from signing in. That's how I know what room you're in."

"Tell me what you look like." The idiot started describing himself to me. I thought, "Good. Just the information I need to give to the police."

Well, I am about 6'2", African-American, there is another black guy and a white guy with me. We think you are so attractive…

"Leave me alone!"

"We just want to have some fun," the tone in his voice changed to a more sinister affect. No! I'm not interested in your stupid party! Stop calling this room! I am calling the police!"

There was silence on the other end for a moment and then he spoke again this time with obvious teeth-grinding anger in his voice.

"Remember, we know where you are; we know what car you drive; we even have the license plate number. You can't get away from us. It won't take us long to get to your room.

CLICK! I hung up again.

The next time the phone rang, I ignored it. But the damage had been done; I was terrified. I did not sleep at all that night for fear that they might just "appear" at my door. The next morning I went to class and talked with three of my professors and my academic adviser about the phone call. I wanted to tell as many people as I could. I didn't mention the dream. Everyone was so nice to me. One of my professors tried to make light of the situation. "Well, these guys certainly have good taste in women," he chided. "That's not funny, professor." "Oh! Ignore him, another professor chimed in; even if he is right."

My adviser was most helpful. "Get out of that hotel," my adviser warned. "Here is my home number. Call me if you need help getting away from there. Also, check with student services for other hotel listings. You need to leave that hotel today." Following his advice, I found a more secure hotel and moved out of the Holiday Inn Express during class lunch break. On my way back to class, I decided to stop and pick up a bite to eat.

I drove down an unfamiliar part of T. Trail; past several strip malls and grocery store parking lots; looking for a McDonald's or Burger King restaurant. Spotting McDonald's off to my right, I crossed over into the far right hand lane, scanning the environment for familiar landscapes. What!? The bookstore; I know that bookstore! Where is the mailbox? Where is the flower shop? The parking area was mostly loose gravel and soft, black asphalt, just like in the dream. I felt chills crawling up and down my arms. Everything was exactly as I had seen in the dream; right down to the "Big Sale" yellow writing on the glass door windows of the bookstore. "Well, there goes my appetite! I'm outta here! And with that thought, I left the area, McDonald's and that strip mall staring in my rearview mirror and never went down that way again.

CHAPTER THIRTY

On one other trip, I had another unusual dreamscape experience. Deep into the night, I dozed off while reading an assignment. I was jolted awake by the feeling of levitating within a humming tunnel of swirling glowing light. It reminded me of the light I was in at the hospital where the little boy had suffered those horrifying injuries. This time though, I was laying flat on my back and my feet were facing forward; like I was waiting to be transported somewhere. "Where am I?" I remembered asking. "What kind of place is this?" I was calm and acutely aware of my surroundings, but not scared in the least. I felt safe and secure, but I wanted out.

Moving my gaze slightly over my body and to the right, I could make out the silhouette of "others" moving slowly forward into this spiraling tunnel of light. There was no sense of fear; there was an overwhelming sense of peace. Then, everything faded to black, I felt a slight bump, as if I had landed on my back, and opened my eyes to find myself laying down in front of the book I had fallen asleep reading. I didn't sleep the rest of the night; not out of fear, but curiosity. I stayed up all night trying to make sense out of what had just happened. Later after class, I decided to visit the town's Aquarium.

Aquariums are so peaceful. After roaming and reading about the indigenous underwater species of that area, I took a boat ride around the bay. I joined others tourists as we circled the island of mansion homes, dwelling places of famous entertainers, watched dolphins swim nearby, docked to learn about native foliage, floated past a smelly nesting place of island birds and played with sea life caught by the host's net as he swept the ocean bottom. As we toyed with life, I asked to see the sea horse.

What a beautiful creature! And it was so tiny; it appeared so fragile, so minute in the vast expanse of the ocean. How could such a tiny creature preserve itself in such an awesome environment? I was intrigued. As I held it around its center, its tail curled and uncurled continuously. So I placed a finger inside the curl and that little tail latched on to my finger so tenaciously that pressure began building in my fingertip and I could not peel the little sea horse off. Its demeanor was one of pure calm as it puffed out its chest, held its head high and steady and did not waver. I was amazed.

This tiny sea horse that had wrapped itself around my finger would not release its grip until I lowered it into a small aquarium of water on the boat. What a metaphor, I thought. This tiny creature, if it did fear me, did not show it. It held firmly to its position on my finger until the threat was no longer a reality and when placed gently back into familiar space, it let go and began to explore the depths of the aquarium. If all humans could meet the challenges of life with such composure, how mighty we would all become.

When the boat docked, the host encouraged patrons to visit the mammalian wildlife rescue area, which was across the street from the Aquarium. Dotted by cute bistros and shanty seafood restaurants, the rescue was visible from the Aquarium, so I decided to visit. Manatees, Sea Turtles, Sturgeons…the sign read like a foreign concept. I had never seen such creatures except on television. I thought "this should be exciting," and it was.

The sea turtles were huge; as large and round as a child's plastic swimming pool. There were two; both had suffered injuries to their shells and had been rescued in order to save their lives. The sturgeons swam in −35 degree water temperature while I shivered just thinking about how cold that water must have been. It didn't seem to bother them at all. There were two giant manatees. One of them was inside a large concrete pool of water behind a wall of glass. This massive creature levitated motionless, gracefully suspended in her tank as if unseen hands were cradling her.

Her only motion was turning her head to grab huge bunches of vegetation in her mouth that dangled just within reach. She was a big girl with a big appetite and ate constantly. The other manatee was inside a large circular pool of water located almost under the floor. The caretakers said she was put there because her injuries were too extensive to be housed with the other manatee. The poor creature had gotten caught in the blades of a speedboat, lost her eyesight and sustained life threatening cuts to her body. She was place in this tank a month ago to heal.

There was a modest window for public viewing. Viewers almost had to stoop down to see her. I first noticed her when I turned away from the sturgeon tank. Halfway inside the floor, just below the humming motors of the tank, there she was swimming inside the clear green water, circling the large filter located in the center of the tank. There were toys at the bottom of the tank, colorful rings and a soccer ball. She didn't play with them; she just swam in circles occasionally bumping into the wall.

That's what the viewing public saw as I walked toward the viewing window. She stayed in the middle of the tank and circled the filter. I felt compassion for this creature. How difficult it must be to circle this hollow structure alone, apart from the world as you remember it. I approached the viewing window with the intention of just watching her graceful movements.

But something entirely unexpected happened. When I approached the window, the manatee stopped swimming around the filter and headed straight for the viewing window; right towards me. I got caught up in the moment, until I saw her face. The manatee's eyes were more than just damaged; they had been ripped from the sockets by the blade of that boat. Ugly scars covered the space where her eyes would have been. She was completely blind. Compassion flooded inside me and I turned away in agony until the words of a tourist, a lady jolted me back into reality.

"Look!," the tourist said as she pointed toward the manatee, "she looking at you." "Looking at who? Me?" I was puzzled. "She can't see me or anything else, " I reminded her. "The poor creature has no eyes."

"Well, the tourist continued, look at her; she's looking at something. Look at how her head is moving. I think she can see you."

When I looked back at the manatee, if she had eyes, they would have been fixed on me. We both stayed very still. She appeared to be "staring" right at me. "That's strange," I thought. "How can she see me?" I moved my head slightly to the right and so did she; I moved my head to the left and so did she. Then she started moving her head on her own, from side to side, as if trying to figure me out. "What the…how does she know I'm here?"

"Perhaps she senses your presence," the tourist chimed in. "Move away from the window and let's see what happens."

"Good idea," I thought. "This is just coincidence." I needed to reassure myself that I was not hallucinating.

When I moved away from the window, the manatee lifted her head slightly as if she was trying to find someone and swam back to the center of the tank, resuming her circular motions around the tank, again occasionally bumping into the wall. The tourist and I both watched as other people peered into the tank and watched the manatee swim in circles, ignoring them.

After about five minutes, when no one else was in front of the window, the tourist waved me back toward the window. She was just as enthusiastic as I was to see what would happen next. I took about ten steps toward the window and stopped. The manatee stopped swimming in circles, positioned herself facing the window, and stayed in that position, motionless in the water.

"Did you see that?!" The tourist was enjoying this.

"Yeah, I did. Wow! This was exciting.

As I got closer to the window, the manatee also swam closer to the window. When I walked up to the window and bent down; the manatee swam right up to where I was and stared right at me…with no eyes. I stood up and moved three paces to my right, stooped back down and the manatee followed. I moved back four paces to my left and the manatee followed.

"She can see me. But, how?" Thoughts were swirling. "She sees your light," the tourist said. In the excitement, I forgot she was standing there. "What light?" I asked. "The light that surrounds you," she said. "She is comforted by your light." And with that comment the tourist walked away. "A light…around me? But how is this possible?" I don't understand. But then I started thinking.

"Could this have something to do with that strange experience I had last evening, when I felt like I was levitating in that tunnel?" Is that the light she sees?" Even as this was as far-fetched as it sounds, this was the only sense I could make of this strange occurrence. The manatee behaved as if she could "see" me. She stayed in the window, staring at me with scarred spaces that used to be eyes and did not move from the window, so I started talking to her.

"Hello there." "You're beautiful". "Thank you for noticing me; I don't know how you can see me, but I feel honored that you can. I have to leave you now, but you will be just fine. God takes care of you, always." I pressed my hand against the window as if to touch her and she came closer, almost bumping her head on the glass. "Take care, friend."

Even as I stood up to leave the building, she levitated motionless at the window, "watching" me walk away. I left the manatee tank feeling like I had been blessed with something special. An animal, blind beyond measure, had honored me with her presence, and it felt good. I didn't need to understand it; I accepted the words of the tourist. Perhaps the light of one who saved me many years ago was still present; maybe the experience of being in that tunnels of light left something to behold. I didn't have any answers.

This was not my only strange encounter with an animal. On a family outing, we visited a pet store one day to buy rabbit food and chanced upon a golden retriever rescue adoption service showing off their dogs for possible adoption. We love animal; so we went to the open pen to play with the dogs. While I was talking with one of the dog's trainers, a large golden retriever startled me when he jumped up, placed his front paws on my shoulders and laid his huge head against my face. The trainers were astonished. This dog was considered antisocial. He had been rescued from an abusive environment and was afraid to mingle. But he found something comforting about me. After a lengthy interview, we took him home.

Over the years other animals would wander into our yard and try to adopt us as their family. We fed them, gave them water and shelter, treated them with respect and then helped them find their owners or good homes. Two Alaskan malamutes jumped a fence and came into our yard. They were returned to their owner after he posted a "lost dogs" sign. A Bassett Hound wandered into our yard off the streets and was adopted by a family friend. A Siamese kitten wandered into the yard and was later adopted by a pet service, and a beautiful little Scottish Terrier wandered into the front yard, one day, muddy, tired and hungry. We fed him and loved on him until he was adopted by a family friend. My daughter says that animal don't just wander into strange yards; they just instinctively know where to find the help they need. That's a good feeling.

CHAPTER THIRTY-ONE

School presented a serious challenge, but I managed. Admittedly, I was tired a lot, but something inside me pressed on. The dreams continued and I stared documenting all of them by date. Stranger things started to happen in these dreams. People spoke to me and asked me questions. Their faces were so clear I could pick them out of a line-up. They talked to me in my dreams about things that went on in their lives. They either gave me information about themselves or I was told and shown phone numbers, addresses, and the names of almost everyone I saw in those dreams. I witnessed lives in review, turmoil, defiance, chaos, and happiness and in death. The information came at me fast and furious, night after night, and I documented as much as I could. Not all of it was pleasant.

But nothing prepared me for what happened one Saturday afternoon in June, 1999. I had worked all night at the hospital. Although I had slept for about four hours earlier that morning, by 1pm I had grown tired again and decided to take a nap. Before falling asleep, I took stock of where everyone was. My husband was outside tending to the lawn; my twelve-year-old son was playing video games in the den; and my fifteen-year-old daughter was upstairs in her room. Everything was normal, so I dozed off.

In the dream, I am standing behind a glass wall, similar to the one I stood behind during my second suicide attempt; watching people enter some kind of enclosure. They were descending down a staircase, landing inside a courtyard. A dark smoky shadow lingered above this courtyard like a thin screen. Many of these people, upon entering the courtyard began to wander back and forth. The courtyard was surrounded by a barrier that they were not allowed to cross. There was one exit; an open doorway with light that flowed away from the darkness.

They would stop in front of it; but nobody looked inside. I don't know where it lead. There was deep and abiding confusion in this place. These people seemed lost, hopelessly, lost and their despondency resonated, as they wandered with their heads down. I could not understand why they would not simply go into the "doorway" of light. It seemed peaceful enough. I stared at these people who levitated rather than walked. They wandered back and forth and I felt sorry for them. I wished I could do something to help them. Off in a distance, I hear a child's voice.

"Mom!" "Mom!" "Wake up! I want to show you something!" I could hear him; but, I couldn't see him. "Mom! Wake u…" and then, my head lifted off the pillow. I don't remember doing this. But I heard my own voice say the eeriest thing imaginable. My son said I looked right at him.

I don't remember seeing him at all. But I heard myself say to him, "Where is your mother?!"

"What? You're right here, mom," I heard him say. Again, my body, in a gentle yet much sterner tone, spoke to my son and said to him, "No, she is NOT here!" "Where is your mother?"

I hear myself speaking and I am unable to stop what I am saying.

"But mom, you're RIGHT HERE!," my son shot back. I could hear the concern in his voice.

"Go find your mother!" I commanded him and my son said my head fell hard against the pillow and I slipped into unconsciousness. In the dream, I remember thinking, the child's voice is gone; why won't these people go into the light? I wake up from the nap feeling a little woozy, but refreshed. My son sticks his head into the door and I notice he is being extremely cautious.

"Mom? Is that you?" he asked with great concern.

"Boy, what kind of question is that?" "Who else would it be?" I was concerned. That was an unusual question.

"No, mom, I'm serious, he began. I woke you up earlier to show you something on my video game and you were acting really weird. You asked me twice, "where is your mother?" And you were laying right there. My mom was asking me "where is your mother." Where did you go?" "Who was that, because the voice was different; that wasn't your voice."

"Probably just having a bad dream; don't worry about it," I tried to comfort my son. But there was no fooling him. He knew things too, strange things. We had experienced an unusual situation with my son just two months after he was born. My husband was startled awake in the middle of the night by an apparition that was staring into our bedroom. The spirit was hovering just outside our door, directly in front of our 2-

month old son's room. At first my husband was paralyzed with fear. He could not move; like he was being held down.

But when that spirit motioned towards my son's room, all fear disappeared and he sat straight up. "No! You cannot enter my son's room!" He spoke with his mind. The spirit motioned again and this time, my husband said he was on his feet and does not even remember getting out of bed. He commanded a second time, "No! You will not enter my son's room." And with that, my husband says it vanished right before his eyes. So, I understand why my son was not frightened by what he heard coming from me; he is a warrior, like his dad. I have been able to steer his focus away from such things, but I worry about him sometimes.

"Is mom still acting weird?" This was my daughter who had just entered the room.

"What do you mean, am I still acting weird?, I asked for an explanation.

She said, "Andy said you were acting weird and that I should stay away from you until you woke up. He said you told him to go find his mother or something." You scare me sometimes, especially when your voice changes."

"My voice never changes!" That was a new revelation. "When does my voice change?" I needed to know.

"When you are upset, very serious, or challenged, your voice changes into this hollow sound; it sounds like you are speaking from deep inside yourself." Areis was insistent. "It scares me because you sound so intimidating." "It's just weird."

"Well, I will have you both know I am certifiably insane at this very moment." I started joking with them.

"BOO!" And with that my daughter let out an ear-piercing scream and bolted for the door. We laughed ourselves to tears until our sides hurt. "Very funny, Mom," she smirked. I put an arm around them both and continued. "Any more dealings with me and you'll end up just like me; weird and weirder. I can't explain what's happening, has happened, or will happen to me; I can't explain any of it. But it won't happen again. In the meantime, I am just fine. Go get your dad; let's go out for dinner."

And just like that, the subject was dismissed. I didn't want to discuss it anymore; not with these two. Truth be known, there was no one I could talk to. Mentioning this to my therapist would have landed me on medication and in a padded room. There was no way I was going to tell this to her. I dropped the subject and never spoke of spiritual things with my kids again. But I quietly monitored both of them.

During the ride to dinner, I was quiet. My mind had drifted back in time to a scene that still breathes life into my birthright." I was at the top level of my home, laying down on a sofa, reading and had nodded briefly, when I was jolted awake by a feeling of sheer panic and visuals of my son dancing in my head. I sat straight up and looked at my watch. Andy! He's in trouble! A sickening "gut" feeling sunk in and I broke out in a cold sweat. Pray! This was all I could think to do. I began to pray. "Lord, my son is in trouble. Please help him." "Hold on, Andy. God will help you. Just hold on." I must have repeated this over and over again, nonstop for at least ten minutes.

All of a sudden, a sense of calm fell upon me and the panic stopped. At around 5pm, my son, who had just returned home from a school field trip to one of the state's barrier islands, comes flying up the stairs calling for me.

"Mom!" "Mom!" "Guess what I saw?" He was bursting at the seams trying to tell me details of his experience. "I saw like, four different kinds of snakes and I touched them! Oh…that's nice; all the while I'm thinking, Yuck! "…And we played with turtles and frogs and picked fruits; some of them were poisonous." And he went on like this for the next twenty minutes. The usual round table dinner discussion centered on familiar topics of school, the day's work, politics and current events- nothing unusual.

But, two days later, my son and I were coming home from the grocery store, when I asked about the field trip again. "So, tell me more about the field trip to the island, I requested.

"The island is just a marshland; there was just one building on it and that's where we checked in," he stated.

"Did you have a good time learning new things?" I asked.

"Yeah, it was fun. But there was one scary moment." He volunteered.

"Uh-Oh. Tell me what happened." I could feel my stomach getting queasy.

"Well, we went out onto the beach area with the teachers to look for "sand creatures. The teachers bought out a big net and said we were gonna catch krill or some kind of water animal that glows in the dark. One of the teachers got into the water and started stretching out the net and called to the group for a volunteer to help him. The other teacher said to me, "you are the biggest of all the boys; go out and help the teacher stretch the net." "So, I did."

By now I am getting that tightening sensation in my stomach.

He continued. "I grabbed the other end of the net and pulled. At first the water was calm and right at my ankles. But then all of a sudden a large wave rolled in and the water rose up to my thighs; then my waste; and before I knew it, a strong current caught my ankles and I fell in the water."

"Your whole body was submerged in water?," now I was getting angry.

"Yeah, and the teacher just stood there looking at me. He asked if I was okay; and since I was able to stand up on my own, I thought I was fine. But when I stood up, the water was up to my neck, right at my chin. As soon as I said to him "I'm fine" another wave came in over my head and another current pulled me under and I fell in the water again. This time I was struggling to get back on my feet and I couldn't see the top of the water." "Andy, about what time was it when this happened?" I asked. Now I'm in full-blown anxiety.

"I think it was about one o'clock. But mom, something strange happened. All of a sudden, I saw a light on the surface, and this hand reached into the water, grabbed my hand and pulled me up. I don't know how, but before I know it, I was standing on my feet and the water was back down to my ankles. The strange thing is, there was no one around me at the time. The teachers and some of the students were running toward me, but no one was near me."

Around 1:00pm; that's the same time I was jolted awake in a panic and began to pray for my son. I didn't tell him about my experience until years later. My son has always been sensitive to spiritual things and at the time, I didn't want to scare him. By now I sincerely believed in the power of prayer. So, I prayed for a divine covering of protection over my entire family. It was my way of feeling secure that they would be protected from harm. Whatever was out there was not going to adversely affect my family.

Nothing like the incident with my son and that strange out-of-body dream ever occurred again; but it shook me. For a long time, I was afraid to go to sleep without my husband laying next to me or at least in the room. I could never get lost behind the liquid wall again because I was afraid I might not find my way back. I believe that recognizing the sound of my son's voice brought me back to myself. That was one of the scariest dreams I have ever had.

CHAPTER THIRTY-TWO

I was at the end of my curriculum, close to graduation and it was time to start looking for an internship. Before I could find one, however, I was introduced to a potential prospect at a convention, whom at first seemed harmless. She was planning to start her own practice and needed help getting established. I gave it some thought. This person was soft-spoken, but "syrupy" sweet.

There was a nagging evil about her that I couldn't shake. So I proceeded with caution. Soon after we started working together, she started asking me about spiritual stuff. Well, I knew a thing or two about the subject, so I volunteered some of my childhood experiences with great-grand mama's old rocking chair. She seemed fascinated. That nagging sense of evil lingered, but I figured it was nothing I couldn't handle.

One day she invited me into her home. She had a nice four-story brick home,…on the outside; but inside the place was filthy. I also noticed the air was cold and stiff and it lingered in a creepy stillness. Something was wrong with this house. There was an unearthly and hostile presence in there. A nagging feeling crept in, warning me that I was in danger. I tried to ignore it, even dismiss it as unfounded, but the harder I tried, the more uncomfortable I became.

Looking down a brick-sided hallway, I saw the backside of a white gentleman, with greasy, black hair, wearing a red, gray, and black-checkered flannel shirt, blue jeans and black shoes, disappear into a room on the right. I remember she said she had a guest staying in the home for a few days, so I assumed that's whom I saw. I never saw his face. She proceeded to show me the rest of the house.

The house looked like it had fallen into disarray. The carpet and living room furniture, were so filthy, I declined all offers to "make myself at home." I didn't even want to touch the walls. When we got near the kitchen, a dark-skinned black, old woman wearing a red and white checkered patterned kerchief on her head and a checkered apron around her black dress, was standing near the dining room table with her hands folded in front of her apron, watching us walk through the house. It was creepy.

"Who's that?" I asked. "Who's who? She inquired with a strange look on her face. "The old woman by the table; who is she? I was curious. "Tell me what you see," she said. "Never mind; it's nothing." I was growing more suspicious by the second. I know she saw the same thing I did because she looked right over in that direction as soon as I asked about the old lady. That nagging feeling grew more intense. Upstairs where I saw the gentleman walk into the room, she showed me five barely furnished rooms.

One room, a very cold space, had only a mattress on the floor and a small black and white television sitting on a makeshift T.V. stand in a corner against the back wall. It was the room I saw her guest go into; only now there was no one here.

"Where is your guest? I asked. I just saw him come into this room."

"Oh, there's no one else here except you and me," she said in a matter-of-fact kind of way.

"No," I said, "I saw someone come into this room as soon as we walked into the house."

I know what I saw and I was starting to get agitated. I felt like she was mocking me.

"Well, there is no one else here," she sang. "Let me show you my room." Her room was colder than the rest of the house.

I remember thinking, "What does she want with me?"

"Look," she said. "I want to show you something." She pulled out a bible. This was no ordinary bible. This bible had a holographic eye on the cover with a pupil that moved when your eyes moved. I had never seen anything like it. This thing was creepy to look at.

"Ugh! That eye is spooky," I was not impressed. "Where did you get this?"

"I bought it at a garage sale," she said. "Isn't it the most unusual thing you've ever seen?"

I ran my fingers over the eye and watched as the pupil followed my finger. It felt like the scales of a snake.

"Have a seat right there, in my chair," she insisted.

It was a large overstuffed chair and the cleanest thing in the house. So I sat down.

"Take off your shoes. Relax. Let's talk," she sang.

She wanted something.

"I think I'll keep my shoes on, thank you." I was not going to compromise.

"What do you think of the bible?" she asked.

"It's interesting, I said. But, I was really thinking, "This thing is creepy as hell." "Here you go. I'm done looking at it." I handed it to her face down.

"No, no, no." she countered, waving her hands in the air like this bible was poison ivy. She wouldn't take it back. Hold on to it for a little while longer," she insisted. I'm going to run to the kitchen and get something. I'll be right back."

"Why does everybody keep disappearing to the kitchen?" I whispered to myself. I was getting upset. Then it occurred to me. The last time a strange person left me alone and disappeared into the kitchen, something weird happened; all hell broke lose. I was not going to let that happen again. This book felt like a Halloween trick and it was frightening to look at.

᾽ By now I am doing everything I can to avoid that creepy eye, and finally, I put the book on the floor, face down. I remember calling out to her, because I was ready to leave. But just as I was about to get up, my head started to feel funny and the room started spinning. I struggled against zoning out because I didn't want to know what was in this house. Before I knew it, she was shaking me by the shoulder and I was awakened by the sound of her voice calling my name.

"Hey, are you all right?" she asked.

"What the hell happened to me?" I was angry for some strange reason.

"You drifted off; but you were mumbling something to me, something about me being afraid to let go and believe. Warning me about a looming darkness, something about a burning pit...I don't know what happened to you; but, when I came into the room, you were not yourself." She seemed more amused than concerned because she had a smirk on her face that made me uneasy.

"So tell me, what did you see?" She said with a big smile and too much enthusiasm. "That's it!" I said to myself. "I'm out of here." And with that thought, I jumped up from that chair and proceeded to leave the room.

"You know what?" Now I was agitated. "I need to leave; it's getting late and I need to get home. I'll call you." I just wanted to get out of that creepy house.

But the next day, after the encounter with the bible, something bizarre happened.

I was sitting in my bedroom chaise around 2pm, when the room started spinning and I went into a zone. Before I know it, these people, at least five or six ghostly figures are standing in front of me. I saw them plain as day through a small crack in my eyes and tried desperately to ignore them. I was also unable to move. It was a surreal moment.

First they stood right in front of the chair I was sitting in and just stared at me. Then I heard them speaking to each other. A woman with blonde curly hair asked another woman standing next to her, "Is she awake?" Another one, a black man looks at both women and asked, "Can she hear us?" A white man, tall, with broad shoulders and black hair came closer to my face and shouted, "Hello?" and then commented to the others, "I don't think she can hear us."

Then one of them started pleading with me, and the others joined in. "Wake up," they took turns speaking. "Please, wake up." "We need your help." "Please, help us." Their voices had a haunting, hollow, echoing sound to them. They sounded so desperate, I felt like crying. I sat very still. This was scary. I didn't recognize any of these people. Finally, after what seemed like forever, they faded away. As soon as I regained my senses, I immediately spoke to whoever was listening. I told them that whoever they were I could not help them; that they were not welcomed in my home; and to leave at once. I felt kind of silly speaking into the air. But it's the only thing I knew to do. I didn't know how to help them and I didn't want any part of this.

I don't know why this happened, but I believe it had something to do with the eye on that bible. This felt kind of like the strange experiences some people have had when they play with a Quija board. Something followed me home that night and I believe she knew about it. I used to see strange people a lot when I was a child. With the exception of a few isolated cases, I had not experienced anything of this magnitude as an adult. I talked to several people about that strange incident. Some of them had seen a bible like that one before and warned me to never touch it again. They echoed each other telling me that this person had bad "karma" and it had collided with my light. All of them warned me to get away from her. A gut feeling told me I should get away from her also; so, I made plans to leave.

During the planning stage, I tried to ignore all signs that I was in danger. When I reluctantly accepted a second invitation to her home, I took my husband with me and he was immediately uncomfortable around her. He did not like her. In addition to the strange occurrence with those ghostly apparitions, other bizarre things occurred while I was in association with this person.

She started introducing me to strange people who wanted to show off personal drawings of heaven and hell. They wanted interpretations. They brought demonic drawings and sketches, prayers and incantations, and pieces of paper that were so heavy with spiritual content that when attempts were made to set them on fire, they would not burn. She also had a habit of going to palm readers, occultists, séances and body healers who did not believe in God.

Other significant details got my attention. Every time we talked, she wanted to sit in the dark as if she was allergic to light. At night, she would turn on a small lamp that produced just enough light to cast dancing shadows on the walls. It was spooky. She was also extremely cynical. No one, including her personal friends was safe from her venom. She mocked everyone and I wondered what she might be saying about me. She even said that she believed some people with mental problems were possessed by demons.

I was walking through a flea market one day and came upon an unusual revelation. Off in a corner, covered in dust was a framed picture that caught my attention. It depicted a man arriving on a boat offering gifts to the natives; but the man had two faces; one face had a smile and the other was the image a man whose smile changed to a sinister grin with his hand on the handle of a hidden dagger. This described her completely. Soon after the incident with that haunted bible, bizarre and dangerous things started to happen to me.

Like one time I was coming out of the shower and the glass door came off its hinges and crashed to the floor, almost crushing me beneath it. What saved me was the towel I was wrapped in got caught on an exposed glass edge and prevented the heavy door from slicing into the jugular vein in my neck on its way down. When my husband put the door back on its hinges, he saw no reason why it had slipped out of its hinges in the first place.

I started sleepwalking and following the voice of someone who kept calling my name and almost fell down a flight of stairs. I woke up in time to find the heals of both feet balancing precariously on the edge of the top stair. I jumped twelve flights of stairs, feeling like I had been pushed and was jolted awake when I landed at the bottom of the staircase, standing up. The contents of the dreams started showing reviews of entities pretending to be one of my children, my husband or other people I cared about. These entities would start out looking like someone close to me.

As soon as my guards were down, they would encourage me to follow them into unfamiliar places. When I did, a door would slam shut behind me; or the entrance to a tunnel would seal shut; or an elevator door wouldn't open sealing me inside a horrendous darkness and I would begin to pray for help in the midst of the dreams. A wall of light would appear and I would step through it, leaving the darkness behind. I would wake up totally exhausted as if I had been in a ferocious fight.

This was a fiendish person and everyone in her circle was just as wicked. She would tell her friends about my spiritual side and soon every one of them wanted to "touch" me; and you know how I feel about being touched. When I refused to let them touch me or pray with them, they got angry. She tried to isolate me from my professional peers, a professional organization I belonged to, using the same manipulative philosophy my mother's husband and all predators use to isolate their victims. She said to trust no one. "The people in that organization are phony," she would say. "I believe they're all sexual predators and you need to get away from them."

I had shared a part of my childhood experience with her so she knew how I felt about sexual predators and child abusers. Her words were carefully chosen to ensure I would have no desire to associate with the people I respected most. She wanted me to shun all associations with the organization. When I resisted all of her attempts to isolate me, she became furious. As a child, every time I dreamed about snakes, I knew I was in the presence of a person who wanted to hurt me.

While I was in association with her, dreams about snakes started almost immediately and they were terrifying. After the first day I met her, in a dream that night, I was looking at a puddle of clear still water. There was nothing unusual at first. But then, the water rippled with such subtlety that I almost missed seeing the huge snake with large fangs that lay dormant and transparent just beneath the surface. I woke up thinking, "Someone in my social circle is trying to hurt me, but is disguising themselves. I need to be careful."

As the dreams intensified, I noticed that sometimes the snake had two heads; one would appear to be asleep and the other was watching everything I did. And always, at the end of each dream, this person's face appeared on the snake's head, smirking at me. In one particular dream, a rather large vicious and hostile snake charged right at me. Just before it got to me, the snake reared back, raised its ugly head, and her face appeared on the snake's head, with a smirk on her face. The more these dreams occurred, the more uncomfortable I became. I was making plans to get away from her, but I was not moving fast enough. I think she knew I was preparing to leave, because she started making phony promises of future success. For a moment, I ignored the dreams and listened to what she had to say.

Everything she said made me uneasy. When she asked why I was so uncomfortable, I started telling her about the dreams with snakes in them and how they always ended with her smiling face showing up on the snake's body. I asked her if she had any idea what these dreams meant. Of course, she said no. But, when I called her one evening and told her about the one dream of the mean snake where it appeared I was going to be attacked, she exploded in anger. I listened carefully as she complained bitterly about my disapproval of her wanting to advertise our potential partnership and my selfish unwillingness to sign a contract that would have obligated me to pay for the entire cost of her destitute daughter's health insurance.

In the midst of her tirade, I said very calmly, "There it is."

"There what is?" she asked with an immediate calm that was frightening.

"You've just confirmed what I suspected all along. Obviously, you are not who you pretend to be. I have nothing more to say." And I hung up the phone.

I sat in silence that night, in meditation, reviewing her venomous words. She sounded enraged. In the midst of relaxation, the Bayou Mystique took note of her ranting and reminisced into my childhood; into the many days spent sitting in mom-mom Suzaaunna's old rocking chair. She took me back into the zones of prebirth memories; precognitions and warnings; heightened awareness; and divine interventions.

She reminded me of something I learned during those times; words I used to read over and over again after writing them down in my diary. I was reminded that "Truth is known when memory is understood." "Life hides behind a veil of gaiety," voiced a subtle whisper. "Always look behind the veil." When I came out of meditation, I knew without a doubt it was time to go. "Forget about her empty propositions," I reasoned, "I had stepped into hell." I started paying close attention to what I was feeling. Both times that I visited her home, I felt like I was walking inside that charred cave. When I looked behind the metaphorical veil, I saw nothing but darkness.

She knew something was up; because her demeanor changed. A few days after that viscous phone conversation, she called and asked me to forgive her for the outburst, claiming to have had a rough day. "You need to stop paying attention to those dreams," she said with that irritating syrupy twang in her voice. "They don't mean anything. Just ignore them." The tone in her voice changed from syrupy sweet to something unrecognizable. I did not trust her and when she tried to be extra nice and invite me to her home a third time, the Bayou Mystique came alive again.

I had two dreams, one after the other that were so revealing, I stopped talking to her immediately. In the first dream, which occurred on a Sunday night, I am an adult sitting in the old rocking chair. Each time I tried to set a foot down to climb out of the chair, an extremely large snake, larger than any pictures of an anaconda I had seen, moved with lightning speed and struck out at my feet with enormous fangs. Each time it pulled back its ugly head, her smiling face appeared. It did this three times and the third time, her face was not smiling. That was all I needed to see.

The next day I went to her new office, gathered whatever belongings I had left in there and drove away from that spooky place forever. I have not spoken to her since then. Details of the second dream can be found in an upcoming book. Some of the most bizarre situations I have ever encountered occurred while I was associated with this person. I saw things that, for the first time, made me question the extent of my knowledge about evil and Christianity. That was a harrowing experience. I have cut off all contact and associations with this person, but the experience highlighted the importance of paying attention to my sixth sense. It has been several years and I have not had one single dream about snakes since I left her presence.

CHAPTER THIRTY-THREE

"Go to the file room; there is something there you must see." The voice spoke with authority. "How do I get there?" I asked. "Pray." On October 19, 2001, while in a semi-state of slumber, just as I was waking up, this dialogue took place. I have no idea where this came from. I didn't even know a file room existed, but I did whisper a prayer for guidance. I have since discovered some of the most fascinating information imaginable. If I had not had this dream experience, I would never know to look into such things.

According to some people and apparently some religions, a chamber exists, a type of file room unlike anything I had ever realized. Edgar Cayce talked about this place. I read his work. It is the place where records are kept; where all that you are is kept on file. Edgar Cayce was a well-respected psychic in the 1930's and 40's. He claimed the ability to locate and read the contents of the files of people who came to him for dream interpretations, healing, predictions about their future, assurance of divine interventions, or solutions to personal problems. From what I've read, he was pretty accurate.

The file room is sometimes called "the place of memory" or the Akashic Files. It is an unusual place where every act, thought, slight, behavior, all words and deeds are recorded and kept in a personal file. Each person has their own. Not only had I never heard of such a place before this dream, but neither had any ministers I spoke to. In all of my years of attending church, not one minister had ever mentioned this place. I didn't want to discount it completely; but it was hard to believe that such a place existed. The Bayou Mystique would not let me languish in my own confusion. She decided it was time to reveal more of her secrets.

On December 10, 2001, on a cold night, I was sitting next to an old electric space heater, curled up in a very uncomfortable chair at a hospital I worked in trying to keep warm. It was a slow night in the emergency room and slow nights meant we could take a nap. It is about 1am and I feel myself getting sleepy and begin to drift off to sleep. In the dream, I emerge standing in darkness surrounded by a strange aura of silver light.

The ground radiated a silver path around the corners of a building, which also maintained this silver hue. I am standing on the corner of a road inside some kind of city. It is nighttime and the city is deserted. The buildings are made of a concrete-clay mixture that looks rough to the eye, but appears smooth to the touch. I fold my arms in front of me and proceed to walk down on the glowing sidewalk, following its path around the corner of the building. Just over my shoulders beacons of light follow me; rays of light emanates from them like the glare of a halogen flashlight, slicing into the darkness.

There is a nondescript wind blowing from my right as I notice a small piece of paper floating in front of me, dancing in the wind that carries it. "What a strange place." I remember thinking. As I turn the corner, to the left, I notice a yellow glow coming from inside a stone corridor. The opening to the corridor has huge round columns on both sides, a beautiful semi-circular ceiling and four steps leading down onto another smooth, well-lit stone path.

The walls, the ceiling, and the path, inside the corridor now glisten with a combination of golden yellow and silver. It is a magnificent sight. Everything is polished and shiny. As I walk down four steps into this corridor, I see a doorway. There is some type of lettering design written at the top of the brilliant white doorpost. It is written in a language I don't understand. This place is incredible.

Entering through the doorway, I find myself standing in the center of a room where the ceiling is made of emanating light. The walls and the floor now glow a brilliant white and I am awed by the magnificence of this chamber. For the first time, I realize that I have shed that silver glow and now stand draped in a glowing white robe.

As I proceed to a semi-round circle before me, movement startles me. WHOOSH!!! Like a rush of wind, something wisps past me. He is moving so fast, all I see is horizontal streaks of light and a flurry blur of gray and white streaks. He moved so fast, my clothing flowed in the direction of his path. I remember thinking, "Wow, someone is in a big hurry."

I turned in the direction of the wind, hoping to see who this is. Just before he reaches the doorway I had just entered, he stops as if frozen in place, turns around and looks at me. His eyes are pinpoint and piercing;

he has a beard and is bald except for the silver gray hair forming a semi-circle surrounding his temples. He is wearing a dark robe, which stood in stark contrast to the beautiful light that surrounded this place. He does not speak to me. He just stares with a menacing look; it was a look that disturbed my peace.

The shadow that surrounded him repelled the chamber's light as if threatening to contaminate the purity of these hallowed halls. He did not belong here. Other than the old man, there did not appear to be anyone else in this room. I notice that he is cradling something under his right arm. They look like pasty gray-colored files. "Where are you going with those?" He must have heard my thought because he gave one last piercing stare, turned around very quickly, and bolted for the doorway, disappearing in streaks of gray and silver. "Who was that?" I remember asking. "I don't think he was supposed to have those." I would see this little man again.

After the little man zipped away, I turned and advanced toward three semi-circular steps that dipped into a sunken floor. I took those steps down into the sunken floor and beheld one of the most magnificent sights I had seen since my childhood dream of the city of gold. In what at first seemed to be a light gray mist quickly cleared up and I found myself staring at a massive set of drawers that resembled files. The file drawers completed the circular circumference of the sunken floor and they were stacked from floor to … wait! Where is the ceiling? This part of the room had no ceiling. The files stretched deep into hovering clouds.

Some of the file drawers' glowed with the brightness of a halogen light; some were brilliant silver, others were bright yellow; still others had a miserable gray pallor to them and some had no glow to them whatsoever. As a matter of fact, the files being carried by the little man either had either a pukey gray hue or did not glow at all. My feet do not touch the floor, but I can feel resistance beneath my bare feet as if I am levitating on a layer of gravity. While inside this semi-circle looking up into the clouds, I watch an amazing demonstration take place.

But then, I am startled out of this dream by the sound of a ringing phone. My head feels funny; like I'm about to pass out. But before I come to my senses, a warm sensation slowly overtakes me and I open my eyes. Everything in that small room was glowing and I felt strangely unformed. In a semi-sleepy state, I stretched out my arms and hands in front of me and saw limbs and hands forming. Fingers were reemerging into recognizable digits everything was encased inside this unbelievable, soft, warm, glowing light. My entire being emerged slowly, lighting in a chair next to the space heater, one arm resumed leaning on a small table, holding up my head; and I watched parts of my body transform from a ball of light back into a recognizable human form, clothes and all.

This dream felt so real that at this point, I felt like I needed to either check myself into a psychiatric unit or just dismiss it as another strange dream. For a week, I considered the psychiatric unit because I was not ready for this level of unreality. But while thumbing through some books at bookstore one day, I came across a similar descriptive experience published by an astronaut. I decided against the psychiatric unit. Perhaps I was still in the dream when this "transformation" occurred; at least that's what I told myself.

I went on with life as usual. The holidays were festive but uneventful. I had to work both Christmas and New Year's Eve at night. So once again, having a boring night at work, on a cold January morning around 2am, I curled up in a chair, in that same little room, right next to the space heater, leaned against the table and went to sleep. It was on the morning of January 12, 2002, that I had a dream experience so petrifying, it haunts me to this day.

During a new internship, the therapist who was supervising me decided to start a group therapy program for women who had been sexually abused as children. Seven women showed up the first evening. As we greeted them into the counseling area, one woman affected me unlike any of the others. When we made eye contact, I stood frozen, unable to move, petrified by what I saw. Something inside me started to shake uncontrollably. This woman had a piercing gaze that took me back to the time I was a small child; when I looked into con-Gwin's eyes and felt that sensation of being punched in the chest. Her eyes were like magnets and I had trouble looking away.

"Look behind the veil," a whisper from the wind shakes me back to my senses. At that moment, I calmed down and turned into a scientist, noting and surveying everything about her. She had the deepest light brown eyes imaginable and a frightened, wide-eyed look of a terrified child on her face. And she trembled like a leaf in the wind, with every step. All of my caution against touching someone or preventing them from touching me went for naught, as she extended her hand without introducing herself.

I responded in kind and I should have seen it coming. I read her fear and I *felt* it. She didn't tell me her name and she didn't say one word for the entire three hours of the session. She simply sat directly across from me and stared at me for long periods without blinking. I was becoming unnerved by her stare because I swear she could see right through me. It was creepy. She wasn't ready to share her story with the group, at least not yet. The therapist had already pre-screened and interviewed each of these women. She knew all of their stories. So, she respected this client's privacy and told her she could share her story when she was ready. This particular client said nothing about her experience the whole night; she just sat in silence.

Two nights later, I was working the night shift at a hospital. It was a slow, cold night, so I sat down in front of an old rusting space heater to keep warm, put my feet up on a chair and dozed off. In the dream I emerge standing in a brightly lit space, staring into emptiness. Then in slow motion, a view emerges. The file room reappears. This time the files, which stretched far into hovering clouds, were very busy.

They opened and closed without assistance, indiscriminately, and information was constantly being applied to the record and filed. I am standing in the semi-circle, just in front of the third step, watching the file drawers open and close when one of the files comes out of a drawer and floats towards me. As it nears where I am standing, a silhouette of a human form appears and he or she holds the file closed in front of me. First there is a glow coming from the closed file; then, the person holding the file flips open. I notice the glow is a halo that surrounds the moving picture in the file, like a circle of energy.

Everything is happening in "real time." The life of this person, someone I did not recognize, is being lived right before my eyes and I am watching the reviews of their life in living color; as if I am watching a movie. I see a child being scolded by a grown woman who shakes her finger in the child's face. I see the angry look in the mother's eyes. The child appears to be her daughter, but she has no love for this child. I see darkness inside her. But, the heart of this child glows. There is so much hate coming from the mother; she has no light in her and light does not surround her. The little girl is visibly scared, but her mother, does not seem to care.

Then I see the mother call out to someone and another young girl shows up; she is smiling. The mother puts her arm around this child's shoulder and they walk off leaving the hurting child standing and staring at them. There is a faint light inside this other little girl; it struggles to stay lit. They are laughing and talking to each other while the hurt little girl, wearing a yellow dress with pretty flowers on it, hangs her head and stands in silence. Then out of nowhere, a man appears. He hits the little girl, punching like she was a man, and knocking her to the ground. She starts to crawl to try and get away from the monster. Her lips are moving and he appears to be yelling, but, I cannot hear sound. I can only observe what is happening. As she tries to crawl away, the monster straddles her from behind and sits on her.

She is screaming, but no sound comes from her mouth. Then he exposes himself and puts his penis inside her rear end and shoves himself inside the little girl. She screams silent noise. I cannot hear her; I can see her and I can feel her. It is disturbing. She appears to be about 8 years old. I am horrified; I do not want to see this, but I have no eyes to close. Then, as if this is not enough, he flips the little girl over and shoves himself inside her, repeatedly. She is being raped again. He is violent and maddeningly evil. I want this thing to stop; I cannot take anymore and I can feel my body jerking, trying to awaken from this ugliness. The scene is violent and his attack is vicious. He pulls her hair; puts his arm around her neck and pounds into her with the violence of an incubus.

"Make it stop! Make it stop!" I don't want to see this anymore! My mind is screaming so loudly, I felt like my head was going to explode. He shoves the little girl down and towers over her, moving his head from side to side, and smiles as if admiring his work. Then the child's mother and her sister reappear at his side and they too are standing over the child's battered body, smiling. The child is laying in a pool of her own blood and she is barely moving. The three of them walk off, leaving the child, battered child to take care of herself. They don't try to help her. I wanted to get out of there and yet, I wanted to help her. But all I was allowed to do was observe. The real time scene starts to fade away and the file begins to close with the three of them standing over this wounded little girl. But, as the scene fades, I saw a brilliant pulsating light glowing inside her broken body. The evil did not destroy her light.

I came to my senses with a massive migraine and tears streaming down my face; rushed to a phone and called the supervisor at 3:00am tell her what had just happened. She confirmed the details of the dream as the abusive environment that the woman with the mysterious eyes, had survived. I stood there clutching the phone in my hand in absolute disbelief. She had to call my name several times before she got a response.

"Are you all right?" she asked.

"No," I said. "I'm not all right."

"Let's talk more about this later on this morning, she sounded concerned, but sleepy.

"Okay, I'm sorry," I apologized, I'm sorry for waking you up." It's just that I've never seen anything like this. That client with those penetrating eyes,…this was her story? Why would this be revealed to me?" I asked in confusion.

"Because, you have the skills to help her," I heard her speak through a yawn. "We'll talk about this later this morning. Call me back at 9am, Okay?"

"Okay, I surrendered. I'll call you back." I felt like somebody was beating me in the head with a hammer so I sat down, held my head in my hands and tried to digest what the supervisor had just said.

At first I felt compassion and a great amount of empathy for her. Then I got mad. This reminded me too much of my own childhood. I didn't want to see any of this. But before my anger increased, a thought entered my mind. "What else do you remember?" A voice whispers from my conscious; and I moved beyond my anger. I remembered at the beginning of this dream, just before the little girl's file opened, there was a lot of activity in this room. I saw a constant influx of information pouring into this room; rivers of energy, dialogues, sceneries, and vibrations. Information seemed to be coming directly into the files straight from the persons themselves and their activities, landing on bi-folded canvass screens.

Everything was being recorded automatically, as they happened, in real time. Without doing a reality test, I remember saying to myself, "So that's why the people in that burning pit and the cave could see their lives in review. They were looking at the contents of their own files." Then I realized I was not thinking straight. "Wait! "Stop!" I said to myself, shaking my head as if to dislodge the cobwebs. "What are you doing? It's just another one of those crazy dreams. None of this is real." I am having a conversation with myself, trying to reason all of this away. But I remembered details in this particular dream that I had not seen in any of the others.

I saw things being imprinted onto the files. Scenes happening in real time would just appear by steady waves of radiating energy and just imprint onto this space that looked two movies screens bonded like a folded canvas. The information looked like varying waves of flowing energy. Like some kind of sophisticated imprinting device everything was being recorded in specific files and each wave seemed to have a different vibe. Some were fluid and smooth; others were wavy and pulsating; and still others were jagged and uncoordinated. And they would just appear as scenes on this folded item that resembled a wide-screen canvas.

No one was physically recording information into the files and I could clearly see the drawers opening and closing indiscriminately. Despite this constant flurry of activity, the room was orderly, peaceful and quiet. As the information continued to pour in, the files took on familiar hues of brilliant light, glowing silver, polished gold, different shades of yellow, blue, pale gray and dark shadow. Everything a person did was being recorded on these folded canvases and settled into a file drawer. That's when one of the files floated toward me and I observed the abuse of the child.

The mysterious woman never returned to the group and the supervisor was unable to contact her. I asked the therapist not to tell me her name because I was afraid the dream would return. I have thought about this woman over the years. Everything I saw about her life of abuse was accurate. I just wished I'd had a chance to talk with her in person.

"Maybe she wasn't real," a friend suggested.

"Maybe not," I answered, but her experience was."

"Even if she was real, how could you have helped her?" my friend asked. "She was horribly damaged and abused. There was no hope in her world. No one cared."

My friend sounded so sad, I wondered...but I didn't ask. Continuing the conversation I said to her, "I cared; the person in the dream showing me this file cared; and the one who took the time to record her pain, cared. If I had never met this person, I would readily dismiss this as just another crazy dream. But experience in life has taught me to pay close attention to strange things.

There is so much we don't know about this life and God and evil; so much we don't understand. But I believe the answer to all things, the key to life is locked up somewhere inside us, dormant like a hibernating power that if unleashed it would provide the ultimate secret to destroying all manner of evil in this world."

"You'll never find utopia here, Suzaunna. It's unrealistic to even consider such a world." I think my friend was getting nervous that may be I slipping into unreality.

"I'm not looking for utopia and trust me, I insisted, "I'm not losing my grip on reality. Lord knows, I've had plenty of chances to do that. But, trying to make sense of such stupefying dream experiences like this can challenge logic to a duel with madness. Despite what I believe, I know what I saw. I believe the light that glowed inside of that little girl's battered body, holds part of a greater truth. In spite of all that predator and his gang of enablers did to her, they could not destroy her light. As a matter of fact, the more broken in body she became, the greater her light glowed." "Why is that?" We both wondered.

CHAPTER THIRTY-FOUR

Based on what I saw in that dream about the little girl, I believe that a person is bound to themselves by all that they do. But what was most intriguing is I saw that predators, enablers and victims were being written on the same canvas, in the same file, as if eternally bound. The file belonged to the child; but others in her world were recorded there. The acts of that predator and his gang of enablers were written on the files of the victims; and I believe the sufferings of the victims will be imprinted on the files of the guilty. Therefore, no one gets away with anything. I thought about Sunday School teachings of judgment day; when the minister said that everybody would be held accountable for their actions.

I have often wondered, "Is this what the minister was talking about?" I reminisced back to the dream about the burning pit because I was angry with the man in the open file who was sexually abusing the little girl. I saw this as his fate. I envisioned him joining my mother's husband and other condemned souls that were lined against the circular interior of this cave moaning and pleading for mercy while a menacing laughter mocked their fate. He'll be there, I reasoned, right alongside my mother's husband, imprisoned, waiting until the justice of their victims releases them into that burning pit.

I believe the condemned will be required to stand in at the hearing of their victims; watch the contents of the open files, this time seeing EVERYONE who was affected by their evil, including spouses, children, extended families, and friends. I imagined that they would attend wakes and funerals of their victims; witness burials and cremations and watch the ascent of purity into the arms of a loving God and their own descent into of darkness and eventually that burning pit.

The life of a child is precious. For those condemned for harming a child, I hope judgment and persecution is especially painful. This evil menace, the man who violated this child so horribly or anyone who violates a child or anyone else, be forewarned. There is no greater evil than to violate innocence just because you can. People who commit wicked acts of violence against others, hit-and-run drivers, unrepentant predators, child molesters, camouflaged child abusers, kidnappers, killers and thieves and anyone who really believes they've gotten away with something; I have disturbing news. You will see yourself again...God is waiting for you. I can't say with certainty how much of the content of these dreams I actually accept. But this much I do believe; no one escapes judgment and all victim(s) will be defended and vindicated.

As if seeing an open file was not enough, on April 15, 2002, during a midday nap, I would have yet another dream. Upon appearing inside another part of this mystical file chamber room of files, I noticed startling details that I did not see the first two times. First of all, in this particular room, there were no files and no walls. Perhaps I was in another section. Inside a familiar semi-circle of the room was a wooden podium that creates within me the desire to kneel and bow my head.

On the podium sat a large open book with writing in it. Next to the podium, slightly behind and off to the left side, if you are facing the great expanse of light that glows inward from an open doorway, emanating from somewhere outside the chambers, hovers a large transparent, angelic being made of what can only be described as "acrylic." Both he and his clothes are one.

He levitates with his head bowed and huge hands clasped and folded in front of his robe. He has no visible wings and no halo; but he has incredibly large hands and the most enormous shoulders I have ever seen. He is huge, a massive form to behold and most incredibly beautiful. His movements are so fluid and subtle, and he pulsates within the light that both glows all around him and emanates from within. "You have found the files," a powerful masculine voice whispers into the silence. "Well done. Use them wisely."

I got the impression that if I wanted to ask questions, he was there to answer and explain all things. I did not ask any questions except for his name, because I was numbed and muted by both the strength of his presence and his awesome beauty. He did not lift his head to make eye contact with me. I don't think I could have handled his beauty. Just quick flashes of his face with eyes that looked like burning coals was enough to make me cringe into submission. I was not allowed to stare at his face. But, he was so beautiful.

There was no other visible presence in this room;…not at first. After a while, I began to make out the silhouettes of others who emerged from the light that flowed in through a doorway, into the room. Their feet barely touched the floor and they just stood quietly behind the podium, like stewards watching me in their space.

These others were wearing white robes. They were transparent, glowing, and had the most alluring smiles, peaceful eyes and the warmest, comforting spirits I had ever felt. They had distinct facial features. The feeling of acceptance was overwhelming. These were good spirits and they reminded me of the people in the city with golden streets. "Welcome," someone said. "You are beginning to understand," someone else whispered.

And with that comment, I woke up. Years later, I was shopping at the local flea market and came upon a painting of a black Jesus carrying a man across the sand. It was the artist's version of the famous "Footprints" poem. A touching scene; but what made me stop in my tracks was the distinct "acrylic" color used by the artist to depict the "Jesus" figure. I was speechless and simply stared at what I considered a confirmation to my sanity.

It was the color of the angel in the chamber room. I could not describe this color before seeing this painting. I bought the print and put it in my home. Memories of a childhood dream came flooding back and I tried to connect them with this one. One day I'll sit down and see if all of these dreams can be pieced together. Until then, the words of the apostle Paul comes to me, "Now we see through a glass darkly; but, one day we will know fully, just as we are fully known." There is more to this life than we know.

While I was in internship, shortly after the third dream, I was finishing up charting medical notes and preparing for a group session. The group assembled, and I was assigned to conduct the session alone on this day. The group was a mixture of men and women who sat around disclosing painful childhood experiences. Today, they were unusually restless.

"There must be more to this than just spilling your guts to a bunch of strangers," one particularly angry client finally blurted out what everybody else was probably thinking. "This is doing nothing for my pain," another person chimed in. Then they all started talking at the same time. "Yeah, this is boring," someone else chimed in. They suddenly started complaining bitterly that this "group thing" was not working.

"Wait, settle down guys," I intervened. "You're right," I surrendered. "This is not working out the way we all hoped it would. Most group therapy is designed to help the client understand that they are not alone in their suffering. But, you're right; it sometimes does little to relieve emotional pain. I have an idea. If you all are really serious about healing the hurt within, then I need to ask you to do something you've never done before. It's going to sound weird, but stay with me. Please everybody, close your eyes. Keep them closed.

Drawing excerpts from a relaxation tape I had to produce while in graduate school, I began the session.

"Take a deep breath. Inhale and hold for three counts, one...two... three...;and exhale slowly as I count to ten, backward." "Ten...nine... eight...seven...six...five...four...three...two...one...and relax. Let's do this two more times."

The group settled down and followed the instructions. Before starting, I gave them a way out.

"If at any time this starts to feel uncomfortable, you have the power to end it by simply opening your eyes," I said. I began the session.

"Just listen to sound of my voice, I stated, and understand the words I am about to say. We've all been through some hard times. Your life has been broken and you desire more than anything to fix the broken parts inside. But you did not just start hurting today or yesterday; the pain started a long time ago when you were a child. Someone hurt you; perhaps someone you trusted; perhaps a stranger.

They hurt you and you couldn't stop them. No one was there to help you or they simply refused to help for their own selfish reasons. You felt alone, abandoned and afraid. Sometimes you found a corner away from that evil world and cried by yourself; consoling yourself; becoming your own best friend. Sometimes you wondered, "Where is God?" Because the "church people" told you that God does not allow children to be hurt. He doesn't.

God does not control choice; people do. Predatory people hurt you. They made a choice to do this. But there is a power within that God has given us so we can help ourselves. It is the power of self-healing. As you sit there with heavy hearts, bowed heads, and closed eyes, allow your memory to drift back to the loneliest time you have ever known as a child.

Go back to that time and space. If there is no door in this lonely place, put an imaginary door in front it. If that time takes you back to a lonely closed room, a closet, even a crawl space, go there. Just stand there for a moment and look at the closed door. Remember, this room holds all that is evil in your childhood world. It is a massive door, but one that will open if you choose to open it. Anxiety will try to scare you. And it is normal to be afraid. There is darkness inside the room. But, anxiety has no power over you anymore. You are different now; you stand in the light. There are no locks on the door. It's okay, just push it open.

Open the door and allow the light to flow inside. Step inside of the silence. Stand there for a minute; look and listen with your heart. The child is sitting in a corner, on the floor, in a chair, or standing alone in the dark. There is great sadness here. Look at yourself, a broken, hurting little child, sitting there, crying, alone in the darkness. Life hurts. Stand back and look at this little person for a moment; he is frail, helpless, and unable to fend for himself; she is hurting, lonely and her spirit is broken; no one comes to comfort her. But, a child's curiosity is stirred by the light flowing into the room and she looks up toward you.

Walk up to the child very slowly. Kneel down to the little one ....a towering figure is frightening. Look into those teary eyes and smile. She may not smile back; she doesn't know you. Introduce yourself. Say to her in a gentle voice, "Hello, I am your future. I've come back for you. Let's leave this place, and you never have to come back here again. From now on, I will protect you."

Move closer to the child; pick her up; embrace her trembling little body and hold her close to you; cradle her head on your shoulder; tell her to close her eyes so she never has to see this place again. Stand there for a moment, holding your child and look around you at the space that once held so much fear and pain. It's not so scary anymore.

Go through the doorway you entered and step into the light; leave this place. Carry your child into the light. Close the door behind you, and lock the darkness inside. Never go back there again. You may open your eyes now." Everyone was crying. This was a psychologically healthy group, so no one suffered a psychotic episode of any kind. I thought about this technique and the transforming power it can have on almost anyone and I wondered what would happen if predators and enablers were to go through this same experience.

I chuckled to myself...that would never happen. Maybe I'm just over generalizing, but I doubt these people would ever allow themselves to trust the environment enough to close their eyes. Even if they got past the fear, I doubt seriously if any of them would dare to approach the door of compassion they sealed shut many years ago. For the sake of argument, let's assume these people find the courage to open the door, allow light inside and go into the room.

Now what? They may see the image of a suffering child; a bitter reminder of their own childhood pain. Most people who want to be healed would embrace such innocence. I don't think these people would do that. I believe that as soon as the predatory child abuser, sex offender, and the enabler see themselves suffering, they will go on the attack. This becomes their opportunity to destroy the innocence they've come to hate, oblivious to the fact that they are really destroying themselves.

They would probably reject all pleas for help coming from their wounded child, ignore his misery and try to destroy all that the child represents. Compare this to what we see them do to innocent children now, especially when we hear the news. Be prepared to watch them storm out of the room, step back into their angry, dreary, and contentious existence, slam the door shut, and leave the child inside to die.

This is probably one of the most detrimental features of the sexual predator and anyone who abuses a child. Once these people allow the wounded child inside of themselves to die and choose violence as a means for revenge, no child will ever be safe from their wrath. It's not the child they seek to destroy; it's the reminder of innocence that every child portrays. And they go on the hunt, prowling for ways to destroy children as a means to an end. In the end, what they want is a world that has no reminders of purity, innocence, vulnerability, and peace, because their dark souls killed off that part of themselves a long time ago and sealed their fate with hate.

One thing I have come to understand is that children are born into a world where some people are used to courting, imitating, protecting, hoarding, and inciting evil. Evil is part of the landscape of this world; a diabolical paradigm and nemesis to all that is good. It's as if most of us come from a place of peace and enter into a caldron of vicious mind-sets that are determined to destroy everything good just for the principle of things, just because they can.

Fortunately, others are here, a remnant of good people, who ensures that this mission of destruction is never completed. The power to heal ourselves from damages caused by predatory mind-sets is latent within us all. And each time we travel back to those rooms of experiences to retrieve a part of our broken past, we see evidence of that healing power. I'm not going to be a hypocrite. I will never like my mother's husband and sometimes when the memories of what he did to me force their way back into consciousness, or I enter my own room of experience, I take back my forgiveness, because the memories hurt and they inspire anger and frustration.

Sometimes I *want* to feel enraged and angry and hateful; all of it is justified. I want to allow these feelings to take root and fester hoping God will understand. All of those emotions are my way of staying in power over the only possession I had when I was abused. My emotions were all that I owned- I determined how they were spent. But the power of anger can be deceitful. Each time I removed forgiveness and allowed anger to dominate my emotions, I lost my peace. And once peace is compromised, trouble is just around the corner. When negative emotions try to consume me in spite of my best-laid plans to contain the rage, forgiveness becomes my refuge.

There were times when I thought about hurting my mother's husband. But I had to keep in mind that I was responsible for every choice I made and I would have to answer for my actions. In hindsight, I am proud of myself for not sinking to his level of stupidity. Because I realize now that doing so would have put me on his debased level of communication. Without realizing it, by not hurting him, I had extended something to him that he never gave to me…the gift of mercy. We all have to give an accounting for ourselves; including those deeds done in secrecy. I am ultimately responsible for all that I say and do. And I will be judged accordingly. Even if I tried to convince myself that I would not get caught, those near death experiences taught me one important fact.

Nothing stays hidden. Someone always knows what you've done. There are no secret deeds, unsolved murders, or unsolved mysteries. Sexual predators, child abusers, and enablers are not hiding from anyone. Based on my experience, we are all on visual display as God observes many forms of humanity folded up in positions of pain or rage somewhere in a corner of bitter reality. Somewhere close to heaven, everything we do and say is being observed and recorded. As the words of the apostle Paul rings true, "Do not be deceived; God is not mocked. For whatsoever a man sows, so shall he reap." It is inevitable.

CHAPTER THIRTY-FIVE

Many people are responsible for doing some evil things in this world. They've committed horrifying offenses against humanity and inspire fear and frustration wherever they go. They live their lives as if there is no God; as if committing evil was their calling. What's interesting however is we blame God when these people do bad things. We even go to the extreme of insisting that horrifying crimes and misfortunes are God's will or God's way of testing our faith in him.

God is not in the crime business. Humans are not chess pieces on the game board of life being strategically moved around by God so he can see how we handle certain situations. Bad things happen because bad people make them happen. Bad things happen to good people because evil does not discriminate. Evil people will not escape punishment. No matter how bullheaded, indifferent, cold-hearted and insensitive these people are, I think many of them are afraid to die.

My mother's nasty husband probably believed that securing my forgiveness would erase the evil he has done. He's wrong. No one can hide from a memory. Memory survives death. No matter how sincere the apology or confession, when he dies he will see his life in review. I don't believe in deathbed confessions and contrary to popular teaching, not all of us can be the "thief on the cross." The thief on the cross met Christ who already knew the condemned man's fate.

Just because a person has been forgiven does not mean there are no consequences for their actions. The thief faced his fate based on his own merits. What happens to your neighbor does not necessarily determine your fate. I believe so-called deathbed confessions and last minute repentance is a desperate attempt for predators and evil people to manipulate their way out of accountability. I think these people actually try to trick God into believing that neither justice nor punishment is necessary.

Fiendish actions committed with cold, calculating, spiteful and deliberate intent are inexcusable. The things some of these predators do leave us shaking our heads in disbelief. In the aftermath of a predator's crimes, we cling to each other feeling resolute, despondent, and disheartened that humans can be both sane and evil at the same time. We sometimes question our faith, which at times seems powerless to stop the evil from happening. When we are left to deal with death, mayhem, and all manner of evil that men do, we want an answer to that gut-wrenching one word question that all but defies conventional wisdom: We all want to know, "Why?" I want to know "Where is God *before* evil happens?"

I've gotten a lot of mean, silent glares and all kinds of answers when I asked this question. Ministers, church people, even the elders in my community did not like this question and most of them didn't know how to answer it. I got statements like, "It's not your place to question God." "God allows evil to happen because it is part of his divine plan for our lives." "God is testing you." "God doesn't see evil." This one is my favorite. "It's not for you to know." I've been told everything from "shut up" to "it doesn't matter."

Well, it matters to me. Judging from the various responses, no one knew how to answer this question. I can only speak for myself when I say it burns to know that the most powerful, omnipotent, omniscient, and omnipresent force in the universe will not interfere with choices of man. Choice is a power man does not always use responsibly. The power of choice is a double-edged sword. I've made several unwise choices. I can't blame God for the outcome. But, I don't want that power taken away. Do you? Therefore, when a person chooses to do evil things, I can't get angry with God. People choose to do evil or good and everyone will have to answer for their own lives. In my opinion, God is not silent; He is waiting.

It was very difficult for me to accept that some people don't want God in their lives or heavenly influences in their choice, including some who called themselves ministers, bishops, rabbis, priests or some other religious title. Some of us remove God's presence from our own lives in so many ways and then get mad at Him when our decisions on things like money, health issues, and relationships result in self-imposed personal chaos. We turn a tempestuous ire in God's direction when we become the victims of someone who does not want God interfering in their lives or decisions, rather than focusing on the reality and power of someone else's choice to commit an offense. This is a very bitter side of reality.

But, judgment is inevitable and I believe the bible when it states there is a place for the destruction of the soul. What I saw in the dream about the burning pit was compelling. Condemned souls were sentenced to watch reviews of their crimes. At an appointed time, each person found himself or herself cast into that burning pit. Everything about them was destroyed. The pit was like the death penalty; once the condemned person was cast inside; they burned and were gone from this life and the afterlife forever. I believe in certain aspects of that dream, particularly that personal choice in this life determines your destiny in the afterlife. But I also had to acknowledge that I could not treat the virtues of God like a menu at a favorite restaurant. I could not continue to pick and choose which parts of God I wanted to keep and which parts of my life I considered off-limits. It was my responsibility for choosing where, what, and who would be the focus of my life; thus securing my fate and my destiny.

For those who have a hard time connecting fact and fate, close your eyes and do this. Imagine yourself wearing a wet suit and an underwater breathing apparatus, standing in the depths of one our vast oceans, observing the environment, when you turn around and find yourself staring into the face of a great white shark; a massive force 5,000 lbs heavier and 1,500 times larger than your five-foot-something frame. Your camera, your harpoon, nothing you carry can protect you from several rows of razor sharp teeth and a bad temper.

He is bigger, stronger, faster and smarter than you are. You have crossed over from dry land into a foreign, watery depth in which you are ill equipped to survive. And now you must deal with a powerful force that does not know you and doesn't want to. You are an intruder; an unwelcome entity whose mission is to disturb peace; a menace that must be eliminated, because your presence only contaminates the sanctity of his world. Just the appearance of such greatness demands immediate respect.

A certain degree of awe, reverence and humility will be expected. Such is the fate of evildoers who will eventually face God. They will stare into the face of grace, mercy, and truth; hostile virtues to an evil soul. Evil and predatory people are defiant to all that God represents. I cannot believe that God will allow their evil to contaminate heaven and nor will he ignore their victims' plea for justice. This passage is not intended to cast a shadow on hope. Because, I believe that just as certain as evil exists in this world; God has a presence, a remnant of his own order, which is stronger than any evil we could ever encounter.

One of my brothers told me an incredible story. He said that one day he and a friend were walking down a country dirt road on their way home, when a speeding truck cut off their path. My brother said the man driving the truck leaned out of the window and pointed a large rifle at him and his friend.

"I know yall did it!" he yelled at them.

"Did what?" they both said at the same time.

"Yall threw eggs at my house!" "I'm gonna kill the both of ya!" and with that he clocked his rifle and took aim right at them. My brother said his friend took off running for his life, but he stood there afraid the man would shoot at them if he ran too.

"I didn't egg your house, man." He pleaded. "I didn't do it!"

"Yes you did! Yes you did! And I'm gonna kill you!" The man was determined to kill someone that day. Then my brother said he was shocked when out of nowhere, a tall man appears and put his arm around my brother's shoulder and said to the angry man, "He didn't do it; he was with me." My brother said he turned around and immediately agreed, "Oh yeah, I was with him," pointing a thumb at the stranger.

He stayed calm; but all the while he was wondering, "Who's this?" The angry man pulled his rifle back into the truck and sped off cursing and vowing to find the person who egged his house. "Whew!" He breathed a sigh of relief. "Aw man, you saved my life. Thank you." He turned to thank his rescuer, but the man was gone. This was an open dirt road. There were no trees or homes in sight. The man could not have gone in any direction without being seen. He had simply vanished. But this is the kind of Godly remnant presence I'm talking about.

I've heard and read a number of accounts of people being helped by strangers who suddenly appear and then disappear. These mysterious beings appear at just the right time to help people in distress. I sincerely believe there is a remnant of good people here that is as good as predators are evil. They probably do more than we understand to help preserve order in this world. Without their presence, evil would destroy everything good in this world.

In trying to explain things in more scientific terms, I would have to say this. I don't know how to explain knowing detailed features and information about deceased family members who died while my mother was still a child. I've never seen portraits of these relatives. As for the dreams I had when I was ten, I believe they were compelling and revealing, because they made up part of the foundation of my childhood.

Everything I learned about life and death as a child was heavily steeped in biblical doctrine. Teachings from the bible were as necessary for life as breathing. My curiosity of heaven, enjoyment of bible school teachings and acceptance by my beloved elders may have contributed to the content of these dreams. The basic themes of deliverance, acceptance, and divine love were enough to keep me anchored in hope when it was time to put my life back together.

The same may be true of the dreams of the burning pit and the images of demons. I was being so traumatized by that predator's abuse, in my effort to make sense of it all and ensure his punishment; I may have conjured up those details of hell in order to feel vindicated. Believing that he would eventually meet this fate may have made me fearless of him. The out-of-body experiences have the sensation of being under hypnosis. The boundaries controlled by the senses became obscured eliminating that critical factor called reality.

Sight, sound, touch, smell and hearing become obsolete and all that matters is what you feel and know. Movement happens by thought. Matter is present, but obsolete. All truth becomes crystal clear. Awareness maintains order; and visuals are images of thought and emotion. Perhaps the images of wandering souls, pretentious ministers, and ominous spirits were visual representations of my displeasure with hypocrisy and I saw what I wanted to see.

Since objects appear by thought, maybe I conjured up the people at the crossroads during my second suicide attempt and forced myself to choose between life and death. I didn't want to die; I wanted my life to stop hurting me. As for the attempted suicide with the gun, what may have happened is I suffered a psychotic episode of auditory hallucination because I didn't really want to die. I wanted peace.

Some might argue that brain chemicals called endorphins created all the heavenly images of peace I experienced. But it is undeniable that mental energy can have a powerful affect on matter. In higher levels of particle physics, such as quantum physics, scientists know that if we let go of the idea that objects are solid and immutable, and instead understand that solid material is made up of particles or waves of energy, life becomes more flexible.

Something as life altering as a near-death experience provides irrefutable subjective proof that life is more than just a body. There are probably hundreds of theories and ways to interpret the dreams, visions, and experiences and the scientist in me would probably understand every one of them. But, at some point in my life, I had to find a way for both science and religion to coexist because some things I experienced defied explanation. I am not a religious zealot because I believe that religion without reason is fanaticism. I've tried to reason away every one of these strange situations; vacillating between rhyme and reason; logic and self-persuasion; even merging faith and fiction only to conclude that I am opinionated, but I don't have all the answers.

CHAPTER THIRTY-SIX

Regardless of the scientific rhetoric or theories, something significant and intriguing happened to me when I tried to commit suicide. I believe I died...both times. Certain things stick out from those experiences and I have learned some valuable lessons. First, someone bigger than you and I is not only watching over us, this enormous energy of magnificent light cares about what happens to us, even after we die.

No one introduced himself by stating, "I am a Christian; or I am a Muslim or Hindu; or I am a Jehovah's Witness or Mormon." Religious zealots who only want to promote themselves and their doctrines as the "only truth," will have a difficult time accepting the realities of eternity. No one religion has **ALL** the answers. Although I believe strongly in my Christian faith, I think on some level, we all worship the same God.

Second, there are entities on the other side, which are not of God. There were dark figures that stayed on the perimeter of the wandering crowd and always stayed away from the light. In the park of wandering souls that I found myself in, these dark entities did not mingle. They stood apart from the crowd and watched everybody. They could also disappear and reappear with ease.

Some people who looked like ministers, had masks loosely held in front of their faces, stood behind a podium, draped in different colored robes and appeared to be preaching. The mask was the face of a man; the image behind the mask was disfigured. There were people who wandered alone. These were dark souls with suspicious mannerism and hostile glares. While others ignored the light, they avoided the light. And still others moved about looking around as if searching for a way to return.

Third, at the untimeliness of my deaths, I understand now that my soul lacked something. There was no connection with this magnificent light, only reflections of what was missing from my own soul. In the presence of this light, I was incomplete. And like many others who have had near-death experiences, I was given another chance to refine my purpose and fulfill my destiny.

Fourth, my pain was greater than my passion for life and that needed to change. I needed to choose a path away from my pain if I was going see the light of life again. I don't know why my life was spared. Sometimes I feel guilty that so many others did not survive. I don't have all the answers. But, I have decided not to question certain things anymore, like whether heaven or hell exists. I believe they do and I no longer tempt fate.

Fifth, memory and emotion survive death. Death is only a subtle transition from one form of energy to another and this energy is in constant motion. Reported sightings of ghosts are common. I've personally seen ghosts. I was visited by what appeared to be the friendly spirit of the old woman. I think it's important that we pray for loved ones who have passed on that they go into the light, including those who commit suicide.

Sixth, I felt a myriad of emotions when I crossed over. Agony was the most intense. I watched as some people stood on the edge of a chasm and stared across a thinly veiled barrier. Whatever they were looking at was captivating. Others wandered around in a space that looked like a park. Memories and emotions of life before death were so compelling that some people didn't even know they were dead. I didn't. And yet I could still see, feel, and think. My awareness was heightened.

And last, pray for departed loved ones that they walk into the light. Present in the midst of this dreary existence was a beam of light which most of them ignored. Ghosts have no place in this world; memory keeps them stuck here. If you encounter a lost soul, trying to get your attention, it might be someone who does not know they are dead. Tell them to find the light and walk into it.

I am a scientist and I sometimes have a hard time listening to myself. None of this can be proven in a laboratory. If nothing out of the ordinary had ever happened to me I would be a determined skeptic, and probably agnostic. But my life experience continues to be a dichotomy of both the mysterious and the practical. I can't pick and choose which one makes more sense, because sometimes faith overrules reason and fact is stranger than fiction.

In this material realm, talking about spirituality is "spooky" and surreal. It scares people. But based on personal experiences, some people understand what I'm talking about. The trainer, Martin, was a self-proclaimed warlock and his wife considered herself a witch. They dabbled in casting spells, reciting incantations, and satanic worship. During one of his trance states, he acknowledged the presence of an entity that he thought was the spirit of someone he knew and invited him in. He was wrong. This was the hostile entity I encountered. I don't believe in the traditional definition of reincarnation or superhuman powers. But a strange metaphysical power exists in this world that is yet to be fully explained.

Perhaps the most definitive truth I have come to understand is this. We all have a space within that no one can touch. It is a place where we put everything we've learned into some kind of perspective. It is a place where personal understanding merges with public opinion; but we decide what we want to believe. This is your point of power; your dominance over presumed destiny. It is the place in your heart where you truly believe, in the words of William Earnst Hensley, that you are the "master of your own fate and the captain of your own soul." Within this space, you are in complete control of your own choices.

It is the place where no one can influence your beliefs, thoughts, or passions because you have developed an understanding on your own. No one can take this away from you. It is that part of you that no one can own or change except you. It is this space that God knows best. This is self-knowledge of things you prefer to keep hidden from the rest of the world. It is the core of your existence; your refuge in times of confusion. This is where you've learned to make sense of situations in this world. This is your truth and only two sources have access to it, you and God. Make the necessary changes and Know thyself.

CHAPTER THIRTY-SEVEN

Great Aunt-Toni used to say to me in her own dialect, "Ever'body should be careful how dey tret peopous; ya nevva know what ya dealin' wit. Dat person could be a angel." I'll never forget those important words of wisdom because I believe she was right. We don't always know who we're dealing with, especially when it comes to children. I'm no angel; but my mother and her husband clearly had no idea or didn't care that they were dealing with an unusual child.

My grandmother knew something was "different" about me. Cousins, family, and friends called me "weird." But where I'm from, weird is acceptable. I think, I'm just as normal as anyone else, with a few quirks thrown in. The dreams continue. As a matter of fact, I had a dream about the aunt who tried to blind me with toe cone remover, soon after she committed suicide. In the dream, I am holding on to a log that is floating downstream, in a river of clear water. I looked up to see her standing on the bank, watching me.

Her face was pasty white; her eyes were sunken with dark circles around the bottom of them; and she was dressed in a white, front-laced, button down blouse and a black skirt. As I floated in front of her, she bent down and reached out her hand as if beckoning me to grab it so she could pull me out of the water. When I did not accept her offer, she withdrew her hand and stood straight up, and watched me float down the river. The stone-faced expression on her face did not change. I don't know what she wanted and I didn't want to find out. Rather than cooperating like I did with the apparition who visited me, I heeded my grandmother's warning, "Do not follow the dead anywhere, especially when they come to you in a dream."

I don't posses any special powers nor can I see into the lives of *everyone* I come in contact with. But there are certain people who affect me more intensely than others. These days I concentrate on strengthening existing relationships. My brothers are cordial and respectful. I maintain a friendly, diplomatic relationship with my mother. I rarely acknowledge her husband. When he's in my presence, he never looks me in the eyes. My mother still tries to mend fences between her husband and I, which infuriates me. I don't like him and I never will. Even if he has changed, I don't care because I don't believe that's even possible. I lost all respect for him when he raped me and I have refused to see him as a person with any amount of decency since the day he burned my diary. My mother has a hard time respecting those boundaries.

As if to reinforce that I am insignificant and meaningless, she brags about how smart he is and tries to manipulate a response from me. She has brought him into my home over my objections. When he is sick, she calls me and puts him on the phone. Sometimes, I'll hear him in the background telling her to say certain things to me and she does. She tries to convince me that he is a good person.

Denial is one of our most primitive defenses against overwhelming pain. Denial and rejection are primitive partners and necessary for self-protection and self-preservation. My mother lives in this kind of denial. She married her husband in good faith. She did not deliberately bring this man into my life knowing he was going to harm me. She did not realize the true nature of his intentions until he violated her trust and raped her child.

In her mind, she may have thought, "I didn't want this to happen. But now that it has, what do I do about it." Facing isolation, loneliness, abandonment, perpetual poverty, and four hungry mouths to feed, she made a choice. She denied her child,…her truth, and embraced a false sense of security. Once a choice is made, particularly one that controls survival, people will go through great lengths to protect themselves and their decisions anyway they can.

For example, I believe if you were to ask any mother who has defended her husband or boyfriend's sexual predatory filth against her own child, would she invite the rapist of her grandchild or anyone else's child into her home as a friend, she would probably say no. She would probably feel justifiably angry and disgusted and suggest justice for that child. The difference is that in defending someone else's child, she has nothing to lose.

My mother was no different. She has insisted that she would never allow her grandchildren to be hurt in any way, by anyone; yet she has never shown any level of compassion or concern for what her husband did to me. Coming to my defense meant losing everything and she chose to abandon me instead. I'm sure this happens in the lives of a lot of innocent children all over the world. We can't force anyone to change. I can only hope that someday my mother and others like her will understand that protecting a monster, is not worth losing your child. She has made some irreversible decisions and egregious errors in judgment that have resulted in irreconcilable differences between us.

My mother turned a deaf ear to my cries for help and a blind eye to her husband's degrading filth. She has been his partner in the defamation of her own child and she acts like there will be no consequences for her behavior. She may never admit that she sacrificed her child for money, companionship and a false sense of security and will not allow anyone to show her the truth of her denial. In her mind, her husband is the victim and she probably finds it appalling that God and most of the world disagrees.

She likes to portray herself as a nice, God-fearing woman and she is active in her church. She used to give away free food from her store to hungry people and provided clothing for the poor. She has always shown compassion toward people in need, including my family. I'm sure in her mind, she has done nothing wrong. She probably believes if she is guilty of any offense, it should be "charged to her head and not to her heart." I often wonder sometimes, "What does God thinks of all this?" For someone who prides herself on the portraying the virtues of Christianity, I wonder, will she be able to stare into the face of God on her day of passing and expect to hear him say, "Well done?"

Both of them have a lot to answer for. Her husband has probably reached an age where molesting children is no longer attractive and now he's pretending to be a model citizen. What he did to me and probably others, was his presumed privilege and they both act as if I have no right to be upset. He will hide behind my mother's excuses until the day he dies. I refuse to believe there will ever be anything virtuous about him.

For a short while, I tried to play my mother's charades, allowing her to talk me into trying to ignore what her husband had done to me and pretending to merge into her family. I tried to mold into her way of thinking and do things her way. Each time I did this I came away feeling very sad, enraged, dirty, used and manipulated. But, the experience was educational. As if scales fell off my eyes, I was able to see exactly what kind of person I was dealing with.

My mother is a good person. I believe she has a kind heart and we still speak to each other. But for reasons known only to her, she prefers to live in a reality that does not hold her husband accountable for any wrongdoing, even the rape and abuse of her own child. I learned that in order to stay in her good graces, I would have to deny every part of my life. I would have to deny my past ever existed, accept that my present was only an illusion, and my future would always be uncertain.

If I accepted her reality, nothing as I understood it would matter anymore. Her main desire was for me to treat her husband as if he were a respectable man and father, ignoring everything in my history. I could not do that; the wounds were too deep and I could not avoid that nagging confusion over my mother's inability or unwillingness to comprehend and accept what her husband had done to me.

I was not going to pretend these horrible things never happened. I would not allow the trauma to force me into an extreme level of denial and avoidance of reality. I could not look at this man she was proud to call her husband and see him as anything but the monster I knew him to be. Her peace revolved around denying that her husband could be so evil. That was the world I saw when I tried to play by her rules and it felt bad. I could not live in her world.

I don't hate my mother, but I stopped hoping for the establishment of a maternal bond with her. I found stronger alliances, relied on the support of my husband and children and adopted God as the most significant part of my support system. I surrendered my confusion and accepted that if she wants to deny her child in support of a sexual predator, then there is nothing I can do to change her mind. I just hope she can convince God that what she chose to do was the only option she had available.

A few years ago, my family and I were visiting my grandmother. My brothers, cousins, and their families decided to meet at my mother's house for dinner and invited my family to come along. With the exception of my wedding, I had not been in that house for almost twenty years, so I accepted the invitation. There must have been at least twenty-five people at the house. After dinner, I decided to get away from the crowd and catch up on some reading. I checked on my kids and told my husband where I was going. I got a book from the car and went to my old room. About ten minutes later, I look up to see my mother's husband crawling toward me, on his knees.

"What do you want?" I snapped.

With tears in his eyes, he said, "I'm sorry for what I done to you. I made your life hell. Please forgive me. I don't want to die knowing that you hate me."

Justifiable rage clouded all thinking. I was not interested in his apology. I sat there and glared at him without blinking. Images of what he had done to me started dancing in my head and a heat wave of rage swept over me. I started counting silently to myself and decided that if he was still there when I got to the number seven, I was going to attack him. I was going to make a scene, because there were enough men around to beat his ass down, including my husband. When I didn't answer him, the expression on his face changed from tears to anger. He got my unspoken message. I *wanted* him to die knowing he was hated.

Just as I reached number seven and was about to stand up, my husband walked into the room. That coward got up and left without saying another word. He didn't even acknowledge my husband. "Give me back my virginity, you sadistic bastard, then maybe we can talk," I yelled at him as he hurried down the hallway. I don't know if he heard me or not. My husband asked me, "Is everything okay?" "No," I said. "Get the kids; we're leaving right now. I hate this place." I packed up my family and left that house for good.

After that incident, my mother and I had a conversation I'll never forget. The content is not verbatim, but this is close. The conversation occurred because I did not want my mother bringing her husband into my home. He was still a predator and therefore, not welcomed in my home. But this conversation would prove to be a defining moment in my life.

"Mom, because of what your husband did to me, I don't want him in my home." I remember saying.

"Suzaunna, I didn't know what was going on when you were growing up. Why didn't you tell me?" she asked angrily.

"Mom, you knew what he was doing to me." "You...she cut me off. Before I could finish, she changed the subject.

Didn't he apologize?" she said to me. I turned the question on her.

"Mother, did he tell you he apologized?" I asked.

"Yes," she said.

"So, you did know what he was doing to me." I responded. There was silence on her end. The ugly truth suddenly hit me. I felt like I had banged my head against a concrete wall as I struggled to make sense of the moment. That's when I concluded without a doubt that she had always known her husband sexually abused me. She had kept it a secret, pretending everything was fine to family and friends. She had ignored everything. First my feelings went numb, followed by a wave of intense sadness and I stared at the floor for a several muted seconds, feeling sick to my stomach. A distant memory emerged and I found the courage to keep talking.

"Did you send him to come and talk to me the day he came in that room crawling on his knees?"

"No," she insisted. "He did it all by himself." I guess he told about that day too.

"Wow, I suggested rather sarcastically, how noble." She didn't appreciate the cynicism "He's changed," she countered.

"He's changed, mother?" I was getting angry. "Changed into what?" "When did this happen?"

"After you left, he changed," she said.

"So, you're saying all of this was my fault; that I caused him to do the things he did to me?" I asked with a hint of rage in my voice. She didn't answer, so I continued.

"Let me ask you something, mother," I spoke through clenched teeth. "Do you think I was his only victim? Predators like him never stop with one victim. I promise you, there are others. I only pray that his other victims can overcome the pain he's caused them. If his nasty ass ever molests one of my nieces or nephews, I'm coming after him. He is a pedophile, mom; a sexual predator that preys on children. People like him don't change. They just grow old and die!"

"If Jesus forgives, you have to forgive too," she continued. Otherwise you can't call yourself a Christian. You are just being a hypocrite. How do you expect to get into heaven if you carry all this hate in your heart? God said you have to forgive if you want to see his kingdom." She was stuck in some kind of religious head game and using scripture to hide from the truth. She didn't comprehend a word I had said.

"This is amazing," I countered. "Now you've got Jesus on his side. Is Jesus blaming me for what your husband did to me, also? Is that what you're telling me? Are you telling me that everything your husband did to me was my fault?" I asked again. By now, I was furious.

"Well, no, not really," she was getting on my nerves. "It's just…you need to leave the past in the past." "Whatever happened, it's over," she snapped.

"It's over for whom?" "For you?" "For him?" "No, mother, I shot back. "It's never over. You may not make him responsible for what he did to me, but I know someone who will. He will answer for his crimes against me and Lord knows who else, and so will you." I was sick of this conversation so I patronized her to get her off the phone.

"Look," I said, "I appreciate every act of kindness you've shown to my family, but I refuse to pretend nothing happened. I won't live in denial, I will not make excuses for his filth, and he is still not welcomed in my home."

My mother lives so deeply in denial that after a long pause she said, "If he is not allowed in your house, then you're not welcomed in mine."

I don't know if that was meant to hurt or not. It didn't. "Okay, fine," I said very calmly. "I'll stay at my grandmother's house when I'm in town." We said our goodbyes and hung up the phone.

CHAPTER THIRTY-EIGHT

It's not like she didn't know about what happened to me. In a desperate attempt to try and help her understand why I hated her husband so much, I wrote my mother an angry letter telling her in graphic detail, everything her husband did to me. I told her how I tried to commit suicide and that during the first attempt, I lay dying on the living room couch, less than 10 yards away from her. I told her how her husband used to lock my brothers in a room so he could rape me without interference. I told her how angry I was at her for not doing anything to help me. I told her everything. She read the letter and made it a point to tell me she had burned it.

Apparently, the letter disturbed her, but not in a way I had hoped or expected. Instead of calling me to discuss the contents of the letter, she called the one brother who is most hostile toward me and refuses to believe what happened to me. She cried over the phone, complaining to him that I was being mean and unappreciative toward her. She got what she wanted; he turned on me. We live less than ten miles from each other and until very recently, had not talked or visited with each other in several years.

The most difficult concept for me to grasp is this. How can anyone, especially a mother step aside and allow someone to hurt their child? This goes against the logic of nature. I cannot imagine a mother bear or tiger simply stepping aside and allowing a hunter to pet her cubs. Anyone threatening to hurt my child has to go through me first. I can speculate and assume whatever behavioral scenarios, explanations and intentions that make me feel less overwhelmed; but I will never truly understand this kind of reversal of maternal instinct.

Unfortunately, this scenario occurs over and over again in the lives of many victims. Some children are orphaned, abandoned, and forced out of the home because they fight against the inhumanity of being abandoned, bartered and betrayed by their own mothers. It is one of the most incomprehensible things I have ever seen. All predators and the women who support them will lie to keep their secret hidden. One of the ways to break this cycle is to listen to what the child is saying, listen for what the parents are not saying, record everybody's behavior and confront all inconsistencies with the facts. Pedophiles, sex offenders, child abusers and the people who support them are as sick as their secrets and those secrets must be exposed. Otherwise, millions of innocent children will continue to suffer from the devastating effects of these maniacal partnerships.

My mother has probably convinced herself that since she never laid a violent hand on me, she is not guilty of abusing me. She's wrong. Standing by and allowing a child to be abused makes anyone just as guilty as the one who actually beats, berates, rapes or kills a child. The traumatic effects of the child abuse are devastating. For seven years, I could read and write music. I had basically mastered four different instruments. But I was so traumatized by what they did to me that today, I can't remember a single note.

Damaged children grow up to become wounded adults who get stuck in a quagmire of confusion. Victims often find it difficult to move beyond the offense because the pain is paralyzing-causing them to become emotionally and psychologically frozen in time. In order to break free of this, I had to get rid of the notion of trying to get back to a feeling when none of this had ever happened. I couldn't act like this stuff had never happened; all I could do was move forward with my life.

Sexual abuse is muting because it violates cleanliness. Many victims get stuck in a vicious cycle of trying to undo, understand or destroy the feeling of numbing frustration. Oftentimes victims struggle to regain their dignity by identifying something in this world as sacred, because we all need something to hold on to that cannot be defiled by human degradation. I discovered that the soul is sacred; the spirit is sacred; and truth is sacred. No one can take these away from you no matter how evil they are and no matter what they do to you.

The journey back to purity was long and agonizing. Since this is a mean world to live in by yourself, it becomes essential that those who've survived the carnage of a sexual predator and child abuse find a support system and form healthy relationships with good, kindhearted people. All victims should share their story with someone who cares. I understand the apprehension. The stories are very painful and personal. If sexual predators can break the bond of maternal instinct to such a degree that a mother feeds her own children to him rather than protect them, then to some victims, there are no sacred bonds.

I understand how hard it is to feel human again when your trust has been destroyed. But I would encourage victims to share their story anyway. One way to become unstuck is to learn to trust again. Someone is always willing to listen. I may have felt like an unwanted child; but I was a sacred soul. I knew someone who believed I was special. In my pain, I cried out for mercy, and someone bigger than my mother and her husband rescued me.

I am not surprised that my mother and brothers treat this monster as if he is the victim. He set them up that way. All sexual predators are classic manipulators. Child abusers and sex offenders in particular already have an identified designated target. So they treat everyone else in their world with such syrupy kindness, people think they walk on water. They do this on purpose so if the truth does come out, no one will want to believe it. Look at what this man has accomplished. By making her world feel secure, even when he admitted what he did, my mother found a way to blame me. That's exactly what he counted on. He needs her to make excuses for him; that way he knows he'll never be held responsible for what he did...not by her.

Now he sits silently on the sidelines, afraid to die. He watches everybody fight over something that is clearly his fault. He pretends to be the victim, because he knows my mother will come to his defense. He extended that phony apology, knowing that my mother would believe him and my brothers would sympathize with him. It was a gesture to keep all of them in his corner; not an expression of remorse. Like all predators, he will do anything to avoid facing the consequences of what he's done, because he doesn't want to repair any damages he's caused. Like all child molesters and abusers, a broken child is his source of power. I was that broken child. But he miscalculated. I didn't stay broken.

His power is gone and now he is on the run. I don't want an apology and I don't care how long he tries to run away from acknowledging what he's done. He will die someday and God will have the final word. Occasionally, my mother and her husband visit my brothers. And since I don't live far away from them, I show up by invitation. Except for a customary greeting, I speak to my mother and ignore him. I have nothing to say to him. He has no positive meaning for me.

This man comes from a family of thirteen children of which eight, including himself has been to prison for one thing or another. Most of them, including their mother that vile woman who used to call me "little black dog" lived to destroy the human spirit in some way. They committed horrible crimes against humanity, destroyed lives, and desecrated anything good in the world.

One of his sisters expressed grave concern that her sibling's lineage, and succeeding generations, with a few exceptions, have either died violently or is plagued by a lingering legacy of violence such as strangulation, crushed skull, one was shot in the head six times, drug abuse, gunshot wounds, stabbings, internal fighting, sibling rivalry, incest, and child abuse. Many members of her family have died violently and she was afraid that her siblings had behaved so terribly, they may have brought bad karma on themselves and their families. Mayhem was their gift to the world and it came back to them.

My faith in God has been healing. But, for many years I blamed God for my pain. I was wrong. God never offended me-that predator did. God does not interfere with the choice of man; but since all offenses cry out for justice big and small, I believe all will be vindicated. My pain was never God's fault. It was during the process of healing from those terrible times that I learned to lean on God for support, not supposition. I never felt like I was being tested. I don't believe that God has a need to test anyone in such a horrible manner. I believe it is sacrilegious to condone the horrors and temptations of life as a test of spiritual commitment.

CONCLUSION

I've come a long way since venturing out from my humble bayou community. My journey is not over. Exploring the memories of a toddler both in happiness and pain; reliving harsh realities that almost claimed my life; and describing the content of dreams and real-life experiences that defy explanation has been exhausting. I have seen so much. These days all dreams, visions, and other "spiritual stuff" are kept in relative perspective.

If I can make sense of a strange experience, I do; if I cannot, I don't worry about it. I document what I see and leave it at that. I am still selective about who touches me and what items I touch. However, I don't avoid eye contact anymore. If I see something, no matter how unusual, I write it down. If someone asks for my opinion, I explain things the way I understand them.

I miss my great-grandmother's old rocking chair. I watched many sacred secrets unfold from the seat of that chair and I'm not sure what to make of the prebirth memories or the detailed memories of a toddler. They are not exactly scientific because some of the details cannot be confirmed. I can only hold them close to my heart as unusual and unexplained. The bayou mystique is a mysterious birthright. She is complex. Sometimes, I became her essence, personified. The elders call this essence "an old soul."

Lessons I learned from the near-death experiences were priceless. There is so much we don't know about the afterlife; but I think it's important to listen to the testimonies of those who have had these experiences. There is much insight to be gained from their stories. And although I don't know how to realistically interpret the graphic dreams of the beautiful city, the cave and its burning pit, and the file room, I'm certain that one day I will understand what these dreams mean, also.

I've thought long and hard about the contents of this book. There are some happy moments in time I would like to recapture. But there were some ominous periods, too. For instance, during adolescence, I would pray for each day to either end quickly or at least let me die before the sun set. So many days sauntered painfully by, as if time was either standing still or playing a cruel motionless joke on me. Like so many other victims, my adolescence was grossly compromised and maligned by a merciless coward. But, I survived.

If you were a victim of incest, child abuse or sexual perversion and you happen to be reading this book, you have survived too. Now, it's time to live. I don't know every victim's situation, but I understand this much. I know how hard it is to piece a broken life back together. I also understand how difficult it is to move beyond the effects of abuse. But the greatest victory a victim can gain over the predator's filth is to become stronger than this monster's need to destroy you. Refuse to stay broken.

Always remember the courage it took for you to make it this far. You are stronger than you realize. Inner strength is more powerful than you can ever imagine. Despite being violated, learn to trust again. It is one of the keys to inner healing. With faith and hope to lean on, learn to love yourself. Courage, inner strength, trust, faith, hope and love are the virtues of a survivor. Hold on them. You will need them when it is time to face your pain. Forgiveness is necessary for gaining inner peace. But remember, forgiveness is only a strategy for containing the pain until you are strong enough to deal with it. Forgetting is not an option.

If someone is telling you to forget about what happened, they are avoiding your pain and your victory. Ask this person if you should forget the evil that was done to you or the courage it took to overcome it. Should you forget the pain that was caused or the healing you found afterward? Should you forget being abandoned or disregard your willingness to trust in spite of it? Are you supposed to just forget your history, cut away everything unpleasant and live as if life was never horrifying? Remind this person that history is like truth, it will not stay hidden in the past. There is no forgetting. Even God remembers.

What most of the world does not understand is that incest, rape and child abuse trauma leaves a victim feeling nasty and/or defective almost every waking moment. Some victims feel detached from society because they feel they have nothing sacred to contribute. The very essence of personal decency has been so horribly violated that life can feel abnormal. I used to sit in class, band practice, among the church congregation, family gatherings, and among friends at school feeling nasty and ashamed all the time. I felt like there was nothing clean about me. I muddled through adolescence with the paranoid delusion that everybody could tell how nasty I was just by looking at me. And I didn't want anyone to hug me or touch me because I was afraid I would contaminate them.

I remember walking into church on Sundays after being raped the night before, hanging my head and hiding my face so God wouldn't see how disgusting I was. I hated every waking moment of my life because I could not get rid of this chronic feeling of filth. I did everything I knew how to destroy my body. In the treacherous stillness of this pain, I tried to end my life three times. I was miserable, but somehow I knew I had to find power within myself to survive or eventually I was going to self-destruct.

The most difficult part of healing was believing it could happen, because when you are an adult trying to undo childhood pain, expressions of childhood anger feel immature. Everyone, including therapists can become frustrated and impatient with silent sufferers, wondering why we don't just "get over it." Spouses and friends grow weary of listening to victims tell their stories over and over again, as if glued to the pains of the past. The reason it is so difficult for silent sufferers to move beyond the pain is because the means to repair the pain is unrealistic. All victims have a burning desire to live life as if this awful thing had never happened to them and it is this wish that keeps them stuck. The cure does not exist; but the means to heal does.

What is needed most is guidance in helping victims trust their own judgment; their own faith; and their own ability to heal from the trauma. I struggled to gain the confidence needed to trust my own judgments. But the survival of my children, my husband, my relationships and my faith rested entirely on learning to trust. I loved all of them enough to try. I now understand that each breath of my life, everyone's life, is lived one precious moment at a time. Having conquered the pain that once controlled me, my chosen path is now paved with peace and good intentions. I can travel as far and as long as I desire.

One other lesson I've learned thus far, is this. Death is not our friend; it is our calling. Let it call on you. Suicide is not a solution, because memory survives death. All you will do is transfer your inner pain over to the other side; because, this emotional pain is not attached to the physical body, it resides in the memory of the soul. The body stays on this side; but, just like love, memory and emotion crosses over with you. Death is not an end; it's a beginning. The present state of emotion, commitment, and loyalty of affairs in which you now live, will become your reality when we wake up on the other side.

You will be more alive and more aware of things there than you are here. What you believe and remember on this side will be your preserver, your anchor or your curse, on the other side. You don't forget what you know; knowledge and emotion are magnified, enhanced and sometimes confirmed. There is no doubt in my mind there is a spiritual realm of existence beyond this physical life. If you believe this, then I offer this humble suggestion.

If in death, you find yourself lost and alone, confused, or in a park surrounded by other lonely, wandering souls; if you find yourself in a dreary gray existence unsure of what to do; if you become aware of yourself as a ghost unable or unwilling to move beyond regrets and materialism; if you feel yourself disagreeing with the manipulative rhetoric of men wearing masks, pretending to be ministers of God; or if you find yourself loitering among dark entities and you don't want to be there, …whatever state you find yourself in, there is still hope. Commit this to memory because it will survive death. Find the light. Go into the light. He is merciful. You will recognize God when you see him.

Life experiences are different for different people and it is difficult to try and cover all of them. This book focused heavily on incest, child abuse, the sexual predator and the enablers who support them. Unfortunately, this scenario is only one of many the sexual predator and child abuser hide in. Family secrets revolve around sons, daughters, brothers, sisters, cousins, grandfathers, grandmothers, babysitters, uncles, aunts, ministers, priests, family friends, coaches, school teachers, principals, psychologists, physicians, etc…the list is endless. Sexual predators can be found in many families, cultures, professions and socioeconomic groups.

However, the message of survival is for anyone who embraces it. Perhaps parts of this book highlight some of the most devastating psychological effects that rape, incest, and child abuse can cause; or maybe it is a powerful testament to the resilience of the human spirit. It could be both. But most of us can agree on one important fact. Sexual abuse of a child or anyone else is despicable and every family member who knowingly supports this kind of filth is just as guilty as the monster that violates the child. No man, woman, or child has the right to use someone else's innocence for sexual release. Therefore, families who support sexual predators must understand that no matter how "good" you try to present these people, what they have done makes them deviant. There is no such thing as a "nice" child molester.

Families who purposely turn a blind eye to this problem need to recognize something. If the child molester can secure the support of family, friends, or peers, he or she will keep molesting children, generation after generation, creating more victims and establishing paradigms and patterns of harboring family secrets that survives for years. These monsters grow old and die, leaving family members whispering among themselves over who will be the next resurrected predator, rather than trying to prevent the next victim. This has to stop.

Victims are people, too. They have a right to evolve into greatness and families who knowingly support relatives who have sexually abused another family member must stop treating victims as if they are a predator's property. Families cannot continue to treat the victim like an outcast of a family sickness and it is wrong to discredit and ignore the victims' pain and cries for help because of what the neighbors might think or how friends might react.

Sexual predators **must** accept the word "no" and understand that a child's body is not their sexual playground. An enabling mother (or any caretaker) cannot continue to hide behind low self-esteem, loneliness, and a false sense of security in defense of these monsters because whether she realizes it or not, she is sacrificing, bartering, and trading her children for personal gain. It's wrong. To families and friends who really want to protect children from this kind of viciousness, ask a victim to tell you their story and I encourage you to listen with your heart. The abuse of children must stop and it will; but not until those of us who have been through the fire join ranks with opponents of this menace, step up and speak out. As one collective voice of everyone who is disgusted by the filthy behaviors of a sexual predator, we all have to speak loudly, clearly, and plainly and proclaim in defense of any potential victim, "NO MORE!"

One of the greatest travesties of justice in all abuse cases is the isolation and manipulation of the victim. Most victims suffer alone and in silence, wrapped in personal shame and disgust. If you were the victim of incest, child abuse, or sexual abuse, you must understand something very important. First, you are not alone. The walls of isolation surrounding you are invisible. Reach through them and tell your story. Someone in the world may understand your pain. Second, you did nothing wrong. Sexual predators and their enablers are the guilty parties. But if they can keep you silent, they know you will turn on yourself. The best way to break free of a personal darkness is to get involved in the healing process of another person. A good way to identify your wounds is by helping someone else heal from their own.

I look forward to the day when no child's heart will ever again serve as a dark room for hiding the family's dirty secret and a predator's perverted lust will never destroy another child's innocence. That day will come. Until then, I will not remain silent. If I don't speak this ugly truth out of darkness and into the light, the evil will continue. If I give in to the demands of enabling family members and keep my mouth shut, future generations will suffer. If I patronize denial and settle for being the family outcast and personify their dirty little secret, I will never know what it means to have pride.

I would encourage all victims to expose a predator's filth and take back the power he stole from you; otherwise you will always be under his control. I will always remind the sexual predator that he should be ashamed to face God. If I remind those who bought and sold my body that they could not barter my soul, I am comforted knowing that God is waiting to have the final word.

Several times I turned on myself to the point of almost self-destructing. I came to a crossroad where I had to decide to find my purpose or spend the rest of my life mourning my past. If I don't fulfill one of my divine purposes, which is to love in spite of my loss, then my life will be meaningless. And I realize now that sometimes victims have to initiate change by refusing to bury their pain in food, drugs, alcohol, depression, promiscuity and self-pity; otherwise, you will die for nothing.

I refused to stay broken and confused and learned to count on God rather than curse Him. My faith has never let me down, but I had to do something else. I had to create passion out of my pain; because, if I don't love myself, heal myself, help myself and nurture myself or if I don't reach into my past deep enough to help another person find their future, then I have failed to fulfill my purpose and God saved my life for nothing.

Refuse to stay in hiding. It is time to speak out. Focus on what you want to create; not just on what you want to change. Change will occur through creation. There will always be difficult days in this life. Sometimes it feels like "you gotta walk through hell to get to heaven." Do whatever it takes and never give up. Put one foot in front of the other and keep your head to the sky. Make life a journey to remember.

There are so many stormy days in life. Always look beyond the dark clouds. You will notice slivers of light tracing the darkness, forming jagged cracks in the menacing hue and rays of a hidden light breaking through. Follow the streaks of silver linings across a darkened sky and notice its rays breaking free. Though darkness blocks the light…for a time; suffer peace, and be still. The light will find its way to you.

Just Stand

Judgment, temper your execution
Wanton souls, do not claim, yet
Soon this malicious war will be won
By the one whom love begat

Oh! That nations would take heed
The cries of every Wednesday's child
To the honor of their beleaguered souls
We beg the mercy of the files.

It is the right of every man
To play folly with his soul
But tis the menace of his deeds
Which thus solidifies his goal

What price, freedom
What is your sacrifice laid?
Where is your loyalty?
By whose authority do you trade?

Does your anchor hold
Against the consequences of choice
Railing with indifference
Does it matter that you have no voice?

In vast numbers, the sands of the seashores
Multitudes follow prosperity's dream
It is deception disguised as wisdom
And sins, yet unredeemed

Some will consider His armor
Very few will put it on
The question is simple
To whom do you belong?

A simple mission, I think not
To rescue fallen angels, repairing broken wings
But a noble necessity to save the soul
Considering what price to darkness it may bring

Sometimes you are the last person standing
In life's dark arena; a wretched nemesis to the goodness
of man.
Abandon all fear in this shadow of death
When you've done all that you can, just stand.

C.S. CLARK

Please send all correspondence to:

Attention: Dr. Clark
Village Community Services, Inc.
5295 Highway 78
Suite D-301
Stone Mountain, GA 30087
Email: consultant@villagecommunityservices.org

ABOUT THE AUTHOR

C. S. Clark holds a Doctorate of Education in Counseling Psychology; a Master's degree in Clinical Psychology; a Bachelor of Arts degree in Human Relations Psychology; an Associate of Science degree in Medical Technology and consulting specialties in forensics, counseling, education, and community programs development. She is also licensed as professional counselor. She and her family live in Georgia.